SHORT STORY COLLECTIONS BY JOYCE CAROL OATES

Extenuating Circumstances: Stories of Crime and Suspense

The Ruins of Contracoeur and Other Presences

Night, Neon: Tales of Mystery and Suspense

The (Other) You: Stories

Night-Gaunts and Other Tales of Suspense

Beautiful Days: Stories

DIS MEM BER and Other Stories of Mystery and Suspense

The Doll-Master and Other Tales of Terror

Lovely, Dark, Deep: Stories

High Crime Area: Tales of Darkness and Dread

Black Dahlia & White Rose: Stories

The Corn Maiden and Other Nightmares

Give Me Your Heart: Tales of Mystery and Suspense

Sourland: Stories

Dear Husband,: Stories

Wild Nights!: Stories About the Last Days of Poe, Dickinson, Twain, James, and Hemingway

The Museum of Dr. Moses: Tales of Mystery and Suspense

High Lonesome: New & Selected Stories, 1966–2006

The Female of the Species: Tales of Mystery and Suspense

I Am No One You Know: Stories

Faithless: Tales of Transgression

The Collector of Hearts: New Tales of the Grotesque

Will You Always Love Me? And Other Stories

Demon and Other Tales

Haunted: Tales of the Grotesque

Where Are You Going, Where Have You Been?: Selected Early Stories

Where Is Here?: Stories

Heat and Other Stories

Oates in Exile

The Assignation: Stories

Raven's Wing: Stories

Wild Saturday

Last Days: Stories

A Sentimental Education: Stories

All the Good People I've Left Behind

Night-Side: Eighteen Tales

Crossing the Border: Fifteen Tales

The Poisoned Kiss and Other Stories from the Portuguese

The Seduction & Other Stories

Where Are You Going, Where Have You Been?: Stories of Young America

The Goddess and Other Women

The Hungry Ghosts: Seven Allusive Comedies

Marriages and Infidelities: Short Stories

The Wheel of Love and Other Stories

Upon the Sweeping Flood and Other Stories

By the North Gate

Zero-Sum

Zero-Sum

Stories

JOYCE CAROL OATES

ALFRED A. KNOPF, NEW YORK, 2023

THIS IS A BORZOI BOOK PUBLISHED BY ALFRED A. KNOPF

www.aaknopf.com

Knopf, Borzoi Books, and the colophon
are registered trademarks of Penguin Random House LLC.

Page 253 constitutes an extension of the copyright page.

Library of Congress Cataloging-in-Publication Data
Names: Oates, Joyce Carol, [date] author.
Title: Zero-sum : stories / Joyce Carol Oates.
Description: First Edition. | New York : Alfred A. Knopf, 2023.
Identifiers: LCCN 2022031406 | ISBN 9780593535868 (hardcover) |
ISBN 9780593535875 (ebook)
Subjects: LCGFT: Novels.
Classification: LCC PS3565.A8 Z39 2023 | DDC 813/.54—dc23/eng/20220708
LC record available at https://lccn.loc.gov/2022031406

Jacket image: *Zeno's Arrow.* 1964 by René Magritte © 2022 C. Herscovici / Artists Rights
Society (ARS), New York. Photo: Banque d'Images, ADAGP / Art Resource, NY
Jacket design by Kelly Blair

Manufactured in the United States of America
First Edition

To Kate Hughes

Contents

I

Zero-Sum

1

K. has been invited. But only barely.

2

No more! Can't endure it.

Excuses herself from the convivial gathering, enters her hosts' house blundering and blinded in the shadowy interior after the dazzling outdoors above the lake.

Invisible she is not likely to be noticed.

Near-inaudible when she (rarely, hesitantly) speaks she is not likely to be missed amid the bright chatter like flashing scimitars.

In search of a bathroom, most plausibly. A wounded heart requires privacy.

Of course: she might have simply asked the Professor's wife where the bathroom is but too shy, sulky-shy, damned if she will interrupt a conversation, draw attention to her*self*.

Also: could not possibly have asked Professor M. with whom she has not exchanged a single word beyond *Hello!* since arriving at the gathering a little more than an hour ago.

Just—not—*possible*—to utter the vulgar word "bathroom" to Professor M., to whom words are so important . . .

And so, inside the unfamiliar house. Stumbling, like one with a prosthetic leg.

Blinking in the shadowy interior, like a nocturnal creature.

A single large room with a peaked ceiling, well-worn sofas and crammed bookcases and a fireplace opening onto a dining-kitchen area, long butcher-block table cluttered with pans, kitchenware, printed material—magazines, books. She stares, she is dismayed, evidence here of the eminent philosopher's domestic life, jarring intimacy in the very casualness with which books are mixed with household items. On the rough-hewn plank floor beside the fireplace a wavering six-foot row of back issues of *American Philosophical Journal.* Nearby, a single very soiled girl's sneaker.

Sharp smell of raw onions, cloying-sweet smell of wine.

Steeling herself for a twinge of nausea.

How *he* has disappointed her! He will never know.

Beyond the kitchen area there's a door, surely the bathroom she thinks as her hand reaches out, turns the doorknob but opens the door startled and abashed to discover, not a bathroom, not even a room, just a kitchen closet—canned foods, cereal boxes, jellies and jams, Tabasco sauce . . . Quickly she shuts the door. *What am I doing!*

Blunders along a hallway. The T-shaped log house above the jewel-like lake is built into a hill at its rear, pine boughs casting a filigree of shadow against the window at the end of the hall.

He'd referred to it as a *cottage.* Far larger than any *cottage* she has ever seen.

Resenting this. Resenting *him.* Inviting her out to the lake to insult her in front of the derisive others.

Should have discovered a bathroom by now, obviously she has missed it. Boldly passing an opened door, glances inside to see a screened-in porch, must be at the (older, more run-down) rear of the house and not visible from the terrace above the lake and so she steps inside squinting—but seeing then, to her embarrassment, that there's a person on the porch, seated in a wicker swing with chintz cushions, reading.

"Hi!"—K. is quick to preempt the situation since the girl, presumably a daughter of the household, has seen *her*.

The girl regards her coolly. Vexation like a shimmering reflection on water, in her small pale face.

A face in which, if you look closely, there is something wrong: a subtle asymmetry. The left eye rigid in focus, the right eye more alert, alive. Unusually dark eyebrows nearly meeting across the bridge of her nose, thin resolute lips.

A girl as like K. herself at the age of twelve or thirteen as a mirror image.

3

Come help us celebrate the end of the term. RSVP appreciated. Thank you!

How does K. *know* that she was invited to the gathering at Professor M.'s house on Lake Orion *only barely*?

Well—she doesn't *know*. Not with absolute certainty.

However, she has reason to (strongly) suspect that others in the seminar, Professor M.'s favorites, were invited several days before she was invited, a deduction based upon evidence inexplicable otherwise, overheard remarks in the seminar room and in the hallway outside the room, murmured replies, cautioning smiles (for *she* was near, though staring intently at her cell phone, still they seemed cautious of her, or wary of her: the two motives were often mixed in her experience, indistinguishable; though among her relatives another motive, a wish to *protect*, might be involved); a fact that, assuming what she'd deduced was true, at least several others received invitations the previous week, perhaps not everyone in the seminar (fifteen) but certainly several, thus it follows that she can *know* that her invitation was belated: arriving in her inbox at 10:28 a.m. Tuesday morning.

Of course, only the arrival of the invitation allowed her to know, in retrospect, what those (certain) others, Professor M.'s favorites, were talking about the previous Friday.

At the time *she* hadn't a clue. Nor even a suspicion.

And there is no disputing this: the invitation to the end-of-term party was an email invitation, presumably the others' invitations were email also, so, her brain spins tirelessly, the delay of a day, or two, or three could not be attributed to the U.S. Postal Service, obviously her invitation had been sent in a different/later mailing, impersonal, that's to say *not personal.* Though addressed to her.

To clarify: addressed to *S. L. Karrell.*

Not by Professor M., she is certain. By his assistant. Issuing the invitation in Professor M.'s name.

Shameful: instead of declining the invitation, the insult of the invitation, for certainly the invitation came *days after* the first invitations were sent out, she, *S. L. Karrell,* eagerly accepted; worse yet, in an appropriated voice, a voice not her own, blithely cheerful, giving not a hint of the hurt she felt most justifiably, and most righteously, typing the breathless reply

Thank you very much. I will be there!

But thinking it over, calibrating the punctuation, deciding to amend to a less manic

Thank you very much. I will hope to attend.

And again thinking it over, considering the slovenly illogic of the future tense, deciding to amend to a more precise

Thank you very much. I hope to attend.

4

For always, K. *gives in.*

For rarely, K. will *hold out.*

As Professor M.'s (clearly precocious) daughter does not *give in* just because a stranger is smiling inanely at her. As instinctively perhaps, the daughter resists the urge of firing neurons in her brain triggered by the other's smile, to smile.

She has thought she'd mastered such resistance(s). The (ill-advised) journey to Lake Orion has unsettled her defenses.

Seven miles from the university. Meaning that those without vehicles (like K.) will have to beg rides with someone with a vehicle.

A forced mingling. Conviviality. With K.'s rivals. With those who, if they could, would tear out her throat with their teeth.

Where of necessity K. is *out of place.*

Where she (alone) is *out of place.*

It is always thus. Once *out* of place, one can never be *in* place.

For once *out,* the concatenation is broken.

A corollary: those *in* have no idea that they are *in.* For they have no idea of *out.*

Only those *out* have an idea. For *out* sharpens the brain like a razor-sharp scimitar while *in* is a browsing meek-necked creature in a herd in a pen oblivious.

5

Oh! That's it.

Seeing, on the girl's left leg, not visible from the doorway, an aluminum brace.

Noting that the left leg is considerably thinner than the right leg, which appears to be normal, though slender.

And how the asymmetry of the girl's face is mirrored in the thin slight body, so careful in its movements; reserving its strength (K. sees now) as the face reserves its expressions.

Feeling an immediate kinship with the girl. *Like me. Like me.* No brace on K.'s leg but an (invisible) brace enveloping her body.

She has been trapped inside the brace, she has grown stunted inside the brace.

Not sympathy for Professor M.'s daughter, sympathy for her*self*.

"If you tell me your name, I'll tell you mine."

In her soul, K. is no more than twelve, thirteen. All the rest is subterfuge.

Startled, the girl laughs. Her eyes are veiled, reluctant. But seeing that K. is waiting expectantly she says, with a shrug: "Hertha."

"Hertha! That's a beautiful name."

Vehemently the girl shakes her head.

"It is *not*. I hate it."

"But it's unusual—'Hertha.' I've never met a 'Hertha' before."

"Of course you haven't! No one has."

"Are you named for someone in your family?"

"Yes. A great-grandmother on my mother's side. Or great-*great*-grandmother. The claim is Tuscarora blood."

Smiling, seeing that she has made her visitor smile. Relenting a little, not so annoyed now at the intrusion, but wanting K. to understand that she *is not* impressed with her own ancestry, or with the pretensions of her mother, only just embarrassed.

"So, what is your name?"

Out of nowhere, a feather blown on the wind, inspired by the Native American reference—"Kestrel."

"Kestrel." The girl repeats the name, doubtfully. "Isn't that some kind of bird?—hawk?"

Meaning to be exact, even pedantic, K. explains that *kestrel* is just some syllables, in English, meant to identify a certain species of predator bird; but *Kestrel* is also a surname, her father's family name.

The girl's lips twitch in a smile. She suspects that she is being teased.

"But what is your first name?"

"Kestrel."

"Oh, that's silly. You are—Kestrel Kestrel?"

"No, just Kestrel, Hertha. There is just one of me."

They laugh together. Gaiety leaps between them like an electric current.

By which time K. has stepped onto the screened-in porch. Uninvited but not not invited, either.

6

Game theory is a paradigm of life, unless life is a paradigm of game theory.

In game theory, a *zero-sum* game is one in which there is a winner and there is a loser and the spoils go to the winner and nothing to the loser.

And the sum of the benefit/wealth gained by the transaction is zero.

Rawest of economics, Darwinian natural selection. The weak fall by the wayside, the strong roll their carts over the bones of the dead. Take no prisoners, no negotiations. A Hobbesian universe, tyranny of might makes right.

Vulgar American soul: Winner take all!

Of course, there is the possibility of the non-zero-sum game.

In theory, all knowledge posits a *non-zero-sum* situation. For one person to acquire knowledge does not subtract from another's acquisition of knowledge. For one person to acquire an appreciation of "culture" does not subtract from another's acquisition.

K. has never been sure what "love" is though she has been hearing the word, the soothing/seductive syllable, for as long as she can remember. In its purest form—(if there is indeed a purity of something so lacking form)—love is the quintessence of the *non-zero-sum* game. For two can love equally, it is claimed, and their love is then doubled, not halved; neither player "wins" and neither player is doomed to "lose" and nothing is lost. In theory.

In reality, however, "love" has seemed to K. the very quintessence of the *zero-sum* game.

No idea how to play this game, so K. steers clear. No trust, no hurt. Cannot even imagine another person laying hands on her body.

Penetrating, entering—*no*.

It's humiliating enough, her wounded heart, her disappointment in Professor M., who has failed to acknowledge her as she should be acknowledged, but (she is sure!) she is not *in love* with Professor M.

In a Ph.D. program highest ranked in the United States, notorious for its savage competition in which weaker students are in constant danger of being *winnowed out,* Professor M. confounded his seminar by announcing, at the first meeting, that he was proposing a *non-zero-sum* model for the term: so far as he was concerned he had no interest in "grades" and would happily give everyone in the seminar just one grade at the very end of the term, and this the identical grade for all.

"Here is my proposition. To curtail competition, and the 'negativity' that, I am told, accompanies competition, which mitigates against the joy of exploring philosophy that is the primary reason for exploring philosophy, I propose that everyone agree to receive the identical grade."

Stunned silence. Nervous smiles. Glances about the long oak table, quizzical, frowning.

Each individual at the table gripped by *thinking* as by migraine.

Was this proposal a variant of the prisoner's dilemma? A trick? A *joke*?

Until at last, after an excruciating silence, one person raised his hand to inquire which grade this would be?

"A minus."

A minus! Uneasy laughter, weak smiles. Professor M. benevolently oblivious as the Buddha gazing upon them all equally.

Each thinking: *But I—I am not A minus. I am A.*

And among them, negligible in size, easily overlooked, frowning, deep-set eyes grimly moist, K. sat with her arms tightly folded across her narrow flat chest as if to hold herself very still, willing her rapid heartbeat to subside.

Not me. Not me. I am not one of you.

Seeing the expressions in their faces Professor M. assured them that they could vote on the proposal—anonymously. Secret ballot!

"No one should feel pressured to vote one way or another, or even to vote at all. Our subject for this seminar is 'the philosophy of mind' but of course it is *philosophies,* and *minds,* in the plural, that is our true subject. I will pass out ballots"—busying himself, like an earnest kindergarten teacher, carefully folding and tearing rectangles of blank paper, passing the ballots around the table for each to take one, shielding their vote from the eyes of others as anxious children might do.

K.'s hand trembled as she block-printed NO on her ballot and folded it over.

"Thank you! Let's see how you have voted."

Gathering the ballots back, frowning as he sifted through them—all (fifteen) ballots in a single pile.

"Well, it's unanimous—'No.'"

Around the table, nervous laughter. Relief, excitement. But also dread.

"So you have rejected 'non-zero-sum.' You have rejected the safety of a guaranteed grade in the hope of earning a higher grade for yourself. Though it is probably the case that some of you will regret this decision, still it's a worthy decision. Rejecting the safe harbor of 'socialism'—casting your lot with 'taking your chances'—that is all you can do."

K. was vastly relieved. For what would her grade be worth if all the grades were equal? *She* did not want to be equal to anyone else, there could be no merit in that.

Still more, a grade of A minus had little merit.

"However, my seminars are not 'zero-sum.' I do not confer a victory on one person, and defeat upon the others. That is not a principle of mine. I have no objection to giving all A's if that grade is deserved—not likely, but not impossible. My indifference to grades—my contempt for 'ranking'—will not interfere with my professional duties. The future lies all before you—to make of it what you can."

Later, as the seminar disbanded, someone asked Professor M. if other seminars in the past had voted differently and he'd laughed, saying, No. Not one.

And were the votes unanimous?

Yes. Always.

"And yet, I am always waiting to be surprised."

K. went away suffused with rapture, which is an excruciating sort of dread. *She* would be the agent of M.'s surprise.

7

Seeing now, invisible until she has approached more closely, a single aluminum crutch on the plank floor beside the wicker swing. And the girl's (bare) left leg, (bare) left foot, so white as to appear, in the shifting filigree of light, luminous.

Too young for multiple sclerosis, K. thinks, shocked. Not polio, surely. A birth defect? A rare neurological condition?

Yes K. is shocked but also gratified. For her first impulse has been to feel envy, jealousy. That this (flawed) girl is *his*.

And always he would love her more than me, if he loved me.

The wife—maybe not. But the daughter, yes.

Difficult to absorb the fact that M. has a family. Wife, now a daughter—a household like any other.

Out of the womb of the wife, the daughter. So banal!

That M. is (after all) a biological being, sexual, sensuous. While nothing of the *biological being* is suggested in the Professor's mastery of words, the surgical precision of his reasoning.

A side of the great man that is ordinary. Nietzsche would say— *Human all-too-human.*

K. cannot help but feel foolishly stricken, betrayed. There have been famously celibate philosophers—Spinoza, Kant, Schopenhauer, Kierkegaard, Nietzsche—but it's naïve to expect celibacy of contemporary American philosophers.

Still, K. is disappointed. Just slightly.

K. asks Hertha what she's reading and is surprised when Hertha shows her the paperback cover—Orwell, *Nineteen Eighty-Four.*

"Isn't Orwell a little too 'grim' for you? I mean—depressing . . ." *She* had not read Orwell until she was much older than Hertha, she is sure.

Hertha laughs disdainfully, baring small child-sized teeth.

A silly *adult* question, K. should know better.

"I *like* 'depressing' things! That's how you know they are true."

"Really! What do your parents think?"

"*Nineteen Eighty-Four* is on our recommended reading list at school. We choose books for extra credit in Advanced Placement English, we write five-hundred-word critiques. I've already read *Animal Farm,* and *Lord of the Flies* . . ."

"What grade are you in, Hertha?"

"Ninth."

Ninth! K. would have guessed seventh grade, possibly eighth. But Hertha is obviously older.

Fourteen? Her physical condition has stunted her development.

Small for her age. Delicately boned. Unnerving asymmetry of the eyes.

K. wonders if the girl has begun to menstruate yet?—probably not.

She had not begun menstruating until the age of sixteen, at which time the experience was something of a trauma, best forgotten. Since then, so-called *periods* do not come *periodically* but intermittently. If she forgets to eat, loses weight, she ceases having periods, which is preferable.

Certainly Hertha is underweight. Thin-boned, with a prominent collarbone, like K.; and those wistful shadows around her eyes . . . K. would guess that Hertha is as appalled by the thought of menstruation as she was at that age.

At the mercy of the body. A female body. What ignominy!

Hertha acknowledges: "It is kind of scary to read *Nineteen Eighty-Four.* You can see how our world could turn into that world—'Big

Brother Is Watching You.' Surveillance cameras everywhere, and people informing on one another. That would make me saddest— that you couldn't trust anyone."

"You could always trust *someone*." K. speaks with a buoyant sort of enthusiasm, guessing that this is the appropriate response to so melancholy a remark from a young adolescent.

"In a dystopia, you could not trust anyone. Because everyone would be terrified and would inform on everyone else to be spared punishment."

Hertha pronounces "dystopia" carefully. K. is sure that she didn't know what "dystopia" meant at Hertha's age.

"Do you ever discuss your reading with your parents?"

"Dad, never. Mom, sometimes. She's kind of busy, she doesn't really have time to sit down and read an entire book. But she knows who George Orwell is, I mean—the kind of writer he is. A 'prophet.'"

"But Orwell didn't really prophesize, did he?—it's many years beyond nineteen eighty-four now, and we are not living in—is it Oceania? There may be cameras in public places but there are not cameras in private places . . ." K. knows that this is probably not true: but she means to sound uplifting. Badly she wants the philosopher's daughter to smile at her again, that quick shy ravishing smile.

Hertha says: "There's something like face recognition in the novel. When Winston Smith comes home and has to check in with the TV monitor. This was before computers, when Orwell was writing. But it's like a computer is scanning Winston Smith."

K. asks why Hertha doesn't discuss her reading with her father and Hertha says with a shrug that her father isn't interested in books like *Nineteen Eighty-Four* or *Animal Farm*.

"Dad wouldn't waste time reading 'dystopian fiction'—that's just fantasy to him. He is contemptuous of fantasy. He doesn't have time for the real world, he says, let alone an 'unreal' world. He doesn't have much interest in history, he says if it has happened once, it will never again happen in the identical way, so what point is there in learning about it? Studying language, logic, mathematics—that's different because it's 'real.'" Hertha speaks sardonically as if inviting K. to laugh with her. "I don't think that Dad has even read George Orwell. He'd call him a 'fantasist.' I think he said, once—he has never finished reading any novel—in his life."

"Really! That's hard to believe," K. protests. But yes, K. believes.

She can barely force herself to read fiction, or most nonfiction; it's the very nature of language she distrusts, ordinary language, which is so imprecise, and used so sloppily by most people to deceive and manipulate one another. Any kind of "reconstruction" of something from experience, and not the experience itself on the page, in words and symbols, with nothing to distract, just seems to her futile.

K. asks if Hertha knows what sort of work her father does? "Philosophy of mind"—"deconstruction"—"semantics" . . .

"He tries to explain, sometimes. But we can't follow him. He gets impatient, and it's worse than nothing, that he's *trying* to make things clear, but we can't understand. There's some simple statement—'It has stopped raining.' 'All Thebans are liars.' 'What is there?' But it never means what you think it means. Some statements are *all-priory,* and some are not. There's the *imperical*—that isn't on a high level. Dad used to give us articles he'd written in journals, but not lately—I guess he's given up. Mostly, Daddy is the man who eats meals with us and doesn't talk a whole lot."

K. is stunned. What a profoundly ignorant—profoundly *sad*—statement for Professor M.'s daughter to make . . .

A daughter unworthy of a father. *She* would be so different.

"Did your father try to explain his work to you when you were a little girl? About language?—sentences? Examining words closely? It might almost have been easier then, I think it would have been easier for me."

"'Easier'? With what?"—Hertha looks at K. skeptically.

"Easier to understand his thinking. When you were younger."

"Why should I care what Dad is 'thinking'? Almost nobody does, including Mom."

Seeing the look of surprise in K.'s face Hertha adds that nobody in her father's own family knows what his work is. They respect him—(she thinks)—but they don't take him seriously as they would if he were an engineer, for instance; one of his brothers is a chemical engineer.

"I don't think Dad even noticed me until I was nine or ten and he could talk to me. Someone said that Dad thinks children are like robots."

"Your father never said that! It was just a metaphor, it was misunderstood."

"Or, maybe: children *are* robots."

"That was a paper on Descartes—'The Body-Mind Problem.' His argument has been totally misunderstood and misquoted. It has nothing to do with actual children, or even robots. It isn't even about a Cartesian principle; the entire paper is a deconstruction of grammar."

Hertha gazes at K. blankly, no idea what K. is talking about.

"Anyway, it wasn't children but animals, considered as machines, not robots."

K. sees that Hertha's interest is fading. To align herself with the father, the older generation, would be an error.

K. tells Hertha how gracious it is for her father to invite his students to a farewell luncheon—and in such a beautiful place, on a lake. No other professor of K.'s has ever done that.

K. asks why Hertha hadn't joined them at the luncheon?—she was invited, surely?

Hertha rolls her eyes, shrugs. As if to say *yes, sure, so what.*

"Your mother prepared a wonderful buffet . . ."

Wonderful buffet. K. hears these puerile words with disdain. Trying so, so hard to flatter this girl!

Thinking: the ear of the other corrupts us. We speak to be *heard.* Words corrupt. Words speak *us.*

Why K. avoids such occasions. Avoids people. Cannot control

these others, who so intimidate her, overwhelm her, existing as they do apart from her and with no reference to her . . .

Airily Hertha is saying: "Sometimes I do come out to meet them. Dad's 'graduate students.' But I didn't feel like it today."

So casual, the disdain. Hertha is a haughty spoiled brat but what bliss, to be *her.*

Taking wholly for granted that the great Professor M., a younger colleague of W. V. Quine, a colleague/rival of Donald Davidson, is, to Hertha, merely *the man who eats meals with us.*

For M.'s graduate students this occasion will be one to remember through their lives, for the spoiled daughter of M. it's perceived as a boring waste of time she'd managed to avoid.

"I spend a lot of time alone here at the lake. I don't need to be talking to people all the time. I hate school!—it's too *noisy.* Dad is like that, too—he'd rather be alone. Inviting you all here, once a year, it's what he does, some kind of tradition from Harvard. He's always saying how his philosophy professors invited him to *tea.* But he doesn't really *like it,* he hates it. When you are all gone he's exhausted. He goes into his study and shuts the door and leaves Mom to do the cleanup. We won't see him again until tomorrow morning."

K. laughs, hurt. "Does he hate us—or just having us here, at his house? But he invited us."

Hertha shrugs. "I don't know, who is 'us'?—Dad won't remember any of you, it's all erased, anything he does, anything he says to people, it isn't real to him. 'Says' is just nothing to him, only writing matters. And only just a teeny part of what he writes because he throws most of it away. When he goes into his study and shuts the door—that's real."

K. has to consider: Who is *us?* K. isn't included in any *us.*

The graduate seminar, comprised of rivals, is no *us.* Certainly!

K. tells Hertha that she isn't surprised. She understands. Of course. Her father must be thinking of his work continuously, he has defined his work as a Möbius strip of problems, anything else would be distracting.

Hertha asks what's a "Möbius" strip; K. explains: "Essentially, something that has no end. Just goes on forever."

Hertha says, that's Dad.

Aligned for the moment, sister-daughters thinking of Dad. Rueful smiles.

Perhaps it's a perfect moment, in its way. Amid so much that is imperfect.

Should leave, K. thinks. Soon. Now.

Awkward with greetings, K. is yet more awkward with departures.

It has been the purest chance that she'd encountered Hertha and yet of course it is also true that there are no accidents in the universe: all that *is* had always been inevitable.

K. is thinking uneasily that Hertha's mother had probably noticed her slipping away from the terrace. Just possibly, Hertha's mother might follow her into the house. Wouldn't approve of a stranger wandering through the house. Wouldn't approve of a stranger cornering her (disabled) daughter like this.

Of all Professor M.'s guests K. is the elusive one who'd failed to look Mrs. M. full in the face, failed to smile appreciatively, scarcely mumbled a greeting to her hostess, shied away from shaking hands.

Rude!—they are whispering of her.

Maladroit, misfit. Autistic.

Does she think she is superior to us?—or, does she think that she is inferior?

The thought of returning to the flagstone terrace is repugnant to K. The eyes of strangers moving upon her, a collective gaze like a net thrown over her . . . And if *he* is present, *he* won't notice her at all.

Far more pleasurable to remain in the screened-in porch. Where K. is a match, and more than a match, for Hertha.

Marveling how like K., this girl. This daughter of M. Beneath the child-face, a terrible adult yearning. Pale thin mouth no one will ever kiss.

I will kiss you! Trust me.

But no.

Time for K. to leave: locate the damned bathroom, her excuse for entering the house. In dread that she will act with Hertha in a way that is irrevocable, unforgivable. For there is no one to stop her.

Go away now. Now!

But Hertha has a serious question to ask of K.: "Is Dad a good teacher?"

K. stares in disbelief, for a moment unable to reply.

"'A good teacher'—that's like asking, was Einstein a good teacher."

"What do you mean? *Was* Einstein a good teacher?"

K. is laughing not in mockery of the sweet naïve question but at the absurdity.

"Nobody cares if Einstein was a 'good teacher'! That's the least important thing about Einstein."

8

Brilliant, very young, skipped grades, not a good idea but it had been her parents' idea, and her teachers' idea as well, pointless to argue otherwise since she'd have been bored, sulky-sullen if forced to remain with "her" class.

So, very young. "Precocious"—"prodigy." Through high school, college. But suddenly not any longer so young: twenty, first year in graduate school.

Stricken with panic in the seminar titled *Problems of Philosophy of Mind.* Taught by the famous Professor M., protégé, collaborator, critic of V. Quine.

For though K. has no doubt that she is the most brilliant of the fifteen students enrolled in the seminar, all of whom are older than K., several of whom are second- or third-year students, the condition of *brilliance* is an essence, not an action; and not precisely an action but a sequence of acts, performed by K. herself, before an audience of others.

Like a top spinning. Impossible to gauge in which direction the top will spin, how precisely the top will fall over. When its frantic spinning will *stop.*

Though the universe is determined in every minuscule detail yet nothing can be predicted beforehand.

Not the movements of the most elemental flatworm, with just a few cells in its brain. Not the trajectory of the human brain, the most complex mechanism in the (known) universe.

"S. L. Karrell"—this name Professor M. pronounced at the third seminar meeting, glancing about the table quizzically, with a vague smile, clearly no idea which one of them *S. L. Karrell* was, only that a paper written by this individual the previous week had impressed him, and so—"Will you read your paper for us? Thank you!"

Each week they wrote brief papers, critiques of their reading. This week, the subject had been W. V. Quine's theory of "empty names." These critiques were not graded, nor were many read to the seminar, for M.'s seminars were conducted like Socratic dialogues, with M. in the role of Socrates, provocative, playful, unpredictable, demanding, and exhausting, never cruel but sometimes sardonic, solicitous toward those who performed badly, so that one dreaded M.'s *kindness* more than his critical remarks.

K. will remember how her heart ceased beating for a long moment, when M. pronounced her name; how her very being seemed to detach itself from her body, like ectoplasm; quivering in sheer shock that is indistinguishable from ecstasy, as she was made to realize—*He is singling me out! It has happened.*

For K. has always known, in any gathering, that the strongest personality in the gathering, likely to be an older male, is keenly aware of *her.*

Seeing that "S. L. Karrell" was K., the child-sized figure at the table most likely to be overlooked, all but hidden from view by larger persons seated on either side of her, M. did not betray any glimmer of surprise, or disappointment; though others in the seminar had been more impressive initially, and were known to him from previous semesters; S. L. Karrell was new to the program, a stranger to M.

The paper on "empty names" was short, succinct. A matter of

less than five minutes read aloud in K.'s rapid girl's voice, a wavering voice, an insecure voice, a near-inaudible voice, while M. listened closely, frowning, eyes shut, nodding with surprising vigor. For usually M. was impassive in the seminar, a benign Buddha presence at the head of the long oak table.

But then he'd opened his eyes, looked at K. for the first time, pointedly.

"Well. *That* was unexpected, by me at least."

She'd made the Professor happy, it seemed. A kind of heat came into his face, which was a large face, heavy-jawed, with pronounced jowls, lines bracketing his soft-seeming fleshy mouth. Between them there passed the look of understanding, rapport.

After a pause the others asked questions of K., hesitantly. They had not—perhaps—quite understood her paper. Seeing how the Professor had reacted they were reluctant to attack. A blunder now by any of them might be fatal. Nor did they wish to betray envy, jealousy. Answering their questions in clipped succinct words shorn of all embellishment or emotional affect K. was suffused with a secret sense of tremendous elation, peace.

Thinking—*Nothing will ever be so perfect again in my life.*

Her life flashed before her, the life to come: she would enroll in each of M.'s seminars, over the course of the three-year Ph.D. program. She would write her dissertation with M., who would guide her in every particular. Perhaps she would be granted a coveted postdoc position in the department. She would be M.'s protégée, as he had been the protégé of W. V. Quine. She felt for the man a breathless fainting sensation. She could not bear to look fully at him, only sidelong. In interviews M. had spoken of the joy of philosophy, which was akin to grace in religion: "Something we somehow don't deserve, yet it comes to us. It comes to us unbidden."

K. had not often felt that joy but she'd felt it in the seminar room, when Professor M. had turned his full attention, his smiling attention, after so many years of deprivation, upon *her.*

9

It has happened. It has been decided.

All of my life.

In the cavernous graduate library K. sought out M.'s early papers published in obscure philosophy journals, not all of which had been reprinted in M.'s hardcover books; she was astonished that the young philosopher had scattered his valuable publications without regard for the prestige of the journals in which they'd appeared—not guessing, perhaps, in his twenties, how valuable these papers would one day be. Little-known philosophical/philological journals published in Trieste, Taiwan, Tel Aviv, Buenos Aires, Winnipeg—if M. visited a university to participate in a symposium, and if he was approached by the editor of a journal there, he'd given his papers freely, prodigiously. Like a man with gold coins spilling from his pockets.

She was so much narrower, more intensely focused. She would learn generosity from her mentor.

Fascinating to K., she was discovering how elements in M.'s earliest work had been pursued, or dropped, as M. developed his major theories of the natural "instability" and "drift" of language; in a curious reversal, M. changed course altogether in his early thirties, influenced by an older contemporary, Donald Davidson, whom he credited in a footnote, but only minimally. (In later work, M. cited Davidson, sometimes critically, but not Davidson's early work.) K. was intrigued by discovering old, seemingly lost papers of M.'s in areas of logical positivism he'd evidently forgotten, or had repudiated; for two or three years, he published papers on Wittgenstein's *Philosophical Investigations,* but never again; by the time of his major work, when M. was in his midforties, he'd lost all connection with this early work. Yet, K. came to think, M. had taken a wrong turn, for all his brilliance. An earlier position he'd taken on "the limits of language" in contradistinction to Wittgenstein had been sound, essentially.

Thrilling to K., she would pursue this early theory, perhaps. She and M. might work together on related problems. As his protégée S. L. Karrell would be of great assistance to M.; if he wished, she could collate articles of his that had been published in journals, to prepare them for book publication; she could edit, revise; she could draw up bibliographies, prepare footnotes, assemble indices, always tedious tasks. Their names would be linked. Their names would appear together on the spines of books yet to be written.

It's customary for older philosophers to include younger philosophers as joint authors of their papers; the protocol is, the younger philosopher's name precedes the elder. But all in the profession understand who is the protégée, who is the mentor.

One day, K. would (possibly) (surely) be M.'s literary executor. Decades from now. M. would live into his midnineties, like his revered mentor W. V. Quine. Like Bertrand Russell. *She* would see to it that she lived beyond her mentor, to care for him if she was required.

10

But then, something went wrong.

Why, how?—K. would never know.

No less brilliant than ever, indeed more confident. Willing to speak in class, to answer M.'s provocative questions. Somewhat daringly, perhaps, K. once alluded to certain early theories of Professor M.'s, of which no one else in the seminar was likely to know, and that M. himself had (possibly) forgotten. She'd cited Davidson, Quine. Is the body, to the consciousness inhabiting it, an "abstract object"—can we have an a priori understanding of our physical beings? She'd quoted Wittgenstein: Can we have knowledge beyond language? Is there *a* knowledge, or is there just—knowledge? Haltingly she'd spoken, softly, yet daringly as only M. would know; he'd had to ask her to repeat what she'd said; and then he'd simply stared at her along the length of the dull-polished table as if not hearing, disbelieving. His kindly eyes had crinkled at the corners, becoming glassy, indecipherable. His mouth twitched but he'd made no comment, not a word. In the uneasy silence no one spoke. Like water trickling shallowly over rock the moment passed.

But then, a gradual shift occurred. Over the course of weeks. M. never invited K. to read one of the weekly critiques again. M. seemed never to *see* K. as his eyes moved restlessly about the oak table; if she dared to contribute to the discussion, he waited politely until she spoke but never commented.

Undetectable as the slow shifting of seismic plates in the earth.

Drift of continents, drift of language. Drift of word-meanings, which cannot be permanent.

One day K. would pursue this feature of mental life, arguably the most mysterious of all: *drift*.

11

A zero-sum game depends upon the actions of others. That is the tragedy of life lived among others.

Definition of *others: not-you*.

12

One of the prominent Dadaists discovered that he wanted to commit suicide.

But he did not want to be "identified" as a suicide.

As a Dada-ritual he suggested a rite of human sacrifice performed by an executioner.

Assembling twelve fellow Dadaists, each agreeing to be a (potential) (possible) victim.

But who would be the executioner? One by one, they declined:

Pas moi.

Pas moi.

Pas moi.

Pas moi.

Pas moi.

Pas moi.

Pas moi.

Pas moi.

Pas moi.

Pas moi.

Pas moi.

Pas moi.

In this way, disappointed, the Dadaists continued (unabated) with their lives.

13

She knew. Before she'd received the final grade for the term: A minus.

That sensation of sinking, collapsing sand. For all is sand beneath one's feet.

A death sentence, A minus. For, in philosophy, you are either brilliant or not-brilliant.

Aristotle might have phrased it:

A grade of A is a necessary but not sufficient indication of a future in philosophy.

A grade of A minus is an indication of no future in philosophy.

In fact it wasn't the grade in itself: it was Professor M.'s judgment of her as second-rate that was devastating.

You are punishing me. I went too far.

Forgive me!

In her bones, icy-radium marrow. Trembling so that her teeth chattered foolishly like castanets.

Approaching the Professor's office on the highest floor of the Hall of Languages. Light-headed from climbing the stairs. (Elevator for faculty only.) Dared not knock on his door, which was ajar, to indicate that M. was inside at his desk Buddha-like, composed.

A heavy oak door with a frosted-glass window on which was painted, in (slightly faded) black, Professor M.'s full, magisterial name.

She knew: he knew. How he had devastated her.

As he'd known, for how could he have not-known, that S. L. Kar-rell was special to him, not only the most brilliant student in the seminar but special in other, more personal ways in his life.

As she'd hurried from the seminar room too crushed to speak. How on that last meeting of the seminar he'd avoided her stricken gaze. The hurt in her face. The others—did they *know*? She could not bear it, surely he'd graded some of them higher than he had graded her. Several were smiling, basking in their high grades. Not a glance at child-sized K., in retreat, humiliated.

For a fleeting hour, M.'s favorite. Like a balloon filled with he-lium rising, soaring into the trees—soon to deflate, descend.

But you know that I love you, you have stabbed me to the heart.

Can you forgive me?

Climbing the stairs to the highest floor of the Hall of Languages. Heart knocking against her ribs. Eyes smarting tears. Shivering, so cold. At the top of the stairs, paralyzed before the door of M.'s office.

Possibly M. had seen her. If not now, previously. In the corridor outside the seminar room. On the stairs, on the walkway. At a dis-tance, at dusk. Exiting the ancient Hall of Languages downlook-ing, stunned. Waxen-white face from which blood has drained. As a sleepwalker might make her way. As a creature might make her way along a cattle chute to slaughter having been struck over the head with a sledgehammer yet still on her feet, uncertain, swaying and determined not to collapse.

Or possibly, more probably he hadn't seen. *Why* would he have seen?

No more aware of the young woman whose chest cavity he'd gouged out than he'd have been of casually dislodging, with a flimsy toothpick, a minuscule bit of food from between deep-set molars.

14

Wraithlike figure silhouetted against the frosted-glass office door. But when the door is pushed open—no one.

Meaning: not *one*. Of a category of possible *ones* there is, outside M.'s office door, for as far as M. can see down the long corridor, not even a singular *one*.

15

"Hello! You are—?"

At last entering the office. Days later but still her teeth are chattering in terror.

He does not recognize her, it seems.

Of course he recognizes her.

Sitting in the heavy chair with the smooth-worn seat facing the massive desk. Almost it seems to K., as to Professor M., observing at a distance, that the girl is too absurdly small for the chair, her slender legs are dangling like a puppet's.

She identifies herself. An abashed whisper.

So light. Her bones so light she seems almost to be floating.

Trying to speak but cannot, not at first. Her eyes are deep wounds in bloody sockets.

He has been thinking of Euripides. The radiant madness of Medea, of a specifically female vengeance. Of an age, in his early sixties, when the mind begins to cast its net backward not only over the life, but past epochs. Old, old stories, but the blood-jet is always new.

K. identifies herself and M. recalls—yes of course: *S. L. Karrell.* In the seminar they'd addressed one another by surnames. No first names, nicknames. The condition of "names"—"naming"—is problematic, bringing with it distracting and unwanted issues of gender. To M., as he has said repeatedly, names of individuals don't always attach to *actual persons;* the arbitrary nature of such "naming" is illogic, but "not a very interesting illogic."

M. does seem to recall the name "S. L. Karrell" with a little grunt of recognition.

"Ah, yes. Karrell."

Gently smiling, encouraging. The heavy mask-face is impassive, betraying no emotion. K. does not wish to think that this awkward *office hour,* so crucial in her life, is of no more significance to the distinguished Professor than pieces of broken cork floating in a stream, fleeting, forgotten.

At last, when K.'s stammered words run out, M. says, in a fatherly voice: "But your premise is faulty, I'm afraid. There is nothing wrong with a grade of A minus. It is entirely respectable, indeed it is entirely inconsequential, as you must know."

Desperate as a drowning girl thinking—*But not for me! No.*

It has been M.'s way, possibly an eccentric way, but his, never to explain grades. He resents having to assign grades, he has declared himself not an *accountant,* a *salesclerk.* He does not believe that philosophical discourse should be graded. He is respectful of effort, diligence, good intentions yet knows that none of these has any bearing upon the rigorous pursuit of truth. He has said: "The greatest among us may be buried in a pauper's grave, like Mozart. There is no connection between genius and its reception and there should not be any expectation of a connection."

In a philosophy department noted for its eccentric professors M. is not the most eccentric. But it is his prerogative, he explains, that if he must "grade" a student, it will be without explanation; anyone who is alert and reasonably intelligent will know perfectly well from his comments in the seminar, and from others' remarks in the seminar, why an individual's grade is what it is.

"Explanations are vulgar. Intelligent inferences are much preferable."

K. hears herself say, not quite pleading: "Professor, if you could reread . . ."

"I'm sorry, no."

". . . I am just wondering if, if . . ."

"No."

But gently, with an air of regret. Faint red nets of veins in the large sympathetic eyes, pebble-gray, fixed upon, not K., but an ectoplasmic figure shimmering just above and behind her, in a year long ago, a sequence of such figures, each imposed upon the other in a diminishing progression of appeals, pleas, disappointment like a palimpsest.

Truly M. makes no distinction between "genders"—whatever claptrap that is. Female, male, indeterminate—each individual is sui generis, not a type. M. is not a sexist, he has no interest in sex. It might be said that M. has no *interest,* he is all *disinterest.*

Brilliant but like Icarus, this one has flown too close to the sun. S. L. Karrell, more clever than wise, locating an Achilles' heel in the very person positioned to judge her, besotted by adoration and so taking for granted the magnanimity of the other, the sincerity of his mission to seek truth wherever it may lead. Rapidly he'd skimmed subsequent work by this person, uneasily thinking that she (for he recalled, Karrell was *she*) was a broken-off piece of himself not unlike a blood clot coursing through his veins headed fatally for his heart, his lungs, his brain; his earliest self, callow and reckless, disloyal to those to whom he owed so much; the earliest self no longer an acknowledged self, an anathema. And so, through the weeks, rapidly skimming the work of S. L. Karrell as rapidly he skimmed all student work with half-shut Buddha eyes, brain idling, awaiting a spark, and a conflagration that so rarely came, the most accurate odds would be *never.*

Silence has fallen upon them like ether.

Time for K. to leave. The (very awkward) conference is over.

Managing to stammer, near-inaudibly: "I see. Thank you, Professor."

"Thank *you.*"

Gracious. A gentleman. Not the slightest irony in this reply.

But for a long moment K. is too weak to move in the oversized chair. How to summon her strength. Weak-kneed, blood draining from her brain. So very close to pleading—*Oh help me, Professor. Don't abandon me.*

Tries to stand, has to lean against the massive desk. Her breath is shallow and sharp. Her eyes are brimming with tears.

"Ms. Karrell, are you all right?"—M. is alarmed, startled bulk rising from the swivel chair.

K. insists yes, she is all right, still she is light-headed, dazed. Turning to exit the office, missteps, almost falls, M. hurries clumsily to grip her arm, steadies her. He is very agitated, K. can sense.

Assuring the Professor that she is all right. Of course! He releases her arm where he has gripped it just above the elbow, harder than he had wished. She is not looking at the man looming over her, she will never look him fully in the face again. Never plead with him again.

And now, exiting the office. With some measure of dignity. Like one who has been eviscerated, holding her guts intact with her folded arms, yet upright, and her head uplifted, retreating without a backward glance.

16

Come help us celebrate the end of the term. RSVP appreciated. Thank you!

K. has never been invited to a professor's home before. Rarely invited to anyone's home.

Having sent unmistakable signals—*asocial.*

K. is all A's: *asocial, asexual, anaclitic, agnostic, amenorrheic.*

In any case all (possible, if improbable) pleasure has seeped out of the invitation from Professor M. for K. understands that the invitation is belated, after the fact. Others have been invited before her, unmistakably.

Also: to accept the invitation means that K. is dependent upon one of the other students in the seminar for a ride.

One of her rivals, who owns a car. Generous of him to reach out to K., who has never said a word to him all term, has never exchanged a smile, a glance.

Murmuring to him now *Yes thank you. All right.*

Even as her insomniac brain is spinning, careening.

Calculating: if the grade of A minus is indeed unfair and unjust, as K. believes, and K. does not further protest, but accepts it, K. is (therefore) behaving unfairly and unjustly to herself, and an asymmetry has been introduced into her life; but if the grade of A minus is actually fair and just, in the larger context of the seminar, of which, unfortunately, K. cannot be conscious, then there has been no unfair or unjust treatment of her, and indeed she should be content, or even grateful, for the grade.

In *zero-sum* terms, however: if K. exacts revenge and it turns out that the Professor has (truly) betrayed her, having assigned to her an unfair grade, then she will have acted justly; but, if she exacts revenge, and it's the case that the Professor has (in fact) not betrayed her, but assigned to her the grade she deserves, no more and no less, then *she* will have acted unjustly.

If K. fails to exact revenge and it's the case that the Professor has (truly) betrayed her, then she will have acted unjustly, and she will (probably) not get another chance quite like this chance to revenge the injustice; but, if she fails to exact revenge, and it turns out that the Professor has (in fact) not betrayed her, then she will have acted unjustly.

For, if she exacts revenge upon the Professor, and the Professor is (in some way: professional, personal) destroyed, and it is the case that he'd betrayed her, then K.'s act of revenge will nullify the betrayal; but, if K. exacts revenge upon the Professor, and the Professor is (in some way: professional, personal) destroyed, but it turns out that the Professor has not betrayed her, then her act of revenge will have destroyed the Professor and, to a degree not calculable by her, *her.*

Lying awake, thoughts careening. Shallow but ferocious mountain stream rushing over sharp rocks, scintillant in the sun, froth of white water, radium-fulgurate, ceaseless.

17

"Of course your father is a 'good' teacher, Hertha! And much more than merely 'good.'"

K. takes pleasure in assuring the Professor's daughter. It's touching to K., the sweet-naïve Hertha looks to *her* to assess her famous father.

"Is he funny? Ever?"

"Funny!"—K. considers this. Silly question but then Hertha is only fourteen years old.

K. has no idea what *funny* could be in philosophy. Laughter is a kind of mental weakness—isn't it? In the seminar, if there is an outburst of laughter, there is also the patient wait for the laughter to subside, so that serious matters can resume.

M. sometimes smiles, but rarely laughs. K. cannot remember M. even trying to make a joke.

"Well—sometimes he's funny. He has a very subtle sense of humor. Most people wouldn't get it. Is he funny at home?"

"He is! He tries to be. Like, dropping things, or not knowing how something works like the remote control for the TV, that kind of thing. Some things Dad gets wrong aren't intended, like pulling the ice cube drawer out of the freezer and not being able to get it back, or setting the controls for the dishwasher so wrong, Mom can't fix it."

Hertha giggles, a daughter who loves her bumbling old dad. A TV family! In that instant K. feels a blade of sheer hatred slice her heart. She says:

"Your father 'teaches' us by allowing us to observe him thinking. He examines language, syntax—it's like dissection. You know what that is: an autopsy." K. makes a gesture as if disarticulating a body, disjointing a (phantom) body, Hertha winces and laughs, sure. "We are really taught to *think*."

Hertha has closed the paperback *Nineteen Eighty-Four*. Done with it, for now.

"You asked if your father is a 'good' teacher, Hertha—but in fact he's a brilliant teacher. Also, he has written brilliant books. He's famous for elaborating aspects of game theory."

"Is that, like, 'games'—video games, card games? Dad used to try to play tennis . . ."

"No, it's more like a calculus of competition. What we've done this semester is explore a priori and empirical statements. Analytic and synthetic. Analytic statements are essentially tautologies— 'There are twelve apples in a dozen.' Synthetic are more complex— virtually anything else you want to say. It's new to philosophy of mind, to consider the actual human brain. 'Where is a thought?'— 'When is a thought?'—'Who is thinking?' Professor M. has been exploring the 'evidence of the senses'—'scientific method.' This isn't a priori, this is scientific research. Genetics. 'Broken genes'— 'neurological deficits.' "

On the wicker swing Hertha stiffens. Her face is suddenly grave, stricken.

". . . nature, nurture. Eugenics, euthanasia. D'you know what 'euthanasia' is? If an X-ray detects that a fetus is abnormal, should parents be allowed to abort? Do parents have the right to extinguish the life of a 'challenged' infant? Is the child better unborn? If a child is 'challenged'—'disabled'—it may be that three people are adversely affected: the child, the mother, the father. Following the principle of utilitarianism, 'the greatest good for the greatest number,' it would be ethically logical to abort in the womb, to avoid suffering. For some individuals, born with neurological defects, may feel that they would be better off not being born. There is a growing movement in philosophy—'anti-natalism.' *Against* bringing children into the world. These ethical questions your father explores courageously; he has written several controversial papers on the subject."

None of this is remotely true. M.'s papers are famously obscure and, when not obscure, indifferent to the vulgarly *empirical.*

Still Hertha says nothing. Her thin lips are pressed together, drained of blood.

K. says, in a lowered voice, as if someone might be eavesdropping, "Your father is the most remarkable person I've ever met, Hertha. He defies convention. Naturally there are jealous people who would tear him down. There are rumors about him that are totally unfounded. Because your father singles out 'special talents'—has 'favorites'—some of us he initiates into intimate relationships, and not others. He is an outspoken *elitist*. He can be demonstrative in his affections—he can be surprising. He'll put his hands on you so hard it leaves a bruise—then make a joke of it and say, '*You* surprised me.'"

Hertha regards K. with an air of frightened apprehension. *Nineteen Eighty-Four* has fallen to the porch floor.

"He must put his hands on you too, sometimes. You might not remember, afterward—that's called 'amnesia.'"

"What do you mean—'amnesia'?"

"The human mind can't tolerate too much reality. What can't fit in is forgotten."

Hertha regards K. with rapidly blinking eyes. Saying, weakly: "I don't believe anything you're saying. I think that you are lying—you are making this up."

"No. You know that I am not."

"It's all just—it isn't true . . . Daddy never said that—what you said."

"Well, you can ask him. Tell him that 'Kestrel' told you. Watch his face—that will tell you everything you need to know."

Dazed, elated K. leaves the screened-in porch. Never will she forget the expression in Hertha's face.

There! I have done it, I have struck the blow.

18

Just standing there looking lost.

Forty minutes later the Professor's wife is surprised to discover a solitary figure in the rear hallway of her house, one of her husband's guests whose name she doesn't recall, just standing there vacant-eyed and lost but seeing Mrs. M. like a guilty child quickly explaining that she has been looking for the bathroom or maybe she'd found the bathroom, asking now if Mrs. M. needs *help? Help clear the table?*—and before Mrs. M. can reply the girl is bringing platters inside from the terrace, scraping leftovers into the garbage disposal, running water in the sink eager, excited, and not seeming to hear when Mrs. M. tells her thank you but that's not necessary, lunch is ending, guests are leaving, the sun has shifted in the sky, which has become mottled and bleached of color like a pebbled shore seen at a distance and the surface of Lake Orion, usually placid, still as shining glass is shattered by small jagged waves; and still the (excited, white-faced) girl is reluctant to leave insisting upon *helping out* clearing the picnic table (in fact: two picnic tables pushed together on the terrace) of dirtied plastic plates, plastic cutlery and cups, paper napkins, festive paper tablecloths, *helping to clean the kitchen* including even kneeling to scrub at the sticky linoleum floor that hasn't been cleaned (Mrs. M. will joke, recounting the incident afterward to friends) in thirty years until at last Mrs. M. tells her sternly please stop, no more, her friends are leaving now for town and she should return with them, and the girl says in a hurt pleading voice that those are not her friends, she doesn't have any friends, please don't make her leave just yet and Mrs. M. replies she is *so very sorry,* the luncheon is over, the last car is leaving for town, she should please leave now; and at last the girl has no choice but to acquiesce, vacant-eyed and smiling inanely as one might smile facing a firing squad, moving off to join the others in the driveway so slowly and stumblingly that Mrs. M. has to call to them—*Wait! You have one more passenger.*

Mr. Stickum

AFTER SCHOOL we began to hear. Certain incidents at night in the old mill town on the Delaware River.

Pop-Up Parties—for (adult) men.

Girls from Eastern Europe, Asia, Central America were available for a fee. These were girls between the ages of ten and sixteen. Or maybe six and sixteen. They'd been transported by night. Initially, some of them, in the (fetid) hulls of ocean vessels. Then, in the (fetid) hulls of cattle trucks. Kidnapped? Or sold into bondage by their parents? single mothers? state-run orphanages? They did not speak English. Which languages they spoke, the beauty of these languages, the sorrow of these languages, how *love* was uttered, how *grieving* was uttered, how *loss* was uttered in these languages we did not know. In the (fetid) hulls into which the girls were herded by men who did/did not speak their languages they must have whispered, shuddered, moaned, wept, and sobbed in one another's arms but in languages we did not know.

Their skin that should have been as soft as ours was rubbed raw. The hair on their heads that should have been lustrous as ours was thick with grease like gristle. Lice scurried over their scalps, stung, and drew blood. Their eyes—oh, you had to know that their beautiful long-lashed eyes were luminous despite burst capillaries and that they stumbled and groped in daylight like the blind after the long solace of the night.

Informed that they would be tortured—"cut to pieces"—if they did not obey. Their families, whom they would never see again (they knew), would be murdered if they did not obey.

(Were there translators? In our imagining, there would have had to be translators.)

(Translation is the most tender of all the arts. Yet, in this case, translation must have been crude, cruel.)

Most of the *child sex slaves* (as they were called) had been abducted in Eastern Europe, then shipped to the West. There was a smaller contingent of Asian girls, including the very youngest (and smallest—some of them reputed to be toddler-sized). Other girls were captured at the U.S. southern border, where they were separated from their families by Border Patrol agents, housed in barracks-like camps behind razor-wire fences or, in special cases, delivered into the custody of Homeland Security Defense consultants who arranged for them to be transported in windowless vans to far-flung parts of the United States.

Sex slaves taken into custody at the U.S. southern border were believed to differ significantly from those from Eastern Europe and Asia because their families had not given them up voluntarily or sold them; indeed, these girls were taken forcibly from their families, who were not likely to forget them, though they had no means, legal or otherwise, of locating them once they were shipped away from the border and into the heartland of the United States.

Sex slave trafficking was a lucrative business, we learned. Sizable cash payments were made to local officials who oversaw the border patrols as well as to the politicians whose decrees made possible the (legal) breakup of families and the subsequent transportation of the girls in a network of Pop-Up Parties through North America.

Rumor was, such Pop-Up Parties took place only a few miles from us. In the night as we slept in our tidy clean-sheeted beds *child sex slaves* our age (and younger) were forced to endure disgusting *sex acts* in motels at the outskirts of our town on the Delaware River.

Which motels?—we thought we knew. On the curving River Road were Days Inn, 7$ Motel, Rivervue Motor Court, Holiday Cabins. Some of these derelict hovels were no longer open for customers but available for short-term (Pop-Up) rentals.

In the night. We'd been told.

Rumors that made us shudder, and grate our teeth in disgust. Rumors that made us shiver, and hide our faces in our hands. Rumors that made us sob in disgust, and laugh uncontrollably. Rumors that made us *scream* into our pillows.

Rumors that bubbled and smoldered like molten earth underfoot where the soil is poisoned by toxic waste—yet when you search for such a place you can't—exactly—find it.

Though with every fiber of your being you know it exists.

Rumors that stuck like glue in our guts. Rumors that would not be dislodged. Rumors that excited us, made the hairs at the nape of our necks stir.

Out of such stirrings—*Mr. Stickum.*

At our table in the school cafeteria leaning our heads close together so that our long rippling hair(s) mingled. Hot wet palms of our hands smacking the sticky table in balked fury. *Disgusting! Perverts!* Gagging sensations, choking our vehement words.

One of us, not the oldest but the most indignant, the very one whose father had not long ago abandoned his family—("Be sure Dad had another way of expressing it")—seized a ballpoint pen, began sketching in a notebook.

Swine! Deserve their throats cut.

Deserve their peckers cut—off.

Laughing wildly, joyously. Earthy braying laughter not "feminine"—"girly." Every other table in the cafeteria dimmed, our table in the corner shone with a radiant light, levitated. For we were the hottest girls, and we were the smartest girls, and we *did not give a fuck* who hated us for being who we were and not who they wanted us to be.

One of us, pen in hand, rapidly sketched the spiral device to be known as *Mr. Stickum.* As the others leaned over staring in amazement.

Where was *Mr. Stickum* coming from? Out of the ballpoint pen? Out of our friend's hand?

A small-boned hand, fingernails bitten to the quick. But the deft unerring hand of the artist.

See, here?—Mr. Stickum.

Hours/days of exacting work and coordination required for the ingenious creation—*Mr. Stickum.*

Deciding upon the material. For girls not accustomed to making crucial decisions (beyond clothes and shoes we wore to school) this was the great challenge.

What would be most practical for our purposes?—we wondered.

Not paper, even thick paper. Not cardboard, even thick cardboard. Not wood, even plywood. No.

Because the material would have to be resilient, would be required to bend. As the captives struggled, the material would "struggle" with them but not snap or break. *Brittleness* must be avoided.

It would have been helpful to ask an older girl for advice. A woman teacher. One of our mothers . . .

No! Better not.

The fewer who know about Mr. Stickum, the better.

Stealthily we rummaged through the basements and attics of our homes where (cast-off, forgotten) things were stored. We had not enough money among us to make extensive purchases but we could not find anything quite right for *Mr. Stickum* as he was imagined in the sketch.

One windy autumn day after school riding our bicycles to the county landfill three miles away. For much of the trip the headwind slowed us but the last ten minutes was glorious gliding down-hill standing on our pedals like Valkyries with our hair rippling behind us in the wind.

One of you/them might've seen us. That is possible. We like to think so!

How distracted you/they were by the sight of seven girls on bi-cycles pedaling single file on the shoulder of the county highway. Coasting downhill exquisitely balanced on their pedals.

So distracted, you'd almost turned your vehicle around to follow us . . .

No. Better not. American girls, white girls, girls with families, might be relatives, friends' children, can't touch. Not these.

What a surprise, the county landfill! Acres and acres of cast-off things, trash, yet also clothes that looked still wearable, furniture, kitchen appliances, garbage bags torn open, spillage that stank even in the open air. As we tramped about the landfill holding our noses scavenger birds fluttered upward on wide beating wings. Turkey vultures—were they? (We shrank from their red eyes, cruel hooked beaks fashioned for tearing flesh.) Also crows, smaller and more animated than vultures, though still large enough to seem dangerous to us, cawing and crying at intruders in the trash.

The angry birds beat us back. Still, in our cautious way(s) we persevered.

That first search, defeated by sudden rainfall, wind. Hasty retreat.

Second search took us into dusk, flashlights were required but the spirit of *Mr. Stickum* must've smiled upon us: we discovered a fresh mound of debris including sheets of (scrap) vinyl.

In all, a half-dozen sheets of badly discolored vinyl of which not one was entirely whole. But we would need that many sheets at a minimum.

Not easy transporting the clumsy vinyl sheets on our bicycles to a secret place where we could work together—but we managed.

———

By this time the original sketch of *Mr. Stickum* had been enlarged on sheets of that thin but tough paper used for architectural drawings. (Paper purloined from the home office of one of our fathers, an architect.) By this time we'd acquired an essential piece of equipment—a powerful staple gun (borrowed from the workshop of one of our fathers who "wouldn't miss it"—"he hardly goes out in the garage these days even if he's home").

Plan was to create a giant flypaper strip in the shape of—oh, what's it called—

Möbius.

Mö-bius. When there is no end to it, a loop, a spiral, spinning, infinite . . .

But no, *Mr. Stickum* was not *infinite*. With the vinyl strips stapled together, by the time we were finished, and it did take time, *Mr. Stickum* measured twenty-three feet from top to bottom. *Finite*.

Strictly it was not a true Möbius strip we were creating out of scrap vinyl but rather a pseudo–Möbius strip—according to the one of us who knew math, or anyway knew more math than the rest of us did. For a three-dimensional model of a Möbius strip is not a Möbius strip. A true Möbius strip is a two-dimensional surface with length and width but no thickness. *It has only one side.*

The pseudo–Möbius strip to which we would give the appellation *Mr. Stickum* was identical to the two-dimensional strip except—it existed in three dimensions.

We were anxious that the strip was supple enough to be given a half twist, and the ends of this (single) strip could be stapled together. Without this crucial feature in the design, *Mr. Stickum* would not be realized.

Though it sounds easy, it was not easy. Much effort went into the creation of *Mr. Stickum* in three dimensions.

This was only the start, however. Greater effort came next.

(No. We never inquired *why,* or *where* Mr. Stickum came from. We never doubted that *Mr. Stickum* came somehow out of the night and yet dwelt within us like a luminous spirit. For we were of that age when an appetite for justice is fierce as an appetite for food when you are starving.)

(Where were our parents, you are wondering? Our parents were where they'd always been: in our lives yet oblivious of us.)

(Were our parents *not aware*? *Not—suspicious?*)

(Very easy to convince them that we were at one another's houses doing homework, having supper, sleepovers.)

(Were our parents somehow *not real*?)

(Fact is, *Mr. Stickum* was far more real to us than our parents.)

(No one is *less real* than parents. A "parent" is a sort of full-body mask that presents itself to you as a complete entity when in fact, as common sense will tell you, if you take time to think about it, this "parent" is but a parenthesis in the life of an individual who is essentially a stranger to you, who lived for many years before you were "born"—who had no idea who you would be, or even that you would exist, for virtually all of those years. Then, when you are "born" this individual employs him-/herself as a "parent" assigned to you, for an indeterminate amount of time. The "parent" may be present through all of your life, in some cases. Or, in some cases, the "parent" disappears in time, as you become employed as a "parent" yourself, utterly bewildered, perhaps bewitched, but never doubting that you must don your full-body mask in the presence of your child.)

(No, we were not cynical! We were idealists. We never doubted our mission to protect our *child sex slave sisters* whom we'd never met and would in fact never meet. We never doubted *Mr. Stickum,* who was hyperreal to us, and always with us, and spread out like a spirit inside us. Like God.)

In stealth, in secrecy, by night. In the deserted no-man's-land by the river.

Shuttered factories, mills. Rubble-strewn lots, sites of buildings razed decades ago and their stone foundations open to the night

like gaping mouths. Fading signs on tilting fences—NO TRESPASS-
ING DANGER.

Close by, the rushing river. After a rainfall, the water level was
high and of the hue of mud, bearing with it churning and spinning
debris like living things.

Down a weedy incline from the road, hidden from view by underbrush and small trees, broken brick walls. One of the boarded-
up mills, decades ago a ladies' glove factory . . . With some effort
we forced the door and stepped inside and—here was the space
we'd envisioned!

Here, *Mr. Stickum* was (vertically) established in the shadows
of the partially collapsed first floor. Taking care not to plunge
through rotted floorboards into the cellar below we worked with
flashlights, for it was dusk, and then night. Taking care that our
flashlight beams didn't shift upward, toward the broken windows,
and someone driving past on River Road might glance up, and
see, and wonder what on earth was going on in a deserted factory.

We were short of breath, we began to perspire inside our jeans
and pullovers. Nothing in our lives had prepared us for such a
challenge, and such a risk. Securing *Mr. Stickum* to a substantial
rafter overhead, that the Möbius strip might hang straight down
into the cellar, unencumbered. All of us wearing gloves, taking
care to protect ourselves as, awkwardly, but conscientiously, we
applied glue to *Mr. Stickum:* the strongest glue we could purchase
in a hardware store.

There are ordinary glues, including what is called cement glue,
and there is *epoxy adhesive.* Claimed to be strong enough to bind
together plastics, wood, metal, human flesh.

In this way, in a succession of nights, working together as a team
we created *Mr. Stickum,* in design a gigantic (and ingenious) strip
of flypaper.

Next, we created rumors of Pop-Up Parties at the outskirts of our
small town on the Delaware River.

Like wildfire the rumors spread online. A day, and a night. And another day, and now dusk.

Drawn by the promise of a Pop-Up Party. Drawn by the promise of *child sex slaves.* A customer would enter the passageway between the brick walls and descend downward hesitantly, stumbling in the rubble, yet determined to achieve his goal. *Hello?—hello? Hello—*

Greeted tantalizingly by glossy cutouts of young girls in short shorts, short skirts, skin-tight jeans. Younger than we were, ten to twelve years old with luridly made-up faces, long straight (usually blond) hair falling past their shoulders.

We mingled with the cutout girls. We wore cat masks with stiff horizontal whiskers. High-heeled boots.

Living girls giggling, tittering. *Yes! You have come to the right address, mister!*

The men saw, their eyes glared red.

They came individually. They respected one another's privacy. They did not wish (perhaps) to identify another, that they not be identified themselves. All very careful! Not at all reckless. Discreetly they parked their vehicles as far away as they could. Practiced in this sort of deception and had not (yet) been made to pay for their crimes.

We were excited. We trembled in expectation. Behind our silken cat masks we stifled our laughter as the first of the customers came eager and ardent into the shadows of the derelict old factory and was guided through a doorway, a step down—("mind the gap, sir")—a sudden fall—a cry of alarm—within seconds secured to *Mr. Stickum.*

Flailing to escape *Mr. Stickum,* whose gluey surface stuck in their hair and on their struggling hands and bodies. At first incredulous— *What is this? What—* Trying desperately to pull away, pushing and shoving against *Mr. Stickum,* who only seized them more securely in his grip.

W-What is this? What can this be? Gigantic strip of flypaper upon which the predator thrashes, beats his arms like flies' wings beating in desperation only to bind faster, more securely in the glue.

Crying for help. Writhing, convulsing.

The first customers were middle-aged males—unfamiliar faces—then, a face that looked familiar—contorted, terrified—yet somehow familiar: someone we believed we'd seen in town, or somewhere—whose name we did not know. But then—on the third night—*Mr. Perry!* We were shocked. We were stunned. We could not speak at first for Mr. Perry was one of the teachers at the high school, who taught driver's education and boys' gym and coached the girls' track team . . .

But we recovered. We kept our distance, detachment. We were very excited, we trembled with dread of what we'd unleashed . . . Of course, we did not take pity on Mr. Perry, who was stuck on *Mr. Stickum* practically upside down, a foolish figure, kicking, flailing his forearms, upside-down face flushed with blood, eyes virtually popping from their sockets.

Help me! Help me!—but there was no help.

On the following night—our first customer was also known to us, and even more shocking: Mr. McCreery.

Oh, this was awful! Ceci's father, some of us thought we'd known very well . . .

Behind her cat mask Ceci was very still. We could hear her breathing, we could feel the pain of her heartbeat.

Taking no note, not staring after her, as Ceci slipped away into the night stricken with shame.

But it was too late for Mr. McCreery, as soon as he'd stepped across the threshold, and into the Pop-Up place.

Piteously screaming, begging—*Help! Help me! What is this—No* . . .

We laughed in derision. Might've been tickled by rough daddy fingers, how we laughed. Howled. Recalling how in fact, yes years ago, Mr. McCreery had tickled our ribs, we'd squirmed to escape, and never said a word.

The next shock, next night, a man whose picture was often in the newspaper—a local politician on the town council—Mr. Steinhauer . . .

He was furious, thrashed so hard, plunged and lunged at us cursing, he came close to detaching himself from *Mr. Stickum* with sheer force—but in the end the powerful glue held fast and he was rendered helpless as a fly that gives up the struggle of his wings and is resigned to his fate.

The next shock, Dora's uncle . . .

And there would be several other shocks: "dads" . . . uncles, cousins. Neighbors. Teachers (social studies, boys' basketball coach).

Our town was a small town. We'd had to realize that some of the customers/captives might be known to us but still, you do not truly expect to see the face of a man whom you know well, a man in your own family for instance . . . You do not expect such a man to be a *sex pervert*.

Behind our masks, hot tears streaking our faces.

Tears of sorrow, rage. Tears of humiliation.

But: no one forced these sex perverts to come prowling here in the night for *child sex slaves*.

Ceci returned to us, for Ceci understood. In her household, there was a gaping absence. No one knew where Mr. Perry had gone. (Except Ceci, who grieved with the others.) Mr. Perry's car was found in the parking lot of the old train depot a mile from the river, locked.

The train depot was no longer in operation for trains no longer stopped in our town. But there was a bus stop nearby and so it came to be believed that Mr. Perry had taken a bus and in this way vanished—though no one could remember a man of his description getting on the bus at the time he was believed to have departed.

Fascinating to us how each of the customers/captives generated a (plausible) narrative in his wake and in each case it would be believed that the man had left of his own volition and not as a consequence of "foul play."

A sweet sort of knowledge, to know that what others adamantly believe or wish to believe is mistaken and to have not the slightest impulse to correct them.

Having no mercy too was sweet to us.

For always it is expected of girls, as of adult women, that we will be loving, forgiving, merciful. But *Mr. Stickum* has taught us that is a losing zero-sum game. That has been a prevailing mistake of our sex.

We took pictures of the captured perverts on our iPhones. We recorded their howls of rage, pain. Their pleas.

These were just to share with one another. We deleted all evidence within hours. We were not so foolish as to risk being caught.

What we recall most vividly of those fevered nights: the way we moved secure and swaggering in our masks and high-heeled boots along the rafters of the derelict old factory. Sure-footed as actual cats.

Safe behind the masks gazing down at our pathetic captives strung below us on the vinyl flypaper. Laughing to see how their agitations made the strip turn jerkily, as in a parody of a dance. How certain of the captives were so frantic to escape they'd torn off swaths of skin, leaving raw flesh oozing and dripping blood; but still they could not free themselves from *Mr. Stickum* for other parts of their bodies were stuck fast in the lethal glue.

The most pitiful, one or two captives who'd managed to free all but their heads and were hanging by their hair, in terrible agony.

Bleating, braying, whimpering, murmuring—*Help me! Let me out of here! I will pay you* . . .

Pleading with us as we passed just out of the range of their flailing hands.

One of us said—*Someone should put him out of his misery* . . .

Another said, mishearing—*No mercy! Not for these perverts.*

Several captives became berserk, their brains boiled, convulsing, froth at their mouths. Several suffered heart attacks, strokes and hung limp and lifeless like giant flies whose wings have stilled. One comical fellow managed to strangle himself, having twisted his body around like a pretzel in his zeal to escape the embrace of *Mr. Stickum.*

It goes without saying, all of the captives soiled themselves. Not the most disgusting thing about the perverts but yes, disgusting to our sensitive nostrils.

However, we made no effort to clean any of their messes. In the grimy cellar of the glove factory, where their waste fell, more filth did not matter.

With time we grew more experienced. You might say crueler.

Losing our capacity for *surprise, shock,* which diminished as each of us had been *surprised, shocked* more than once by who turned up writhing and whimpering on *Mr. Stickum.*

One of the perverts calling to me, in his distraught state barely able to speak, head downward, limbs askew as in a crucifixion, tears glistening on a pasty-pale face—*Help me, I am begging you . . . I'm not a bad man, I have a family, I have daughters . . . I am in such pain! Oh God please . . .*

In panic I thought: *He knows me!* But he never uttered my name.

He could see only the cat mask. He could see only the eyes in the cat mask. He could not see *me.*

I walked away trembling, where I couldn't hear his pleas. But I walked away.

Soon, we lost track of how many captives/perverts were stuck on *Mr. Stickum.* The pleasure of observing them, counting them, taking pictures on our iPhones and recording their cries of misery began gradually to fade.

Success is like stuffing your belly. Hunger fades to nausea.

And so after a few weeks we decided to remove all Pop-Up notifications from the internet. Our "virtual" identities vanished. Our chat room friendships came to abrupt ends. For fewer customers were showing up to stumble and fall onto *Mr. Stickum,* and one night no one came at all.

Hard to say if we were relieved or disappointed. Though this was good news—of course.

All of the sex perverts in the vicinity are now captives of Mr. Stickum and can harm no one else.

We wanted to think this. We didn't want to think that local perverts had simply become more vigilant and did not wish to take a chance on a Pop-Up Party at a time when a number of men in the area had "vanished."

We debated what to do with the captives who were still living, or did not (yet) appear to be dead. At first we'd feared that their howls of rage, fear, distress would draw attention but the deserted glove factory was far enough from town; no one heard. There was too the murmurous sound of the rushing river close by, which muffled much sound.

We had never fed the captives, we had never given them so much as a paper cup of water. Not just that we were heartless—we were cautious, and wise: to come too close to the desperate would be to be trapped in their desperation. Especially, we feared the slightest touch of *Mr. Stickum*—we knew that would be lethal.

If we abandoned the factory our captives would die—eventually—of thirst and starvation, which seemed to us a (relatively) painless death, considering their depravity and the wickedness in their hearts. In time, their befouled bodies would be devoured by scavengers—turkey vultures, rodents. Insects. In time, their skeletons would fall into the murky cellar. Their bones would be mixed together in a common grave.

On the last evening when we returned it was to discover that every captive was dead! Their bodies hung limp and lifeless from the gigantic flypaper strip and something dark—blood?—streaked the length of their bodies. In the dark there were slow dull dripping sounds.

Someone had come surreptitiously and slashed the captives' throats!

One of us, we had to suppose. But which one?

We never knew. At least, I never knew.

She'd succumbed to mercy, whichever one of us it was. For slashing the throats of perverts was a merciful, kindly act. A gesture that must have involved a good deal of effort from one unaccustomed to wielding a razor-sharp butcher knife, let alone wholesale slaughter.

Hastily we departed from the factory, and never returned.

We have no pictures of *Mr. Stickum*. We have not even the original plans, sketched in a fever of inspiration in our school cafeteria.

All evidence linking us to *Mr. Stickum* was destroyed.

All of us remained friends—that is, *we remain friends*. Our bond is *Mr. Stickum* though we never utter his name or include it in any email or text message.

We all went away to college. We were good students, in the wake of *Mr. Stickum* we were mature and self-reliant students who did not have to be urged by parents or teachers to excel.

Eventually, we suppose the deserted glove factory will be razed, and a mound of skeletons discovered in its cellar—but that has not happened yet.

The same old derelict buildings remain on the river behind semi-collapsed wire fences that warn NO TRESPASSING DANGER.

Most of us return to visit our families several times a year. We were always dutiful daughters and we are scarcely less dutiful now. We lie in bed in the night in our former rooms, with at least one window open. Some of us lie sleepless beside deep-sleeping husbands, awake and alert and suffused with yearning for the time of *Mr. Stickum,* which has faded from our lives. But if we listen closely we can hear faint cries borne on the wind from miles away—*Help me! Please help me . . .*

Nothing sweeter than falling asleep to the beautiful music of sorrow, heartrending pleas in strange languages. The wind, the rippling churning river, the cries of the damned.

Lovesick

A N UNKNOWN PERSON, male, has left phone messages threatening to murder her, E__ tells me. He'd used the actual word—*murder.*

In a lowered voice E__ tells me this, within seconds of our meeting in the café. A quivering voice in which I can discern, I think, a *frisson* of pride.

Murder!—this is a shock.

Not what I expect E__ to confide in me when she'd asked the previous night if we might meet at short notice.

Seeing what must be a stunned expression in my face E__ adds quickly that she has no idea who it is, who is threatening to murder her, for of course this would be my first question: *Who?*

No idea!—E__ repeats as if I might have to be convinced; for it does seem doubtful to me, that a woman as intelligent as E__ wouldn't have "any idea" who might care enough about her to want to murder her, or to make that threat.

I don't say this, of course. Not yet. Nor do I interrogate E__ about the alleged threats for she's looking fragile, distracted.

It's sympathy E__ wants. Someone in whom she can confide who isn't in her life.

That's to say, in her *intimate life.*

Terrible, I tell her. Just—outrageous . . .

Laying my hand atop hers to comfort her. Not seizing her (small, chill) hand in my (larger, warm) hand, nothing like that. Only just a neutral sort of comfort that won't be unnecessarily protracted.

. . . so sorry to hear this, E__. You must be terrified . . .

E__ has often surprised me with remarks I could not have anticipated but never anything quite like this, which has nothing to do with me, and no relationship to our (tangled) history together.

As soon as I'd sighted E__ approaching the table I'd reserved for us on the café terrace I understood that something was wrong: oversized dark glasses hid her eyes, her face, which is usually "radiant" in social situations, was stiff, masklike. E__ was even walking oddly, with a curious sort of caution, like a drugged or drunk person, as a blithely smiling hostess led her through a maze of tables.

And her stylish Issey Miyake clothes fitted her loosely, as if belonging to another woman. A cream-colored pleated top with one flaring sleeve longer than the other, a matching mini-pleated skirt with a jagged hemline.

Was this E__? Her face was very pale as if drained of blood. Her mouth was too brightly red and her smile was wan, weak.

This was not our usual greeting. This was a very restrained greeting.

As I stood, awkwardly jarring the table, E__ leaned toward me, somewhat off-balance, and awkward also, lightly brushing her (chill) lips against my cheek.

Well—hello!

Hello . . .

Slithering-sinister as an eel the thought came to me—*Something crucial has happened between us, something has changed.*

I had no idea what this might be. With E__, much could happen *in absentia.*

Where once we'd seen each other rarely less than once a day I hadn't now seen E__ in nearly five months. A seismic shifting in my life to which I'd adjusted, to a degree.

(Admittedly I'd occasionally seen E__ at a little distance, by chance, without waving to her, or identifying myself; indeed, shrinking out of sight before E__ could see me.)

When I'd written to E__, last March, not a lengthy email or a terse declarative message indicating that a reply was expected, simply a casual, friendly email veiling no deeper meaning, E__ hadn't replied.

(On principle then, I'd declined to write again to E__. If our relationship is a zero-sum game I am hesitant to put myself in the humiliating position of knowing unmistakably that I have lost while, if I resist writing again to E__, I might console myself with the possibility, actually a likelihood, that E__ hadn't received the original email or had lost it amid her daily flood of emails; but if I'd written a second time and didn't hear from her it would mean that E__ was deliberately not answering.)

(In this sort of absurdly petty zero-sum game what is risked isn't money but pride. To risk so much, and to lose—some of us, grown canny with age, have learned to retreat from playing.)

Of course I tell E__ that I am very sorry to hear her shocking news. And very concerned for her.

Asking her if she'd told anyone else. If she'd notified the police.

No, and *no.* E__'s response is vehement.

Certainly she hasn't told anyone in her family, E__ says. (But why *certainly*? I don't understand.) She did notify the police. Just once.

Despite knowing that police officers are likely to be indifferent to women who report threats from men, even from men who've already abused them; and that the threats she was reporting could be dismissed as mere harassment, intended only to frighten.

So far, E__ has received five or six messages. (She isn't sure about the sixth, and maybe there was a seventh, she now deletes messages without hearing them unless she knows the caller.) After the third message she called the police, asked to speak with a woman officer but none was available, or so she was (rudely) told, was put on hold for five minutes or more. The (male) police officer who took the call asked few questions of E___ and didn't seem very interested in hearing the contents of the messages; E___ realized it was hopeless and hung up, angrily.

For a day and a night (she says) she'd worried that someone might call her back from the police station or even come to the house unannounced but of course no one did, no one cared in the slightest, and that made her angry, too.

They ask: Is this someone you know?—E___ says. They're convinced you must know who it is, who's leaving threatening messages. As if it's some kind of stupid game. Or flirtation. As if you're to blame for being threatened.

Blame the victim—you can hear it in their voices.

E___ laughs bitterly. It occurs to me, I have never heard anything remotely resembling a bitter laugh from E___ before.

Yes: *blame the victim.* Especially if the victim is a beautiful woman.

Lightly I say this, not at all accusingly. Sympathetically. For it's true: E___ is a beautiful woman, and has lived her life behind the protective scrim of beauty. And so there's the temptation to blame E___ for her beauty attracting the wrong sort of attention, like expensive gems held out carelessly in the palm of a hand.

E___ hides her face in her hands when I make this remark. For a moment I think she might burst into tears.

But no, E___ recovers. Her pale skin is looking mottled, as if I'd actually spoken harshly to her, or slapped her.

No one thinks I'm beautiful, E___ says quietly.

Hesitating then, for surely she meant to add *except you.*

To this, I make no reply. When I'm in an emotional state I distrust words, especially my own, for a misspoken word cannot be retrieved, and is irrevocable.

E___ reverts to the subject of the police, a safe subject about which she can be incensed, indignant: how like a fool she felt, what a fool she *was,* calling them, what had she expected?—local police officers barely investigate sexual assaults, rape. They're hyper-vigilant to peaceful protesters, Black Lives Matter, crimes against property but have no time for crimes against women or mere messages left on an answering machine, which, E__ says, she'd deleted, out of disgust.

Deleted?—so you have no proof, now . . .

My voice is sharp with disapproval, disappointment. But I must be patient with E__, she has been frightened, and isn't thinking clearly.

Yet, how exasperating E__ can be! I am remembering, now.

E__ says defensively she hasn't wanted anyone else to hear the messages, they are so ugly, obscene.

She'd thought of calling 911 but the situation wasn't *literally* an emergency, there wasn't *literally* someone in the house trying to kill her. The last thing she wanted was a squad car with a blaring siren pulling into the driveway of her house . . .

E__'s voice trails off. Awkwardness here, that E__ should speak of a house, a residence, which, so far as E__ knows, I haven't seen, and certainly haven't been invited to enter.

(In fact, I do know exactly where E__ is living. I do know the address, which I have memorized. But E__ doesn't know that I know.)

To deflect this awkwardness I ask E__ when the most recent message was?—and E__ tells me, just yesterday.

Late afternoon, she'd discovered it when she returned home. Like all of the messages from the unknown caller, left on the answering machine after three p.m., of a weekday, and before six p.m., as if he knows that no one is likely to be home at that time.

Some sort of gloating distorted voice, E__ says with a shudder. Definitely male. Not a boy, an adult.

In no way recognizable?—I feel the need to ask.

Of course not! No.

E__ asks if there's some sort of device you can use to distort your voice over the phone?

Yes, probably, I tell E__. There's every sort of surveillance device and spyware available now to civilians via the internet. But I don't actually know of anything specific.

I'd thought that *you* might know, you're so skilled in the new technology.

E__ speaks with a cryptic smile, an air of reproach. A weak echo of what would have been, in other circumstances, a flirtatious remark: as if E__ were blaming me for the fact that I happen to know more than she does about the "new" technology.

To be older than twenty-five in the America of the twenty-first century is to be confronted, confounded by the "new" continuously; and both E__ and I are much older than twenty-five.

But this is a moment of, if not actual flirtatiousness, mock-levity, a wan allusion to days past when E__ did indeed tease me about my so-called technology skills, which were (she'd seemed to be suggesting) provinces of male knowledge inaccessible to one like herself.

I assure E__ that I could only seem "skilled" in comparison to an individual who has never made any effort to keep up with technology because she knows that if she needs help, someone will always help her.

E__ laughs; this is an oblique kind of flattery.

Much of our mutual discourse *is* flattery. At least, on my side.

Our drinks are brought, not a moment too soon. Exhilarating to me, to see that E__ *needs* this drink.

Why hasn't she changed her telephone number?—I ask E__.

I am not scolding. I am not being reproachful. This is a perfectly logical question.

E__ stares at the tabletop with a faint wan smile as if trying to articulate a plausible answer.

Explaining, then: it's the landline he calls. The house phone. "Unlisted"—of course.

Not E__'s cell phone and so not *her* phone, exclusively.

Something about this reply seems wrong to me. Off pitch.

E__'s warm beating heart in my hand, a trapped bird. I *will not* take advantage.

Assuring E__ that of course I would help her, in any way she requires help. In any way possible, plausible. Unspoken between us, the changed circumstances of E__'s life, which should have rendered such an offer redundant.

And *of course* I would help her if she needed help with her computer.

To this, E__ seems too moved to reply. A glimmer of gratitude, gratification in her face.

For during the most intense years of our friendship, now nearly a decade ago, I'd often helped E__ with her computer, printer, iPad, cell phone. Of course!

We'd never lived together, that was a (melancholy) fact. But often I was at E__'s apartment—(she'd lived in an apartment then, the top floor of a beautiful old Edwardian mansion converted to a multiple-dwelling building)—through the night.

Night begins to end not with a lightening sky but before the lightening sky with the first tentative calls of birds, not *calls* so much as *queries.*

In our part of the Northeast, the first birds to wake, to utter these *queries,* are cardinals.

Granted that elsewhere, the first morning-birds are likely to be seabirds.

E__ concedes that yes, she supposes the person who has been threatening to murder her would have to be someone she knew, or had once known; (possibly) an old acquaintance, or someone she'd known professionally; (possibly, though she didn't like to think this) someone associated with her husband . . .

So now, E__ is acknowledging H__. Until this moment, not a hint that H__ exists.

Referring to him as *husband.* As if I didn't know the man as H__.

Even as E__ speaks in a breathy confiding way she isn't exactly looking at me. Nor am I looking at her.

In a (tangled) relationship there are protocols that must not be violated. No more than one would touch the eyeball of another with a forefinger. You just *would not.*

(But could one acknowledge these? Dare one take the risk?)

(The unspeakable is a category that should be respected: Do. Not. Speak.)

Still, it seems to me a sort of subterfuge, a false note, that E__ would refer to her husband H__ as *husband* and not *H__* since both E__ and I knew H__ before H__ became her husband; and that, since E__ (certainly) knew this, speaking in this way could only be a kind of cruelty toward me, a provocation.

(Is all provocation between male and female sexual in origin? Intention?)

I find this impasse disturbing but I am gentlemanly enough to be determined not to acknowledge it.

Let E__ imagine that I haven't been annoyed, still less wounded.

Shaking my head as if to clear it. To clear it of *her*.

As E__ continues to speak, in the vague tones of apology, I glance about the (buzzing, thrumming) café with the sort of general benign bland interest with which one glances about a café, as if with the expectation of seeing a familiar face. Though not, in this instance, a *familiar* face.

For all I know, the "gloating" would-be murderer is observing us.

Certainly, keenly aware of us. As a couple (?). (But this unknown person would know that E__ has a husband, and surely the husband's identity.)

Quite possibly, he has followed E__ in her car. To this very café.

(As in a movie. A certain sort of movie—a "thriller." The kind of movie, an old-fashioned melodrama, vintage Hitchcock for instance, in which the slow-witted viewer is alerted to suspense, danger, romance, terror by the tone of the music.)

(The kind of movie in which the glamorous female lead behaves with inexplicable recklessness and naïveté while the stoic male lead bears the burden of behaving responsibly, plausibly. Protectively.)

When E__ called me, last night at eleven p.m., to ask me to meet her for lunch today at one p.m., she'd suggested this café as *neutral ground*. As if, in our (tangled) relationship, which never failed to remind me of Laocoön and the ghastly serpents, there are carefully calibrated territories in the city: hers, mine.

In a way this is probably true. And there were—are—those places we'd often frequented—restaurants, museums, coffee shops, cafés like this but not this café in an unfamiliar hillside neighborhood where no one is likely to know us, in theory at least.

Among the patrons in the café, no one seems likely to be the "unknown" caller. No one makes an impression on me. But of course I can't see every face clearly, and I don't want to appear to be staring.

Our waiter, hovering near, seeing me glance about, comes to take our lunch orders. He has approached us, and been subtly rebuffed, not once but twice.

It makes me smile, E__ orders exactly what I expect her to order while (very deliberately) I order a specialty of the day E__ could never have predicted of me.

E__ smiles, too. Quizzically. On the brink of asking why on earth I'd ordered what I'd ordered but hesitating as if, at this delicate point in our lives, such a question assumes an intimacy we no longer share.

All this time I've been wanting to ask E__ why she'd invited me to meet with her, why she'd wanted to confide in me, after her silence of months. A deafening silence, it has seemed to me.

But of course, that's the kind of question I can't bring myself to ask, for reasons of pride.

Lovesick is an insipid word, still more an insipid condition. No dignity in *lovesick*.

Sickly sweet like the odor of gardenias. Frosting on hot cross buns, a sugary assault on the tongue.

E__ knows how I adore her. How she can rely upon my adoration never to waver, wear out. Weeks, months, even years might pass, E__ can depend upon me to remain unswerving while E__ herself might change utterly, if she wishes.

It is unfair, unjust: *lovesick*.

But a fact: if love is a seesaw, unevenly weighted. One side *up,* the other *down.*

In love, one is loved more, the other less. This can never be doubted, never contested, rarely acknowledged.

Still, I am capable of irony, even sarcasm. I do not treat E__ like a fragile butterfly with brittle wings. Remarking that it isn't surprising the police would be suspicious, expect her to know who cared enough about her to want to murder her, isn't that only logical? And isn't the spouse, ex-spouse, lover, or ex-lover the first suspect in a murder?—everyone knows that, from watching TV. E__ must know that.

But E__ repeats, really *no.* She has lain awake nights miserably sorting through the men she knows, virtually everyone she'd ever met who might be capable of such behavior, fastening upon someone, then discarding him; fastening on someone else, then realizing that it couldn't be *him.*

The first thing they ask, E__ says, by which she presumably means the police, is *could he be a lover? Ex-lover?* In this case, E__ says, very carefully, I told them the answer is *no.*

A pause. I make no reply, neither frowning nor wincingly smiling.

Nor do I say, with heavy irony—*Darling, thank you!*

It is certainly possible, E__ says, that (in fact) she doesn't know the person but he knows her, or has seen her somewhere, has fixed upon her, become obsessed with her, God knows why.

God knows why. But why *is just the excuse.*

Whatever pretext for a random obsession that feels like fate.

Lifting her wineglass E__'s hand trembles. This is painful to see. I admit, I'd felt a little *frisson* of satisfaction that E__ is in distress, thus needing me, or imagining that she needs me; but this initial feeling has quickly faded, I am feeling upset on her account, and concerned.

Asking E__ what can I do for her? (For obviously, E__ must have some reason for contacting me, yes?)

E__ laughs uneasily. What could I *do* for her?

Not sure that there is anything anyone can *do* for her, E__ says. Practically speaking.

To protect herself totally she'd have to keep indoors, or hire a twenty-four-hour bodyguard, or move away to some secret place.

Uproot her life, change her life completely. None of that is possible.

For, in situations like this, you really can't know if the threats are serious. You should, it's said, behave as if they are serious, and yet, for practical reasons, how can you?—simply, you can't.

To this, I listen gravely. It occurs to me that the "threats"—(of which I know nothing specific)—might not be serious, only just intended to terrorize E__; at the same time, of course, they might be serious, and E__'s life might really be in danger.

Either/or. No (plausible) way to predict.

Which is exactly what the "unknown person" wants, no doubt.

E__ is saying that she is anxious much of the time, but still, un-expectedly, the fact that someone wants to "murder" her has had the effect of making her feel, well—*special.*

Because, E__ says, hurriedly, seeing the look in my face, it means that this "unknown person" is thinking of her, in a particular way. In a way no one else has thought of her. Or has ever thought of her.

As if she were *important.* In some way *unique.* Needing to be punished, cut down to size.

Oh, she knows this is a bizarre thing to be saying, ridiculous, shameful, she can tell no one except me; but it's a fact, in her entire lifetime she has never been so singled out, never has she meant so much to another person that whoever it is would risk so much by threatening to "murder" her, leave such messages when he might be caught, might actually be arrested . . .

Ridiculous! Rudely I interrupt saying that she erased the mes-sages, didn't she?—thus has no proof. Even if the police were inter-ested in investigating.

In a way, E__ is protecting the "unknown person."

E__ stares at me, stricken. *Protecting—!*

Well, yes. *De facto.*

No disguising it, E__ has annoyed me. Plenty.

But persists saying she knows it sounds wrong, she is trying to be candid, honest, which (she'd thought) she could be safely with me, admitting that since the messages on the answering machine she has been feeling as if someone were watching her at all times, she is never *alone.*

Because *he* is thinking of her, whoever *he* is. In some way she could never imagine and could never think of herself.

Jesus!—shaking my head, this is so—repugnant . . .

I know, I know, E__ says hurriedly, I hate hearing myself. I am just trying to be accurate. None of this is anything I can tell anyone else.

Well, this is touching of course. Calculatingly so.

I've finished my glass of wine. A blazing sensation falls upon me, from the opalescent sky. For a confused moment, a streaking comet in daylight.

I am beginning to see why E__ wanted to confide in me: she knows that I won't judge her; and even if I did, even if I judged her harshly, unlike members of her family I would never cease adoring her.

Lovesick is *foolproof.*

There is love, ordinary love, normal love, E__ is saying, but beyond this love there is a kind of *fated love.*

Fated love!—(is she joking?).

Seeing my look of exasperation E__ tries to explain: not that the object of such an obsession can return the feeling, but it has to be *love* of a kind, doesn't it?—*fated love.*

Ridiculous, I am thinking.

Just—*no.*

Glancing distractedly about the café another time to see if anyone is watching us. For now I feel that yes, *he* is.

Of course, if *he* were present, *he* would be too cagey to watch us openly.

When I'd first arrived the café terrace was nearly empty. Now, most of the tables are taken. A popular, trendy place in an upscale shopping area where I'd reserved an outdoor table in a corner. In such circumstances I make it a point to arrive early and position myself with my back to the wall so that I can scan the scene. No one can come up behind me, or beside me, taking me by surprise.

E__, seated across from me, seems grateful to have her back to the patio.

My eye is drawn to men, in particular solitary men. Reasoning that a man in the company of another person, especially a woman, isn't likely to be the "unknown person" desperate enough to threaten E__.

For there has to be desperation in such threats. Recklessness, rage.

As I am beginning to feel, not rage, but anger, exasperation, as E__ continues to speak haltingly, yet with that subtle air of pride, about this ridiculous notion of hers—"fated love."

Meaning, E__ says earnestly, that whoever it is thinks about her a great deal, (probably) more than anyone has ever thought of her.

It's different from being *loved*. There is such risk in it, such hatred.

On the tabletop, E__'s hand. Tremulous as a wounded bird.

The temptation is to cover the hand with my own. Squeeze hard!

Hard enough so that the rings cut into her fingers, diamond-sharp. Wincingly sharp.

This temptation, I am determined to resist.

But you know, I tell E__, as if I'd just thought of it, not meaning to be cruel but just candid: it isn't all that unusual—*stalking*.

E__ recoils a bit. Is that what it is?—*stalking?*

Well: what else would you call it? Not *romance*.

Now just slightly there's bitterness in my voice. The set of my mouth. So, forcing my mouth to smile.

With her fingertips E__ wipes at her eyes behind the dark-tinted glasses. Right hand, right eye; left hand, left eye. At the brink of emotion E__ manages to be poised as a ballerina. As in our love-making: at the very brink of climax, resisting, retreating, the poise that comes with fear, if not terror.

E__ has laid down her fork, the Waldorf salad has been scarcely touched.

A pause. Neither of us speaks. My heart is beating quickly, erratically.

Again, I feel an impulse to seize E__'s hand. To prevent her from leaving, if she jumps up from the table, to flee.

Unexpectedly, E__ squints and smiles at me. For indeed I have been cruel.

(*Had* I ever been cruel, in the old days? Truly, I can't recall.)

Wondering, she says, what I am thinking?

Thinking? I'm not thinking anything, I protest.

Transparent in my emotions, through my life. Like a glass. In which you can see emotions emerge like bubbles in water. Like breath.

Lovesick. It's obvious. She can see.

Insisting to E__ that I'm not thinking anything. Except I am upset, agitated thinking of her.

The useless police! The madman leaving her messages . . .

Though (in fact) I am wondering if she has told me everything.

If, just possibly, there's something she has left out.

What's the fancy word—*lacuna*?

E__ stiffens. E__ tries to laugh. A revival of her old flirtatiousness like a butterfly stunned by cold, managing to lift just one wing.

Asking me what I mean? "Lacuna . . ."

How would I know? Seeing that it's a *lacuna*.

Maybe you're thinking, E__ says slowly, that I'm not telling you the truth, exactly.

Why would I think that? *Should* I think that?

Because you're a "deep thinker"—not shallow, like some of us. Not easily fathomed.

Once, I'd wondered if this *deep thinker* accusation had a ring of anti-Semitism to it but now, probably no. E__ is, if you can be such, sincerely disingenuous.

E__ laughs, her spirit reviving. The stunned-butterfly wings beating a little harder.

What I'm thinking, E__ says, is that you don't believe that I don't have any idea who he is—the unknown person.

Like the police, you *don't believe.*

You've been pretending to agree with me, out of politeness. You've been nodding, you're "sympathetic," a habit of yours, our friends love you for it, it's comforting to them, but sometimes, to me at least, it's annoying, because it seems, sometimes, to me— (maybe not to others but definitely to me)—mechanical, perfunctory. Being "sympathetic" is a kind of mask that allows you to think what you truly think in secret. Which you're careful never to reveal.

This is confounding! This, from E__, in a not-accusatory voice.

Watching me closely. Cruelly. Actually leaning forward, across the table. Lightly laying her hand on my arm, a shudder runs through me.

She knows! Of course, this is a game to her.

I'm just being objective, E__ says with a shrug of a shoulder.

And I, I–I'm being objective, too . . . But my voice is weak, unconvincing.

E__ says reflectively, when we were together—(speaking matter-of-factly in this vein, like an anatomist wielding a surgical instrument)—you know, in those days, years—you didn't think of me much. I mean—the closer I was to you, the more I loved you, the less reason you had to *think* of me.

Always there was something distracting you, at a distance. Something "major." Because I was so close to you, it's as if we were a single person, you no longer had to be concerned about me, in a way I *was* you.

A kind of annexed territory, E__ says, laughing. Showing her small white teeth.

Like Puerto Rico: not a state, but not free, either. Under the authority of. Under the jurisdiction of. A *territory*.

Was this true? In some way, true? Not now but, well—then.

A man requires a woman about whom he doesn't have to think constantly so that he can think about his work in which he competes with others, notably men.

E__ is saying, not at all bitterly, that she understands. No one wants to *think constantly* about anyone, not even children.

In her own childhood, she'd been a kind of *lacuna* in her parents' lives. They were high-achieving research scientists at Penn. They could spend as many as one hundred hours a week in their laboratories. Each became a consultant to Pfizer—"Big Pharma." And when an experiment or a project ended they sought out lovers, desperate to catch up with the life they'd been missing. When not working researchers have an excess of nervous energy they have to discharge. Like powerful motors, idling.

So, E__ had been left alone. There'd been a succession of babysitters. Watching TV or on cell phones. Distracted by boyfriends who'd come into the house, surreptitiously.

E__ speaks bitterly but brightly. Of course I'd heard much of this before, in a different context.

No wonder she takes pride (she says ironically) in a deranged person fantasizing about her, imagining that she is important enough to "murder."

All this, I've heard in silence. I've finished my second drink, and have ordered another; and another for E__ as well.

Our lunches are scarcely touched. Platters of expensive food, on colorful Mexican-glazed plates.

This is a small smug pleasure: knowing that, when E__ ordered a Waldorf salad, she would instruct the waiter with a prim little frown—"no walnuts, please." And knowing that, when I ordered a portobello mushroom "steak" with avocado, E__ would blink in childlike amazement.

My fork has fallen askew across my plate. E__'s fork too, at an odd dissolute angle.

Quietly I tell E__: he is probably someone you know. This "unknown person."

E__ says yes, probably. She knows.

If she were hypnotized, possibly she could identify whoever it is, E__ says, with no interference from her conscious brain.

The police will say: just tell us *who you think it might be.*

Just *name names.* Quick, without thinking. The first person you suspect will be him.

In fact, you probably know him too, E__ says, peering at me. A light touch, a tap, perhaps a reprimand, her fingertips touching my wrist.

Surprising me now, as (surely) she has intended all along: taking, out of her elegant woven bag, several sheets of paper.

E__ has, she says, transcribed the phone messages. Like scripts. She'd listened to each message before erasing it, typed it out, printed it from her computer.

You see, E__ says, showing me the first page, I've marked it "disguised voice"—as in a play. Would you read it for me?

Clumsily I take the page from her. This is happening so quickly—unexpectedly—I am not prepared. Thinking more clearly I'd have laughed and pushed her hands away.

Will you? Please? Read aloud? Not loudly of course. Just—to me.

I am staring at the neatly printed words. My throat closes, this is not possible.

Cunt. You know who you are, don't you.
Yes, you—"E_." Tell me you don't deserve to be murdered.

Hey—"E_"? Are you listening? (Sure you are!)
(unclear words) deserve to be murdered, don't you.
Any objections?
(muffled laughter)

Hello hello!
I have been watching you cunt & you are aware as you
    should be.
(unclear words) "garrote" prepared. You will like this.
(unclear words) you will "call the shots"—with your own
    body-weight.

Hairs stir at the nape of my neck. I am unable to read these hateful words aloud. My eyes sting with tears, the words blur.

E__ is watching me closely. Is this a test? (Does E__ suspect *me*?)

A sensation of cold washes over me. A rivulet of sweat running down my side, beneath the peach-colored Zegna shirt.

(E__ hadn't purchased this shirt for me but we'd shopped together at Neiman Marcus. Fancy men's shirts on sale, 70 percent marked down post-Christmas of which year, I could not say.)

The printed pages fall onto the table. There are more, too many. Clumsily I push them toward E__.

No, I don't care to read these sick stupid words aloud.

Just rip the transcript up, I tell E__. Change the damned phone number.

Tell H__ you're receiving too many robocalls. Solicitations. Change the number yourself, that will solve the problem.

E__ laughs airily. Oh, will it! Just changing the phone number.

Get rid of the landline altogether. All you need—you and H__— are your cell phones.

Don't be ridiculous, E__ says. He'd just find another way to threaten me. This way I can monitor the threats, at least.

Like walking past an attack dog, behind a fence. I can see the dog, I can hear him, I know where he is. I know that there's a fence.

Jesus! You should avoid provoking him, at least. Avoid public places.

Not that I am scolding E__, I am not. Nor am I passing judgment, that is not my role in E__'s life.

Sweating inside my clothes. Shivering. E__ has been watching me closely.

E__ agrees, of course I'm correct. But after the pandemic, the long quarantine, she has been too restless to stay home.

Some risks, you have to take.

Some risks, you have to take. Where'd you get that, a Chinese fortune cookie?—such wisdom?

I am trembling, so angry. But of course, *I am not angry.*

Calmly—frankly—asking E__: You want to live, don't you?

No. Yes. I don't know.

Telling me: I mean, if whoever it is is serious he'd have tried to kill me by now. He'd have killed me by now. That seems obvious.

No. Not at all. You can't assume that. A mentally disturbed person can't be predicted.

Oh, I doubt that he's "mentally disturbed." He seems plenty organized, calculated. He certainly knows *me.*

Enjoying intruding in my life. My private, personal life. Knowing that I'm thinking about him. Talking about him. Confiding in someone close to me, about *him.*

Almost, I feel a stab of jealous hatred, for this *him.*

Asking E__: If you have no idea who the hell he is, what satisfaction is there in that? For him? It's all so abstract.

It isn't abstract at all, E__ says. It's close as a heartbeat. He can know that he isn't alone, just as I know that I'm not alone. There's a connection between us, invisible to anyone else. Even if it's sick, perverse.

Well—it *is* sick. Perverse.

And how would *you* know? The "deep thinker"—E__ laughs, with startling hostility.

The terrace is beginning to clear. We have been lingering over our uneaten lunches.

Not far away, a gaunt man of youthful middle age with a spade-shaped beard is sitting alone, food on his plate only partially eaten. He has been typing furiously away on an iPad. White shirt, sleeves rolled to his elbows. He has been "busy" as if performing.

Is this *him*? E__'s *murderer*? Risking detection in this way?

Elsewhere on the terrace is another solitary man, thicker-bodied, with a shaved head, earring in one ear, a black T-shirt tight-fitting over a fatty-muscled torso. Some sort of *artiste,* tattoos on both arms. He has been joking with the waitress. A local celebrity, is he? He has glanced in our direction, perhaps thinking he knows me.

(Well, I too am a "local celebrity." I guess. And maybe we know each other, through mutual acquaintances. Possibly.)

Probably he isn't the type, I'm thinking. Too at ease, relaxed. If he's an ex-lover of E__'s he wouldn't be circuitous, he'd come right over to confront her.

Others in the café, of lesser interest. My heart is still beating erratically as if I were in the presence of danger.

The waiter is removing our plates and glasses, he has brought our check, which I take from his fingers.

Of course: I'll be paying with a credit card.

E__ makes a feeble offer to lay out her credit card, I won't hear of it.

Don't be ridiculous. Really!

You are so old-fashioned, E__ says, embarrassed. You are so predictable.

Is that why you called me last night?—because I'm so predictable?

Tediously predictable. Of course. Why would you even ask . . .

We laugh together. If the iPad man, or the tattooed man, glances at us, he can see that we are a couple.

On our feet, leaving the table. Crossing the terrace naturally I guide E__—my hand against the small of her back (which feels alarmingly warm, the pleated fabric must be thinner than it appears, like paper).

It gives me a spiteful sort of pleasure to know that the "unknown man" might be watching us: the iPad man, the tattooed man? Another?

E__ too glances nervously about the terrace. Her gaze is fluttery as a hummingbird, daring to settle nowhere.

Reminding me of a conviction I'd had frequently, years ago: a beautiful woman accustomed to being *seen,* and isn't so practiced in *seeing.*

The shallow soul, doomed. Depth of a teaspoon.

In the parking lot E__ leans to me, in farewell. Daring to brush her lips against my cheek as before. Except now her lips are warm. Her breath is warm with wine.

If I move to embrace her, E__ will draw away. This, I know.

Brittle butterfly wings, self-protective. Beauty as camouflage.

In a tender/affable voice assuring her: I will call her, soon. I will email her. If there is another message, one of those obscene messages, she must let me know *immediately.*

Vaguely E__ promises, yes of course. Her manner is becoming abstract, she is thinking ahead to *home.*

In that instant, I am seized with despair. Yet, the more determined to seem tender/affable.

D'you promise, darling?

Oh yes. *I promise.*

Reluctant to leave each other. Each reluctant to turn our back on the other.

So we must turn away *each at the identical moment.*

What I would like to do: return to the café terrace to see if either of the men is departing, now that E__ has left.

Possibly, one of them is in the parking lot already, poised to follow E__ in her car.

But I can't really do this, for E__ and I are walking to our separate cars, she will notice if I don't drive away.

(Though if I linger in my car, to wait for one of the men, and if E__ sees me, she will know absolutely that I am not the "unknown man"—if she has any doubts, that will dispel them.)

Of course, I may never see E__ again. In the sense that E__ will see *me:* for I can always see E__ at a distance. And I know exactly where E__ lives.

Unless the story, never in my control, swerves yet more wildly out of my control, and I see E__ again, very soon, unexpectedly soon.

Sparrow

T HE MOTHER'S MEMORY was failing. It was a season in which much was failing. The economy, the weather, the earth, marine life. Invasive species were moving in, pitiless and efficient: fish, birds, plants. Karin's father had taught environmental law at the University of Michigan from 1974 until his death in 2017. She'd continued his membership in the Great Lakes Environmental Protection Association and knew from its ominous online postings that more than 180 invasive species had been identified in the lakes in recent years: sea lampreys and alewives of which everyone knew but also more exotic Eurasian ruffes, zebra mussels, spiny water fleas. And invasive birds in Michigan alone!—mute swans, Eurasian collared doves, a hardier subspecies of North American sparrow driving out gentler song sparrows as well as house finches, chickadees, cardinals. At the sliding door to her rear deck in Charlevoix, Karin stood staring at a snowy scene in which deceptively small dark-winged birds fluttered out of dense evergreen foliage in sheer numbers, emptying out feeders within a day or two, ravenous with appetite.

Thinking, if my mother doesn't remember me, what will become of me?

The mother, once so formidable, sharp-eyed and sharp-tongued, continued to live in the family home in Ann Arbor, alone now, since the father's death, overseen by caretakers with whom she was often dissatisfied; in the aftermath of aggressive chemotherapy following colorectal cancer, she was said to be slipping into frontal lobe dementia, though Karin hadn't seen much evidence of that, yet. Calling her mother on the (landline) phone, saying in the buoyant teenaged voice she'd cultivated for such occasions, "Mom, hi! It's—," and her mother would interrupt instantaneously, "I know it's you, Karin. For God's sake!"—with a hurt little hissing laugh.

Since the father's death Karin had become the family chronicler. Relaying droll little tales to a dwindling number of relatives, anecdotes designed to entertain while passing on information, news. *Keep in touch, kids*—their father had urged. Karin spun amusing self-deprecatory tales out of professional frustrations, disappointments, knowing to downplay her (considerable) accomplishments as a poet, translator, editor so that no one in the family was likely to resent her: she had two younger siblings, sister and brother, who seemed perennially on the verge of disappearing from her radar, both living on the West Coast, though nowhere near each other. It was like Karin to send accounts of "invasive species" in a group email to relatives, friends, a litany of ravaging insects in her trees (spongy moth, emerald ash borer), rapacious weeds on her property (poison sumac, ten-foot giant hogweed), marauding sparrows at her feeder . . . Between the lines, the recipients of her emails might conclude that Karin hadn't personal news to tell them, or to wish to tell them. No news in the life of an unmarried woman in her midforties means exactly what it suggests: no news.

Resolutely, she kept her emails nonpolitical. She didn't want to lose contact with anyone out of disgust with their political choices.

Now it seemed that Karin's mother no longer checked her email, had ceased sending email altogether. Karin had no alternative but to telephone her, hoping that one of the caretakers would pick up the phone, to bring it to her mother with a useful explanation—*It's your daughter Karin.*

Strange to have become, in recent years, hesitant to use the phone. She thought it might be generational—few of her friends called any longer, the sound of a ringing phone was jarring. Only a very few people knew her cell phone number and they preferred to write or text. Any sort of surprise had come to be a rude and unwanted surprise, an invasion of privacy.

But when you don't call, and you don't visit, you imagine the phone ringing. A stranger's voice with a Hispanic accent. *Hello? Is this Karin? Mrs. Arhardt's daughter? I'm afraid there is bad news . . .*

The plan was for Karin to help her mother pack, preparatory to moving into an assisted living facility in Ann Arbor. From Charlevoix in northern Michigan to Ann Arbor in the southern part of the state was a distance of about 260 miles, a drive of four hours, not long as road trips go, yet Karin kept postponing the drive.

Too sad!—moving her mother, essentially against her will, into Stonebridge Manor, or Stonehenge, whatever it was called, the facility at the far end of State Street where, during Karin's childhood years, it was said "all the professors ended up"—sooner or later.

But not Karin's father. He'd avoided the assisted living facility by dying in his early seventies.

On the phone he'd assured Karin that he was well, nothing to worry about, on the very eve of entering hospice he'd told her not to be concerned, not to take time out from her work, there was plenty of time, he was sure. And so she'd believed him, or half believed him, until finally, when it was almost too late, she'd driven to see him one last time, still in disbelief that he was truly, seriously ill.

In March of this year, she'd planned to drive to visit her mother in Ann Arbor but had to postpone at the last minute because of a sudden snowstorm. A few days later, she'd started out but after twenty minutes encountered a multi-vehicle accident on the state highway and had to turn back; another time she'd been determined to make the drive but on the eve of her departure fell ill with flu that left her dehydrated and weak, and so she'd postponed the trip again, until now: early April, spring thaw, more daylight, hope lifting like mist from the earth.

Ridiculous that her sister and her brother had so exaggerated their mother's power over them, they'd moved out of state to escape her. *You can't win, with her. Only she can win.* Karin had moved north to Charlevoix, but for other reasons. (A romantic relationship that had begun with much intensity but faded by degrees over a decade as the other, the man, older than Karin by eight years, had had health problems that he hadn't wished to share with another person, or at least with Karin. Not an actual loss, not a tragedy, but yes, a disappointment.) Was it significant, none of the mother's children had married?—sister, brother, Karin. And no children, nor the likelihood of children. Though they felt "young," they were well into middle age—Karin especially.

She didn't want to think that they'd abandoned their gentlemanly father to their mother's sharp-edged personality, it would break her heart to think that she'd betrayed him. Yet, at the time, she'd seemed to feel that her father would live forever. *Why don't you come visit, Karin? We have plenty of room, you know.* The wistful voice, the disinclination to plead.

She hated it! Driving alone, too much time to think. She would listen to Italian language CDs—enunciating words as she drove, sibilant and fierce. To learn a language is to declare a life beyond the immediate life: a future in which she would travel to Italy, with a friend. A new friend. When her mother was no longer a responsibility.

Of course, I know who you are. How would I not know my own daughter!—that hissing laugh, like the warning cry of geese.

Fearing her mother's memory loss but fearing the sharp tongue even more.

Always uncanny to approach the place that is *home*. The smallest changes leap to the eye, disconcerting.

Of course, State Street in Ann Arbor has changed over the years. More chain stores, clothing stores, fewer bookstores. Karin's father had lamented, once there were more than twenty bookstores in Ann Arbor, now there were only three or four. Legendary Borders Books had begun here, in the early 1970s.

But the tall beige-brick house on Sixth Street seems unchanged, at least its exterior. Only the first floor of three floors is used now: a hospital bed for the mother has been moved into the father's former study with its floor-to-ceiling bookshelves, its wide windows overlooking a deep back lawn.

To be born is to step through a doorway. Blind and trusting, the child steps inside, the door is shut to protect the child. But when the parents die, the door is opened. There is no shutting the door a second time.

Always a relief, seeing that the house is all right. If one doesn't look too closely.

There has been some storm damage to the ash trees, limbs scattered on the front lawn; perhaps one of the trees is dead, devoured alive by the invisible ash borer. In the moist dull-dead grasses of winter, a flock of small birds is pecking, which scatters as Karin approaches the front door.

Here is a surprise: the foyer is untidy with boxes. Karin has been prepared to pack boxes. Has it happened already? Has the mother—died?

The young Hispanic caretaker is kind to Karin as if seeing something in Karin's face of which Karin is not aware. Smiling, encouraging—"Your mother has been waiting for you! She keeps saying, 'My daughter is coming to see me.'"

And: "She keeps asking me, 'Is my daughter coming today?'"

Karin wonders if the mother will remember that it is she, Karin, who is coming to see her and not the other, younger daughter whom the mother had seemed, in her whimsical way, to favor. She steels herself for the mother's disappointment, which is likely to show in the mother's face like something straining through a mesh.

"Mom, hello! You are looking just great"—Karin's voice catches, but it is her exuberant girl's voice, which never fails her in these circumstances.

Stooping to kiss the soft lined cheek, a softer skin than she recalls. Breathing in the yeasty smell of her mother's body, bed-clothes that might need changing.

Awkward hug, Karin is out of breath, panting. Feels a rush of blood to her head, a sensation of faintness. The mother is sitting up in bed, large floral pillows behind her that give the room a festive air. The mother accepts Karin's hug, her arms lack the strength to lift and close about Karin in turn.

It is clear that the mother expects Karin and knows who she is, several times speaking the name "Karin."

Still the mother's eyes retain a certain luster, only slightly di-minished. Like dregs of sherry left behind in glasses, Karin recalls from a startling line of Emily Dickinson.

Karin is vastly relieved, the visit goes well. She sees that her mother has lost weight, her cheeks are thinner, pale. Her hair, rav-aged by chemotherapy, is growing back in feathery white strands that remind Karin of fledgling birds just out of the nest, some of them fallen to the ground, quivering with a feeble life, vulnerable to predators.

Karin always remembers to bring her mother a gift from the most upscale Ann Arbor food market: today a wicker basket of exotic imported fruits including fresh figs, strawberries, mangoes, kiwi, seedless black grapes the size of plums. Such delicacies please the mother, who has always appreciated gifts.

To think that they were once frightened of this frail person!—Karin, her sister, and her brother. How much is imagination, Karin thinks. The child's magnification of the parent's power.

She is laughing, and she is crying. Wiping surreptitiously at her eyes.

She does love her mother!—of course. Her heart is suffused with love for the elderly woman, she is deeply grateful to be here.

In fact, the mother isn't *old*. Not by contemporary standards, when people live well into their nineties, and the age of one hundred isn't uncommon.

In her midseventies, Karin thinks. Seventy-four?

Not age but health matters. One can be stricken with cancer at any age and suffer what are called cognitive deficits.

If Karin asks how the mother has been, she knows the reply she will receive: "I don't know. They don't tell me." It's a flat, bemused accusation Karin has heard many times. Still, she must ask. Listen politely to the reply.

If she wants to know how her mother *is,* she will speak with the caretakers and her mother's physicians, as she does routinely.

In a few carefully chosen sentences Karin sums up her "news"— always vague, upbeat, not *too* upbeat, not too specific. Her mother's face will brighten if she mentions that her next book will be published by Harvard University Press, but her mother will soon lose interest if she identifies it as a translation of a short novel by the contemporary German writer Hans-Ulrich Treichel. Her mother has even less interest in Karin's own books of poetry, published by Graywolf Press; the last time Karin gave her a copy of a new book, she'd taken it reluctantly from Karin and said, "Don't I already have this? You gave me this already."

Karin steels herself for the mother to ask about Karin's long-time companion as she so often has, but this time, for some reason, she doesn't ask.

She has given up. She knows better. You will have no good news for her.

No news of a lover, a companion, a fiancé, but news of cousins, aunts, and uncles and neighbors once household names, some of them still living not far away, others far-flung, even if her mother probably can't recall some of these individuals clearly, wouldn't be able to remember when she'd seen them last. Still, these are subjects about which Karin can chat with her; there's satisfaction in noting how, when a name comes up, a cousin of Karin's, for instance, Karin's mother will invariably say the same thing she always says—*Oh, that one! She was always flighty.*

Or, when Karin speaks of her brother—*Him! Don't tell me about him.*

Always satisfaction, when a sibling is found lacking.

Karin is hesitant, speaking of her father. Her tone shifts, she finds herself emulating him, his voice, his seriousness, telling her mother that she often meets people who'd studied with her father and recall him with much admiration, his lectures, his generosity with graduate students; she means to entertain her mother, telling anecdotes about "invasive species"—how upsetting, to learn that there's an invading army of mute swans, for instance, even a sub-species of sparrow, not to mention new varieties of weeds, every year . . .

As her mother used to interrupt her father when he spoke of such things, designated by her mother as his "work," thus vexing to her, since it comprised a vast realm of facts, issues, ideas not related specifically to her, so now her mother interrupts Karin, with a provocative little smile: "But they have a right, too, don't they? What d'you call them—'invasive' species."

Patiently Karin tries to explain, as she has explained in the past: invasive species have their own natural habitats, and when they invade others, they drive out native species. For instance, songbirds like cardinals, chickadees, finches can't compete.

But Karin's mother isn't really listening. She never really listens. Enough for her to be provocative, to register a query, or an objection, to derail a conversation, knowing just enough to be brightly contrarian, as she'd been as a young, attractive wife in Ann Arbor decades ago, married to a renowned professor.

She has been eating grapes out of the basket, noisily. Karin should have thought of washing the grapes but now it's too late, pointless to cause a fuss.

From their mother, they'd learned to wash their hands carefully—

"thoroughly"—after using the bathroom or, indeed, coming into contact with anything that might be "contaminated." Which could include, certainly did include, one's own body.

That look in their mother's face, disdain, disapproval, disgust—stooping to sniff at Karin, sweating from outdoors.

Stained underarms in her sweaters, stained underwear.

Rushing back to her now, as an adult. In the orbit of the Mother, who'd dictated so much.

Wincing to recall how, in middle school, she'd stood at a sink in the girls' restroom washing her hands compulsively, counting *one-two-three-four,* scrubbing at her already reddened knuckles. And years to follow, how many years.

Are you sure that those hands are clean? Are you sure that those hands are clean?

No logical answer. Of course, one could never be *sure.*

And now, Karin's mother is eating the (unwashed) grapes, with (unwashed) hands. And eating them greedily, juice glistening on her fingers. As if there'd never been any need for any of it. Those years.

Her brother had warned her—*The woman is just poison.*

Karin doesn't think so. Karin wants to think that, in any case, she is an adult now: she is in control of her life now. In a sense, *she is the parent now.*

Bringing the mother the hand sanitizer. Just in time to prevent her from wiping her sticky fingers on the bedsheet.

"Here, Mom."

As if begrudgingly, Mom murmurs *thanks.*

While her mother is napping Karin examines boxes in the foyer. No reason to feel furtive, inquisitive. But she is curious if there is anything she might claim, anything worth bringing back to Charlevoix with her. In one, she discovers old photo albums—from the 1970s!—she is certain she hasn't seen before; the caretaker has told Karin that these boxes were removed from the attic.

Many of the snapshots have loosened. Most of the photographs are in black and white and many have faded. Among the snapshots are old birthday cards, Christmas cards. What a treasure trove!— if only Karin had time.

One of the loose snapshots, which has been mended with yellowed transparent tape, is of Karin's mother as a young woman. A very young mother. Beaming with happiness, an infant in her arms. Karin has rarely seen her mother this happy. Rarely with such a joyous smile. The infant in her arms is presumably Karin and not her sister or her brother since the mother looks so young. A shadowy thumb obscures a corner of the snapshot: has to be Dad, taking the picture. The background is outdoors, nothing Karin recognizes.

Karin sees on the back of the snapshot the penciled, almost unreadable name—*Karen*. But the date is 1975, which seems wrong, Karin was born in 1977.

When Karin brings the snapshot to show the mother, to ask about the date, and where the picture was taken, the mother takes it from her fingers to peer at more closely. Her fingers are sticky now with strawberry juice; she wipes them on a pillow.

The mother nods, curtly. As if she has been proven correct in an argument.

"That was her—Karen. She was taken from us. 'Meningitis.'"

Karin stares at the mother as if the mother has uttered words in a foreign language.

"Meningitis. There was no saving her."

"But, Mom," Karin says carefully, "*I* am Karin."

"Yes. I know who you are. But you are not 'Karen.' She was taken from us."

The mother smiles irritably as if speaking to a stubborn child.

"Mom, I don't understand . . ."

"There was *no cure*. There was nothing to understand."

Karin's knees ache from having been squatting in the foyer, looking through boxes. Her breath is short. She finds herself staring at the snapshot taken so long ago: A riddle? The very young mother, the infant in her arms. Though it was taken more than four decades ago, the picture is certainly of Karin's mother.

The infant is scarcely visible, a white blur clasped close against the mother.

Calmly Karin tells the mother another time that she doesn't understand. Thinking—*She is losing her mind of course, she is senile.*

As if she can read Karin's thoughts the mother says sharply: "You are named 'Kar-in' because you took her place. She was ours, she was taken from us, she was only five months old. A valve in her heart was not right. My heart was broken. Then, a year later, another baby was born, a little girl, to the daughter in a family in Ypsilanti your father was advising at Legal Aid. No one wanted that baby—that is, you. This girl they said was a 'delinquent,' she'd gotten pregnant and nobody wanted the baby so an adoption was arranged, this baby was given to us."

"Mom, that's ridiculous! I—I never heard of . . ."

"Don't lose this picture, this is a precious picture. Put it on the table here, please."

Karin is on her feet. She is protesting, but she is also laughing. For this is ridiculous, she has fallen right into the trap.

Her sister warned her, her brother warned her—*Don't go near her, she is poison.*

Her father had pleaded with her after all—*Come home, Karin! I am so lonely, I don't want to die alone.*

She has planned to stay upstairs in her old, former room. But now, she will stay in a motel. It is too late to get on the interstate to Charlevoix, that would be madness. One of the motels on State Street—or on the interstate—anywhere will do! Time to leave the mother, in any case. The mother's eyelids are drooping, as if sated. The thin lips are stained with strawberry juice.

Oh, all this was planned—plotted. Even the Hispanic caretaker must have known.

Karin gathers up her things, desperate to leave. Blindly, a roaring in her ears.

Someone calls after her: The caretaker? But what is her name—Maria, Marianna, can't remember.

"Goodbye!"—she shuts the door behind her, hard. She has been rude to the housekeeper, unavoidably. In the sunken wet lawn, a lone sparrow pecks in the dirt.

The Cold

WHEN IT BEGAN, I do not know.

If I kept a journal or a diary, as some of you do, perhaps then I would know.

But I don't, and so I don't.

When *the cold* began to pursue me.

Pursue, I think.

Persecute.

First, should establish: *the cold* has nothing to do with *weather.*

In fact it may have begun as early as last summer. Late summer.

Outside on our redwood deck at the rear of the house, setting down plates of food, taking away dirtied plates, one of our family suppers that's like a runaway vehicle—just keeps accelerating, hang on tight and get through it with my trademark gritted-teeth grin.

Relatives visiting for the day, and their kids. And our kids.

Such pleasure (you wouldn't guess) in that casual remark—*And our kids.*

Two boys, seven and ten. Husky and healthy taking after their six-foot-two dad.

Seeing the boys as others see them—not possible. The mother sees—*I did that? (Did I do that?)*

Offered help in the kitchen (of course) but having others in my kitchen, even my favorite sister-in-law, even my favorite niece, is distracting to me so no thanks. I am happiest when my thoughts are focused like a swarm of bees aimed in a single direction.

No distractions! Best to be alone.

Humid, hot late-August day. Crazy cicadas shrieking. Rivulets of perspiration running from my (shaved, deodorized) armpits down my sides. Two dozen large ears of sweet corn, boiling the corn on the stove in the giant pan, placing steaming ears on a platter. Preparing hamburgers, hot dogs, salmon steaks for my husband to grill. Bag of ice melting fast. Yet when I return outside there comes a draft of cold air like an unwanted caress, making me shiver.

Low-backed summer dress, hair tied back from my flushed face. Just about, my ravaged body has been restored and (judging from men's glances at least) I am looking pretty good again.

If you don't look too closely.

No time to wonder amid the busyness of the occasion why I'd be shivering, where a bone-chilling draft might be coming from on such a (windless) day, temperature at a high of eighty-eight degrees Fahrenheit in the midafternoon (when we'd all been at the softball game watching some of the older kids play) and hardly cooling as dusk came on. Harried, happy.

See?—I can do it. What'd you think!

Yet I was feeling (weirdly) cold, suddenly weak. Ran upstairs to get a sweater, draped it over my shoulders. Loosened my hair so that it covered more of my face, and the nape of my neck, for warmth.

Not the hair I used to have, that was like a mane. *That* was warm, couldn't stand against my neck on a hot day.

Thinking if the redwood deck was some kind of a boat, and everyone having a good time on the boat, drifting along a river, leaving me behind on shore watching the sparkling lights and hear-

ing the (receding, fading) laughter borne off into the darkness—
why would any one of them miss *me*?

That was when *the cold* returned. Clammy sensation, upper
back, shoulders, nape of my neck . . . If I'd been drinking cold
beers maybe that would be why but no, not one beer yet today.

Then I think: back of our suburban acre-and-a-half there's a
wooded area, no-man's-zone between property lines forbidden
to children (poison sumac, sharp briars, ticks and mosquitoes),
marshy land there, presumably cooler air.

Maybe *the cold* is coming from that place?

Forty years old on my last birthday. At such times you think—*Well!*
I made it this far.

Rarely is it uttered—*Do I need to go farther? Why?*

Yes: I married late. Had (two) babies late. (Three pregnancies. Two
"live births.") Eleven years working for a local realtor before I quit
to get married figuring I would never be so lucky again, a husband
who loves me.

At least, as a husband loves his wife. *His* wife.

All that is required for happiness, it's said, is to find just one
person to love you, and to be loved by you.

Out of the billions of human beings on earth, shouldn't be that
hard to find just that one person.

And a child, or two children: shouldn't be hard.

Certainly not—children adore *Mommy*. At least, so long as they
are young enough to need *Mommy*.

(Little love-stabs, sheer happiness seeing the boys hungrily eating what I've prepared for them, and no complaints; husband sig-
naling with a smile he's having a great time—*Hey. Love you!*)

Yet, I am reluctant to provide their names. Our names.

Adult male (husband), adult female (wife), two "live birth" children. (The miscarried sibling was to be given a name if she'd been

born but only if she'd been born.) To provide these names seems risky to me, like boasting that you have money.

Because it's no one's business, who we are. That we are—we exist. That is enough.

No name but I'd thought of her as Hummingbird.

Because so small. Because what there was of her would fit in the palms of your opened hands.

Because hummingbirds' wings are a rapid blur and blurredness is a symptom of tears.

Because the hummingbird is a miniature bird that, if you blink, you might miss. *Here?—gone.*

He's saying maybe not just yet. And I'm saying why the hell not.

Well—it hasn't been that long. You're still on the medication, right?

Fuck the medication. Flushed the medication down the toilet.

(But I don't tell my husband *that.*)

(*That* would sound belligerent, hostile. Reckless and self-destructive.)

Caution in his eyes like light reflectors. Laughter rises in my throat like bile.

O.K. to laugh if not angry-sounding. Light-laughing, girl-laughing, nonaccusatory-laughing. For men fear women laughing at them, that is the true castration.

Make eye contact: lift eyes. Crucial difference between a locked ward and an unlocked ward—*Normal affect, clarity of speech, no evidence of "suicidal ideation" . . . Smiles, laughs. Self-aware enough to be embarrassed.*

So he says O.K. then, but don't drive far, at first. Just in town. Not the highway not for a while O.K.?

Duck my head in submission. O.K.

And not take the kids? Not just yet.

O.K.

Sure I can trust you?

Sure.

Next morning there is the key to the Honda Civic on the kitchen counter.

My car that's been sitting in the garage for three months.

He'd kept the battery alive. For that, I am grateful.

At first I assumed that the (random, unpredictable) drafts of cold air were naturally occurring: door left ajar, window left open somewhere in the house, air vent, furnace fan. (A quirk of our furnace seems to be that, when the furnace shuts off, there comes an emission of air through wall vents, neutral in temperature—just *air*. But this air feels cold.)

At the grocery store where I've shopped for years, streams of icy air in unexpected places: not the refrigerated aisles (which are uniformly cold) but aisles of canned goods, paper products, even counters of hot prepared soups, roasted chickens. In the drugstore, hardware store, café—fingers of icy air. At the mall.

Especially the mall: God-damned stores with their doors flung wide, issuing cold air in waves like an assault on passersby.

Hell, it's an affluent society, air can't be natural but must be *conditioned*. In my husband's Jeep the AC is always *on*.

We joke about it: him wasting energy when there's no need. He admits he isn't even aware of it, his AC is always *on*.

In my car, which is a battered Honda Civic, I have become cautious, jittery. Always check to make sure the windows are shut tight. Front, rear. Except in hot weather the AC in this car is always *off*. Fan *off*.

Yet—still—after a few minutes I (often) feel a maddening stream of cold air against the side of my face or the nape of my neck making me shiver.

Making me shudder.

Double-checking the windows: yes. All are closed.

Fan *off.* AC *off.*

There is no draft inside the car. Can't be a draft inside the car. I have imagined it, clearly.

But then—again—after a few minutes *the cold* returns, like a caress that steals up from behind.

All women know that stealthy caress. That moment of utter panic, then the shudder of revulsion.

No. Stop. Don't. Go away!

The car lurches. Jolts to a stop on the shoulder of the highway.

In a sharp voice the older boy asks what's wrong, Mom?—what has happened?—and at first I'm too shaken to reply then tell him a squirrel ran in front of the car, that's why I braked.

Squirrel? Where is the squirrel?

Neither of the boys sees a squirrel. Anywhere.

Can't see the squirrel, I tell them. It must've run across the road and disappeared.

Demanding to know did you run over the squirrel, Mom? *Is it dead?*

I did not run over the God-damned squirrel and it is not dead.

The shock is: I am not alone in the car. Could've sworn I was alone in the car as usually I am when *the cold* comes over me.

Nights when I can't sleep. Suddenly, most nights.

The cold has crept up on me. It has a smell, I am beginning to realize—dark, mineral-like, the smell of a deep stone well. But also the smell of black blood.

That dark, thready blood. Splotches on underwear after childbirth.

After miscarriage, smelly dark splotches on the thickest sanitary napkins at the drugstore. *Weeks of this. Sneeze, there's a small hemorrhage.*

It is familiar, this smell. Weirdly comforting.

Fall asleep exhausted but can't sleep for more than a half hour waking abruptly as if someone has called my name.

Mom-my!—almost inaudible.

A man sprawled beside me. Naked.

Giving off heat, to counteract *the cold.*

My fingers yearn to caress. It has been so long. Stroking his upper arm, the swell of muscle. Fingers at his groin. Tangle of wiry hairs. Fat soft sea slug that stirs at my touch as if alarmed.

Quickly my fingers move away.

No one so lonely as a wife in bed beside her (sleeping) husband through the interminable hours of the night.

How many nights: prowling the (darkened) house.

Insomnia like the vast Sahara stretching to the horizon.

Trying to avoid checking the boys. Should not give in to (paranoid-Mom) fears.

Yet: Isn't it a mother's right to check her children as they sleep? So long as the children are too young to protest.

Wearing an old wool bathrobe of my husband's, heavy and cumbersome. Trailing to the floor. Scattering of moth holes in the fabric, smell of stale sweat. Coarse gray wool socks on my feet, also belonging to the husband.

It's a thrill—at first. Can't sleep, wandering the house, no one knows, watch TV with the volume turned low, eyes staring. *Is this me? What has become of me?* Driven out of the basement TV room by *the cold.*

Restless then, ascending stairs to the boys' room.

Silent as a lioness prowling the veldt too restless to sleep.

Just this once. Won't wake them.

Reasoning that if there'd been an infant in the house, *that* would have wakened them—maybe.

Needing to see if they are both asleep and of course they always are. Not anxious (for that would be ridiculous) but needing to see if they are breathing and of course they always are.

Don't. Just—don't.

Don't frighten them, haven't they been frightened enough by their mother . . .

What would I do, I wonder, if my children didn't live in this house! When they are older, and have moved away—how will I know if they are sleeping? If they are breathing? If they are happy? If they still love me?

If they remember me?

And how will they remember their mother?

We had a little sister. Supposed to have a little sister. Why'd they tell us she was coming if she never came . . .

Both the boys are sleeping. They share a room of course. Though soon, the older will want his own room. The younger will be heartbroken. Unavoidable.

I am standing over the younger boy. Not sure how long I have been here scarcely daring to breathe.

Though I can see my son's narrow chest rising and falling faintly yet I am concerned that he might not be breathing—really. Might be some sort of optical illusion. Wishful thinking. The brain makes leaps of inference based upon incomplete data, this is well-known—filling in gaps, it's called. So though I can see (clearly) that the boy is alive and breathing yet I am anxious that what I am seeing is a deception of some kind and he is not really alive, and not breathing.

As, in the uterus, the fetus is alive yet not-alive. A living organism, so to speak, yet not an (independent) living organism.

Uterus. Ugly word.

Fetus, uterus. Can't blame men, edging away.

The risk here is obvious: if the younger boy (my favorite, though must not say so) wakes suddenly he will be astonished/appalled to see his disheveled white-faced mother stooping over his bed like a vulture.

And if he cries out, he will wake his brother, too. *That* brother will be astonished/ disapproving.

So far, several nights in succession, I have not been caught. This makes me feel reckless, giddy.

You don't really know how much they know. Adults spoke to them carefully about what happened. With children you must choose your words—carefully.

A relief to back out of the room without waking them. Relief to be free for the remainder of the night of crazy-Mom worry her sons have ceased breathing in their sleep.

Well—no need to check the husband's breathing. *He* is certainly alive.

Sprawled in the queen-sized bed with arms and legs outstretched, big head flung back on a pillow, both pillows, his breath is hoarse and loud and assertive. Here is a being perfectly at ease in his skin. Sometimes a kind of sniggering laughter erupts from the torso, a rattling snore. If I wake him gently he will mutter at me, frowning, yet affable enough, turning from me to fall asleep within seconds.

Help me, don't leave me. I love you—no idea why these pathetic words issue from my numbed lips but no matter, the husband doesn't hear.

Not your fault, never anyone's fault, act of God (you could say)—accident.
  So don't blame yourself.
  Except—

Fact: a certain percentage of babies *fail to thrive* in the womb.

Do we know why, we do not (usually) know why. Well—there is a *how* but not a *why*.

A doctor will explain *how*. As in *how did this happen*.

A doctor will not explain *why*. As in *why did this happen*.

(Usually) it is no one's fault. The very word *fault* is not helpful.

It isn't an anniversary of that death. Indeed, a miscarriage is not considered a death though it is acknowledged to be a loss.

Even a late-term miscarriage, in the sixth month.

Like bringing home plants from the nursery, flowering shrubs, small perfectly proportioned trees, you have faith that once in the soil they will thrive and not instead fade and shrivel to a few brittle leaves and stalks for if you are a gardener you do not think about this possibility. You may be a fool but you are suffused with hope.

A near-fully-developed *fetus, embryo*—yet not what is designated a *baby*.

Grieving for a miscarried fetus, embryo, not-a-baby is not a hallowed custom. It is not any kind of custom. Not a custom enshrined in religious rituals or even observances. The remains of a miscarriage do not constitute *remains* in the usual sense of that word and indeed that word, in its usual sense, is a terrible word I cannot bring myself to utter aloud.

Such remains may be *disposed of.* Not *buried.*

A miscarriage isn't a *death* in the family but a physical event that happens exclusively to the mother, not to the baby. For (as it is explained) there is *no baby*.

But you are doing so well! We all knew you would.

Unhappiness looks to the past. Happiness, to the future.

My husband urges me to drive to the nursery. Now that I am allowed to drive again. Isn't it getting late in the season for planting a garden?

Yes, late. It is getting late.

The husband is the responsible parent. He is unfailingly affable, except when he is impatient, exasperated. As a dad, he can be feverish-funny, but he can also *lay down the law*. In college he'd majored in business administration, and that is his career—vaguely, administering some sort of business in a local company called NeutroLink.

For a man of his size he is surprisingly deft, quick on his feet. He has cultivated a habit of clapping his hands to get family attention, laughing as he does so.

Hel-lo! Atten-tion please!

His eyes glide over me like liquid mercury. He has not *seen me* since the catastrophe or maybe, if I am being honest, he'd avoided looking too closely at me in the later stage of the pregnancy though (as all insisted) I was looking remarkably good, smooth-skinned, with the proverbial "glow" of pregnancy.

Go on, now. You've got your credit card, right? Go. It was a long damn winter. You deserve it.

Squeeze of the shoulder. Gentle shove. Hadn't he kept the battery in the Honda alive, these miserable months?

Yet, in the happiness of the garden, in the joy of working in the garden, in the midday heat of the garden rudely there comes *the cold.*

As if *the cold* is hiding in the soil. Waiting to be released, freed by the reckless excavations of a shovel.

Oh but why am I having such difficulty digging in my garden! (Though the property is *ours,* the house is *ours,* the boys are *ours* yet the garden is *my garden.*) Must be that my muscles are weakened. Stamina weakened. Short of breath for there is something resistant in the soil tough-textured as the muscle of a great beast.

Must be a network of roots, tangled together in the earth. I am eager to clear a way for these young tomato plants, pepper plants. Marigolds, nasturtiums, miniature iris. Quick before they wilt and die.

Stupidly I've forgotten my garden gloves yet continue digging with the shovel until my hands begin to blister. *The cold* wafts upward from the earth smelling of something dank, rotted. Still I persevere—I am desperate to get the soil tilled properly. Sinking the shovel into the earth, leaning on it as hard as I can, as deep as I can into the earth encountering something sinewy and resistant like veins?—arteries?—through which the sharp edge of the shovel cuts.

There! A tangle of roots, severed.

(Do I hear a little cry? Out of the earth?)

By now I am perspiring. Smelling of my body. Hot sun beating between my shoulder blades as there comes an updraft of cold air that penetrates my lungs like a fetid mist.

Because of *the cold,* it is becoming harder for me to sleep.

Or because I am having trouble sleeping, and am jittery and tired during the day, I am more susceptible to *the cold.*

A week. Ten days.

Sleep comes in tatters.

Sleep comes in textures.

Thin gruel of sleep—washing over you for a few fleeting seconds, then retreating leaving you bereft.

Sleep like a teasing/tormenting caress—leaving you aching and bereft.

Sleep that is a thick sludge: muck.

Sleep that is oozing, sticky: sleep-porridge.

Sleep that is sharp, hurtful: sleep-acid.

Sleep that is downy, airy, too light to be nourishing: sleep-feather.

Sleep that is the flutter of the hummingbird's wings, too rapid a blur to be seen though it can be felt . . .

Come to me, don't leave me alone in this place. Mommy!

Hummingbird! Shocking to me, that my little daughter who has never been born, who has never known speech can address me so clearly.

Then I understand—this has to be a dream. The prologue to a dream that awaits me once *the cold* allows me to sleep.

Any idea what I look like, now? No.

My face, eyes. No. I've avoided seeing.

Last I'd seen of my body I had a belly that drew the eye to it irresistibly, the face of the pregnant woman a blur even to herself.

Except—swollen ankles, legs. Shortness of breath. Too old?—thirty-nine.

Soon after, the belly collapsed. Deflated like a balloon. Disappeared by magic. No telling where it had gone, just—*gone.*

Flaccid and bruised, ravaged skin remains, in yellowish folds.

And the taut fat breasts leaking milk—don't even think of what these look like now.

Hadn't known that I was a vain woman, before. That seeing men's eyes glide over me, I'd felt a thrill of excitement, pride.

My son saying to me—*You're the prettiest mommy!*

O.K., I knew I looked O.K. That's enough.

Now, I wouldn't know. Have no interest. The mirror's a blur even if I glance at it unthinking.

Yes: you can even apply lipstick if/when you want to impersonate a normal woman, without really engaging with the mirror-face. You can brush your teeth, hair. Dress yourself. Like dressing a body that cooperates with you, mostly.

Not so hard. Try it. I am proud of myself, for I have become a brilliant impersonator of myself.

So *awake,* my "self" is detached from my body and floats at a little distance from it.

Watching TV news. Seated beside my husband, who wields the remote control like a wand switching from channel to channel impatient to discover what it is he might be missing when he watches a channel for more than a few minutes, or seconds.

A kaleidoscope of "breaking news." Fires, flames, famine, flame-throwers, drought, earthquake, sodden bodies of refugee children washed up on littered shores. I would cry but *the cold* blunts my feelings.

"Disgusting!"—my husband mutters.

"Disgusting"—I hear myself echo.

"How can such things be? How can such things be shown on television?"

Soon then, my husband stretches, yawns, declares it's time for bed. As if nothing were wrong in the world.

And soon, I will have forgotten, too. *The cold* numbs memory.

In the corners of (certain) rooms, *the cold* is drifting like fine white sand. Try not to notice, not to hear the soft hissing sound . . .

Yes I have taken sleeping pills. I have tried.

And yes I have "slept"—a strange unnatural dreamless sleep that leaves my mouth and eyes parched, my brain hurting when I wake up abruptly in the morning like something thrown from a shovel.

My husband has urged sleeping pills of course. When in doubt, prescribe the wife/female pills.

But medicated sleep is not true sleep. This is not the sleep I require, that nourishes me.

Not the sleep we require, that forgives us.

Each night begins with (naïve) hope. Theory is, the next hour, hours, constitute the future, the future is *new*. Absolutely no reason that the future will replicate the past.

Husband sleeps, oblivious. For this, the (insomniac) wife is grateful.

To be sleepless is to wish to be alone. To be sleepless is to be supremely and irremediably alone.

At midnight still the night is new. Still there is the hope, the expectation that *sleep is approaching*.

A big stealthy lanky-limbed cat. Black panther. Elastic spine, rippling as she moves. On padded feet, making no sound.

But minutes pass. Hours. Still awake.

About to drift into sleep, *the cold* shimmers in a corner of the room. At once fully awake again. Alert, on guard.

Will I give up, and slip downstairs to the TV room?

Will I give up, and prowl the house?

No—*must try*.

You have noticed: time moves slowly, even languidly in the hours just past midnight. Two o'clock, two thirty, three o'clock . . . But then at four o'clock, time begins to quicken.

Between four and four thirty—a rapid glide. Between four thirty and five—quick descent.

As soon as the first bird chirps—(a cardinal, usually: tentative, faint cry in the foliage outside the window)—*the cold* has burrowed beneath the blankets.

Shivering, trembling in your burrow. For now the night is coming to an end—inescapably. The night that had seemed so hopeful, so promising, now coming to an end. No way to stop it. Like a landslide that begins with a few dislodged pebbles then gathers momentum, plunges down the mountainside taking the stunned observer with it.

Soon must *get up.*

Superhuman strength is required to *get up.*

Dazed, deathly tired. Yet, I will make the effort to *get up.*

Determined not to give in to (my) weakness. *Get up.*

On my feet. First task is prepare breakfast for the family. Crucial to behave as if all is normal. Husband, sons. Hungry in the morning. A fretful time of day. They rely upon me to care for them, can't let them down.

Examining each egg with care holding to the light to see if there is a miniature gnarly growth inside and not a (mere) yolk. Examining toast for (scorched) weevils. Perusing tiny, near-indecipherable text on the back of a cereal box where the side effects of cracked wheat are indicated with a miniature skull and crossbones.

Once they are gone and the house is quiet I can try to sleep again. Crawl into rumpled sheets of the closest bed. Shut eyes.

Try.

That day, or the next day. Next night.

(How many nights?) (Emptying vessels of water into the ocean. Yes the volume is increased. No it is not calculable.)

Here is a remedy for insomnia: counting down from 1,111. Slow, methodical. Self-hypnosis. Descending a ladder into the Grand Canyon. Except at 1,004 my eyes open wide and dry.

Give up. Get up. Why do you need to sleep?—you don't.

The trick is to remain calm, I am sure. Try counting animals, different species of animals, how many do you know?—cats, dogs, cows, pigs. Sheep, goats. Beautiful high-stepping horses. Wild horses, mustangs. Elephants. Leopards, tigers, lions, cheetahs . . .

The animals are too vivid. In the room with me. I am more awake than ever!

Counting friends in grade school, middle school, high school.

Counting girls I'd liked more than they'd liked me.

Girls I'd liked less than they'd liked me.

Boys (I had thought) I'd loved who did not love me in return.

Boys/men I'd actually spoken with, touched. Kissed . . .

Men I've slept with . . . But there have been so few, no more than three, maybe four—the counting ends quickly.

Suddenly remembering: *Kamachenko*.

Tall skinny slope-shouldered boy with a man's ravaged face in our homeroom, senior year high school. Also in geometry class. Unpronounceable name Mr. Langley printed on the blackboard—*Kamachenko*.

Vasyl Kamachenko was from Eastern Europe we were told. "Refugee"—the word was new to us.

Most of his family had been massacred. He was living with a local minister who'd taken in refugees. Carefully enunciating his name—*Kama-chen-ko*—Mr. Langley was unintentionally comical provoking laughter in some (of us).

Almost immediately the boys who liked to tease called him the Camel.

Kamachenko was a head taller than the tallest of them. Someone said he was nineteen—older than we were. Bony face, deep-socketed eyes, long narrow face bearing the shadow of a dark beard. His stiff dark hair was oddly thin for a boy his age, patches of roughened red scalp were exposed. Not even the brightest of us seemed to understand that malnutrition caused such hair loss. Stress, trauma. In our comfortable American houses we had no clue.

Kamachenko, Vasyl. His English was halting and abashed. When he spoke (which was infrequently) he ducked his head, glaring downward. He stuttered, fell silent. There was a sound he made, a rush of sibilants, like a sound you might make slurping cornflakes. We jammed our hands over our mouths to muffle laughter.

No. I did not really laugh at the Camel as others did. For covertly I watched the Camel with soft admiring eyes.

Through a rain-lashed autumn watching the Camel in the corner of my eye. Never speaking to him, or in his vicinity.

He was a freak—too tall!—too thin. Shoulder blades weirdly bent forward like the wings of a crane. And that ravaged young-old face. You'd think that, up close, he might've smelled of something like wet socks, creosote.

In the senior corridor his locker was just three lockers away from mine. Very easy to observe, covertly. Boys shoved pictures of naked women torn from magazines into Kamachenko's locker but Kamachenko seemed to take no more notice of these than if the pictures were leaves.

They also shoved dried leaves, mud, hardened bird droppings into Kamachenko's locker.

Girls did not observe, girls tried not to know too much.

Yet somehow it happened, Kamachenko could open combination locks easily. If you had trouble opening your lock, getting into your locker, Kamachenko could help.

How d'you know what our combinations are?—Kamachenko was asked.

Kamachenko shrugged saying the combinations were the same, just one numberal different.

We smiled, the word *numberal* was strange to us.

In geometry class Kamachenko could solve difficult problems but could not explain why. No patience for the classroom protocol of *problem-solving*. One day Kamachenko began shivering in his desk. Tears ran down his narrow cheeks, which he tried to ignore. Awkward and embarrassing and even the teasing boys seemed not to know how to react. Mr. Langley came to Kamachenko's desk to offer him a tissue but Kamachenko shook his head, no thanks. Yet his ravaged face glistened, his nose was running. At last Mr. Langley wiped Kamachenko's face as you'd wipe the face of a child.

We were stunned, abashed. We did not laugh nor even smile. We feared that Kamachenko would strike at our teacher with his fists but he did not and somehow the class continued. But we never saw Kamachenko again after that day.

It was said he'd been moved to another city where there were *more people like himself who spoke his language*. It was said that he'd *turned violent against* the minister who'd brought him into his home.

But no—Vasyl Kamachenko had been *claimed by relatives and moved away to live with them*. All we knew was that he was gone from our high school and we never saw him again.

Wouldn't have thought that I'd cared for Kamachenko but the sight of his empty desks—homeroom, geometry class—tore at my heart.

Thinking to outwit *the cold*. To combat (imaginary) drafts of cold air I (deliberately) opened windows, left doors ajar. Turned down the thermostat. Believing in this way that (actual) drafts of cold air would be subsumed by (imagined) drafts and so my consciousness of *the cold* was not imagined.

Yet *the cold* persisted in pursuing me as a *deeper cold within cold*.

Thinking to outwit *the cold*. I have gotten into the habit of wearing extra layers of clothing in the house even in the daytime. Thick coarse wool socks. Gloves. On my head, a cap with earflaps.

In exasperation my husband asks what is wrong with me?—the temperature in the house is above seventy.

This is not true. Certainly not. No matter how I set the thermostat it reverts within minutes to sixty-eight degrees for my husband has programmed it that way.

Insisting upon taking me to see a doctor. But I have already seen a doctor. Too many doctors! Flushing medications down the toilet before I am poisoned by them.

Think of a miscarriage as a correction by nature. Something very wrong with the fetus, which then self-aborts . . .

Did you say—mismarriage?

Staring at my husband as (patiently) he explains to me. Not for the first time. Watching his mouth move.

Unable to recall his name. Very familiar and comforting name—William? Matthew? Richard? Robert? Phillip? White-protector names like stones worn smooth from continuous usage over the centuries.

At the computer I type in my husband's surname. (This is known to me because it is "my" surname as well.)

His employer is NeutroLink. I type this into the computer and a site opens to me but when I type in my husband's name the message is NO MATCH.

There is a telephone number, however. I call this number. The voice at the other end tells me *I am sorry, there is no one here with that name.*

That isn't true, I insist. My husband has been employed with you for many years.

Ma'am I am sorry, there is no one here with that name.

But—when did he leave? Did he transfer to another department?

Ma'am I am sorry, we cannot divulge that information.

But I am his wife. I am Mrs. __.

Ma'am I am sorry, we cannot divulge that information.

World record for staying awake is eleven days. Eleven!

I have stayed awake somewhere beyond twenty days in succession. Over weeks, months I have slept on the average of a few fleeting minutes or seconds over twenty-four-hour cycles though I have not kept a record for I am confident that gradually I will overcome my need for sleep, which (I see now) is just a predilection, a weakness. I mean—wreakness.

Weakness.

Nighttimes are most treacherous. The air is aswirl with *the cold* buffeting my face in little gusts if I don't cover it with a blanket.

(But then I can't breathe.) (But then I certainly can't sleep, panicked by the possibility of smothering.)

Like a pretzel curled to sleep on a downstairs sofa. Hidden from *the cold* beneath blankets. In the morning discovered—Mom! Hey . . .

Pulling the blanket from my face. Of course I am not asleep but fully awake and *my eyes fully open.*

Hesitantly the younger boy touches my face. Mommy—why is your face so cold?

Cold, cold! It is the boy who utters this word not me.

True, my face has become very pale. Icy. Frostbite?

Still, managing to assure the boys with a quick Mommy-smile that I am *just playing* with them, don't be silly.

You're the silly one, Mom! *You are.*

The older boy is abashed, ashamed. The younger is confused.

Asking what kind of game is Mommy playing but the older brother interrupts sneering it isn't Halloween, Mom. News for you.

Yanks the blankets off the mother to discover that she isn't wearing a nightgown or a bathrobe but the same rumpled slacks, soiled pullover sweater, wool socks she has been wearing for days and this is very wrong. This is bad to see. Upsetting to both boys, they back away from her and run from the room.

It is easy to forgive them. Out of oblivion they came, into oblivion they will soon return.

My brain has detached itself from my body and observes me through a scrim, as in a laboratory experiment. It occurs to me that my husband is a research scientist at NeutroLink and this is one of his experiments. *Of course: I am a laboratory animal.*

The cold renders my skin an odd, eerie, incandescent white like frost—frostbite. My lips are very thin, pale, with a bluish tinge so that, if I want to be seen, if I want to be acknowledged, I must darken my lips with lipstick. The redder, the better. I understand that red lipstick—a red mouth—is intended to send a sexual signal but I have no choice about lipstick for otherwise my face will begin to dissolve. The boys, who already distrust their mother, won't know where to look to find me.

Still, my husband doesn't seem to notice. If I don't wear a cap with earflaps, and a fleece-lined jacket in the house, he doesn't seem to be as annoyed with me as he has been. I keep meaning to ask him about his "executive" position at NeutroLink but each time I see him I forget, as if there is some sort of static interference from his direction.

The other day on his way out of the house he brushed his lips against my cheek and recoiled from *the cold* that has penetrated my skin like frostbite.

At any hour of the day there are estimated to be between one and three billion individuals who are *sleepless*—awake at the same time.

Sleep deprivation is an insidious form of torture. For it leaves no (visible) marks, scars.

Indeed it is possible that NeutroLink is a research laboratory, and that I am a research specimen. If so, being kept awake for a protracted period of time, somewhere in the vicinity of thirty days, is having an interesting effect upon my brain, which is becoming ever more alive, alert, *charged.*

It is said that no one can survive such protracted wakefulness. It is claimed that a normal person would have died by now. (As, it is claimed, an individual who persists in sleeping ten, twelve hours a day will soon die, also.) But of all (normal) people, I am not (evidently) in such dire need of sleep.

As time has slowed to a stop, so too the weather seems to have become a single, singular weather. *The cold* permeates everything, rarely is there a burst of sun. Outside the house a stationary mineral-mist seems to have settled in.

I have been hearing the husband speaking on the phone in a lowered voice, behind a shut door. I am not *eavesdropping* for I can hear perfectly well, my senses are sharply alert as knives in a drawer that has been yanked open. And so, I understand that the husband is expressing his concern for me, his fear that *it is happening to her again but worse this time.*

A plan has been made. A trap has been set. Our sons shrink from their mother—she is not *Mommy* now, nor even *Mom,* but *her.*

And so, it is time for Mommy to *go away.*

To *go away* is not difficult. The difficulty is *where to go.*

Packed a suitcase. Clumsily, hurriedly, not sure what I have stuffed inside.

Baby clothes I'd hidden away. In case there'd been a misunderstanding, Hummingbird is waiting at the hospital . . .

In a dumpster months ago, behind the Rite Aid where I'd parked, I'd found a doll in the trash, missing an arm. Missing most of her hair. Had not meant to bring her home, in fact had not brought her home but there she was in the back of the Honda Civic, the husband discovered her with a look of horror—What the hell is this? Where'd you find *this?*

Driving in the direction of Metuchen, New Jersey.

Why?—pulled like a magnet. No *why.*

Avoiding the Turnpike. Two-lane state highway through darkened fields. Ribbon of pavement seems to float. Faint sickle-moon overhead. This interminable day I'd been preparing. Eyes wide and alert, all senses alert. Not clear where I am going but confident that I will get there.

A powdery snow has fallen. That hissing sound. The heat in the car is on full blast yet *the cold* coils about me like a king cobra. Wisest strategy, I have learned, is to neither resist nor give in to *the cobra-cold.*

Entering Metuchen, three twenty a.m. Desolate town. Streetlights, deserted streets. Snow falling so slowly, each individual snowflake is visible in the headlights of my car as I stare through the windshield.

A red dashboard light has come on—gas tank is near-empty. In my lifetime I have never *run out of gas.* But thinking now that I had better find a gas station. More immediately, I need to use a women's restroom.

Looking for a lighted strip of highway. All-night diner. But there is no diner, and there is no gas station. Boarded-up stores, vacant lots filled with rubble. Signs lead to Metuchen train depot. What a melancholy neighborhood! Shuttered warehouses, abandoned vehicles along the streets like decaying beasts. Traffic meters decapitated so only posts remain.

The (deserted) depot parking lot is lighted and so I will park here and look for a restroom.

Down a flight of filthy brick steps, a mound of litter. Dressmakers' dummies amid trash that startle the eye for they resemble human figures tossed aside.

Following a sign—PUBLIC RESTROOMS. But the restrooms, doors defaced with graffiti, seem to be padlocked.

A door marked EXIT EMERGENCY ONLY. I am thinking that the electricity has been turned off here. There are no emergencies here. No one is here. Brashly I push open the door and step inside.

Here, a pungent odor of mineral-cold. Here is *the cold.*

Ah, I have hunted *the cold* to its lair! I am very excited now.

In a vault-like corridor. Dimly lit but I am grateful for any light at all. The mineral smell is very strong. Like raw meat. Creosote.

And then I see, in the corridor ahead as if he has been awaiting me—a tall thin figure with a bald head, ravaged face, and deep-socketed eyes—can it be Vasyl Kamachenko?

We stare at each other dry-mouthed. So stricken with emotion, neither of us can speak.

Kamachenko is an adult now, as I am. Last seen (by me) when he was no more than nineteen years old he does not seem to have aged much in the interim. Not as I have.

Yet, Kamachenko recognizes me! He calls me by name, he remembers my name.

I have a surprise for you, dear—despite his heavily accented English I have no difficulty understanding him.

We have been waiting for you. Good you are here, now!

In his arms, in his big hands—it is Hummingbird!

Kamachenko presents my lost daughter to me in both his opened hands, very carefully.

She is beautiful—yes? She is yours.

Too moved to speak, I take Hummingbird into my arms. She is swaddled in a white wool shawl. She weighs only a few ounces—oh, less than one pound!

Whatever Hummingbird's afflictions were, she seems to have healed now. At the hospital they refused to allow me to view her let alone hold her but now I see that she is a very small baby, the smallest baby I have ever seen, not perfect as a doll is perfect but as a human infant may be perfect. Her eyes are clear, cobalt-blue. Her hair is gossamer-thin, very pale, against the curve of her head fragile as an eggshell.

So suffused with love, for both Hummingbird and Kamachenko, who has brought her to me, I am finding it difficult to breathe.

As an adult man Kamachenko has become tender. The wariness he'd seemed to feel in our high school has vanished. Despite his physical awkwardness he exhibits a gallantry, almost a gaiety that feels foreign—European. We are each shy people, awkward at greeting, hugging. But so happy, hugging each other! Laughing, this is such a wonder. And Hummingbird with her miniature glowing face, in the crook of my arm.

Of course, Kamachenko and I are shy of each other. For not until this minute have we actually spoken to each other, let alone dared to touch.

Let me hold your hand. Let me warm you. You are so cold . . .

You *are so cold.*

It is true, Kamachenko is very cold. His hands grasping mine, his face that looks frostbitten, like my own. But Kamachenko stares at me with a look of love.

The cold washes over us, we will be frozen together, and Hummingbird in our arms between us.

For now I recall that Vasyl Kamachenko was my first love. I'd forgotten, but now I remember we'd hidden away together where no one could see us. I'd dared to drink the whiskey Kamachenko had provided. He'd laughed, he'd sung songs in his native language. He'd called me *moya lyubov* and taught me to call him *moya lyubov* in turn. Tenderly he'd kissed me, the first kisses of my life. My mouth, my eyes, my forehead, and again my mouth he'd kissed with his soft damp hungry lips. Embracing each other so tight I felt that I would faint, and we'd made love awkwardly and excitedly each for the first time in our lives and afterward slept in each other's arms exactly as I am sleeping now.

Take Me, I Am Free

THE MISTAKE must have been, the child woke too soon from her afternoon nap.

Really she knew better, for she'd been scolded previously for waking too early, and interfering with her mother's schedule. And now, coming downstairs unexpectedly, in her fuzzy pink slipper socks, she hears her mother on the phone: "No, it *is not* postpartum bullshit. It isn't physical at all. It isn't mental. It isn't genetic, and it isn't *me*. It's her."

The voice on the other end of the line must have expressed surprise, doubt, or incredulity, provoking the mother to speak vehemently: "It's *her*. She's defective. She's perverse. She hides it—whatever she *is*." Another pause. "You can't see it. Her father can't see it. But *I see it*."

And, as the child stands frozen on the stairs, in her fuzzy slipper socks, groping her thumb against her mouth to suck (though *disgusting thumb-sucking* is certainly forbidden in this household): "Of course my mother-in-law, the doting grandmother, refuses to 'see' it. The woman has a vested interest in denial."

Now, the mother notices the child on the stairs. A flush comes into her face, her green cat eyes glare with fury that the child has (once again) wakened too soon from her nap and come downstairs too soon, intruding upon the mother's private time. "I've told him, it's her or me. Preferably *her*."

Carrying the phone in one hand the furious mother seizes the child by the wrist and tugs her down the remainder of the stairs—"You! Are you eavesdropping, too?"—giving her a small shake of rebuke while continuing to speak into the phone in an incensed voice: "I didn't sign up for this. I didn't understand what was involved—'motherhood.' Before I knew what was happening *she* got inside me and kept growing and growing and now she's everywhere—all the time. Always I'm obliged to think of *her*—sucking all the oxygen out of my lungs."

Guiltily the child tries to apologize. She is a small inconsequential girl, just four years old; tears leave her face smudged, like a blurred watercolor. She should know better by now—indeed, she does know better. *Waking at the wrong time. Coming downstairs at the wrong time. Bad!*

In a flurry of activity, focused as a tornado, the mother gathers the child together with the week's trash to set out on the sidewalk in front of the buffed-brick row house on Stuyvesant Street. In the neighborhood there has been a long-standing custom of setting out superannuated household items—old clothes, chairs with torn cushions, battered strollers, children's toys, occasionally even a toilet seat, or an entire toilet—beside a hand-printed sign reading TAKE ME, I AM FREE. Mocking this phony-charitable custom the mother sets the weeping child down amid a gathering of unwanted useless things, of which some have been on the sidewalk for weeks.

"Just sit here. *Don't* squirm. I'll be watching from the front window."

Trying not to sob, feeling her lower face twist in a spasm of grief, the child sits on the chilled pavement through the remainder of the day as strangers pass by pausing to stare at her, even to (rudely) examine her, or to ignore her altogether, as if she were invisible. Some laugh nervously: "Well—hell! You're a *real girl*." A rusted tricycle, a soiled lampshade, a red plastic ashtray with a plastic hula girl on its rim, a box of old clothes, shoes, books are met with more enthusiasm than the shivering child who remains obediently where her mother positioned her even after a cold rain begins to fall.

If only she hadn't wakened too early from her nap!—the child recalls with shame. *That* was the mistake, from which her punishment has followed.

Each time a pedestrian approaches her the guilty child peers up with an expression of yearning and dread—yearning, that someone will take pity on her, and bring her home with them; dread, that someone will take pity on her, and bring her home with them. Though she should know better she can't help but think that, in another few minutes, her mother will relent and lean out the front door of their house to call her in a lightly chiding voice—"*You!* Don't be silly! Come in out of the rain right this minute."

Eventually it is sunset, and it is dusk. There are fewer pedestrians now. The child has virtually given up hope when she sees a tall figure approaching—"Good God! What are you doing here?"

It is the child's father, returning from work as he does each weekday at this hour. He is astonished to discover his beautiful little daughter curled up asleep on the filthy damp pavement beside the crude hand-printed sign TAKE ME, I AM FREE.

"Darling, I've got you now. Don't cry—you're safe."

But the child begins to cry, clutching at the father's arms as he lifts her and carries her into the house, which is warmly lit and smells of such delicious food, the child's mouth waters.

"Well! Nobody wanted her *again,* eh?"

In the dining room the mother has begun setting the table for dinner. She does no more than glance at the indignant father and the fretting child in his arms—their appearance hasn't surprised her at all.

The father says to the mother: "You aren't funny. You know very well that we wanted this child—we want her."

"What do you mean—'we.' *You*—not me."

"Well then, yes—*I* want her."

"But did you want *her*? You couldn't have known who she would be, could you?"

"Yes."

"Oh, come on—don't be ridiculous. Do we 'want' what we are given, or are we merely resigned to it? In the matter of children it's a lottery—losers, winners—'blind fate.' You can't say that we deserve her simply because we had her, as you can't say we had her because we deserve her. *She* has no say in the matter, either—but she doesn't realize, yet. As one day she will."

"You have no reason to come to such conclusions. In a civilized country like ours—each child is *precious*."

" 'Civilized'!"

The mother laughs derisively. Her laughter is sharp and cruel as a cascade of falling glass.

The father says, stung: "I said—you aren't funny. Just stop."

"*You* stop. You're the Platonist in this household."

Though the mother speaks in a bright brittle accusatory voice she is really not unhappy. She is not in what the child knows to be a *bad mood*. The glassy-green cat eyes gleam with less malice than before.

For it seems that while the child has been outdoors in the rain the mother inside the warm-lit cozy house has prepared a special meal. Moist pink flesh upon a platter sprinkled with fresh parsley, which the child identifies as grilled salmon; wild rice with shiitake mushrooms, Brussels sprouts sautéed in olive oil—a feast. The mother has brushed her lustrous dark hair, brightened her sullen mouth with red lipstick, changed from the shapeless slacks she wears around the house into a soft heather-colored wool skirt that falls to her ankles; around her slender neck is a necklace of wooden beads carved to resemble tiny hairless heads.

How many places are set at the dining room table?—the child blinks back tears, desperate to see.

The Suicide

S HE KNEW. Had to know.
    (But no, how'd she *know*?)

Obviously, she knew. A wife would—a wife would *know*.

Especially a loving wife. Which The Suicide's wife was, famously.

Keeping a close watch on him. Weeks, months.

Days, hours. Minutes.

Had to know, or rather to *sense*. The (young) wife so (famously) empathetic.

This would be the day. This, the morning. Finally, the God-damned fucking *hour.*

Not that he's judging her. What right's *he* got to judge *her.*

First Law of Suicide—*No suicide has got the God-damned right to judge any survivor. Especially not a loving long-suffering survivor.*

So, he isn't. Is not.

Not judging her. No.

Monster of egotism. He's been called.

Or is it master of egotism?—more flattering.

Wanting to inquire: is the meaning that The Suicide is *a monster of egotism* or more particularly that The Suicide is *the monster of egotism.*

Wanting to inquire: is The Suicide in fact the sole individual of his acquaintance, possibly of his entire generation, who *acknowledges frankly and without qualification that HE IS A MONSTER OF EGOTISM while others (so many others!) pretend that they are selfless fucking saints by pretending an interest in the environment, in fucking* birds*! Christ's sake.*

No act more "egotistical" than suicide: self-crucifixion. But where Jesus Christ was honored for His selflessness, The Suicide is chided for his selfishness.

"God-damned unfair."

For half his life The Suicide has been seriously debating: to leave a *suicide note* or not.

The bipolar brain divides all issues handily into *pro, con.*

Obviously, if you leave a note, you had better be eloquent, original, profound. And concise.

He has never been concise. Though (The Suicide has been encouraged to think) he is indeed eloquent, original, profound.

Except the *suicide note* is a genre that invites maudlin feelings. Every sort of cliché. Sentimentality, kitsch. His detractors would howl in derision, taking the case online. Once he's *virtual,* he could *go viral.*

Newest definition of Hell: *going viral not in a good way.*

To a word-master, *kitsch* is as awful, as clownish, as degrading as a splotch of Heinz catsup on your (white) shirtfront.

(Except: Who wears white shirts? Only saps or suckers wear white shirts. Ditto neckties. Cuff links? His insurance-executive dad wore white shirts, neckties, cuff links. One advantage of being an *artiste,* no one expects you to look like your dad if you'd had a dad who looked like a dad should've looked in those mid-twentieth-century dad-years when the dad was living, which The Suicide did, actually.)

He rarely wears a dress shirt if he can avoid it. T-shirts, sweat-shirts. Much-worn, with stretched necks and frayed cuffs. Food stains, or some sort of stains that despite laundering never quite disappear, like fossil traces.

Since discharged from the hospital in Minneapolis he's been wearing a much-laundered, still-beloved sweatshirt from a bygone bachelor era, acquired at Yellowstone National Park: faded-gray with faded-red letters *Yellowstone Supervolcano* on the front and a cartoon volcano erupting in lurid flames like an exploding head on the back.

What's a *supervolcano*?—The Suicide is frequently asked, allowing The Suicide to reply tersely, wittily—*May we never find out.*

(An archivist of arcane doomsday information since he'd been a bright, bratty kid younger than ten The Suicide will inform you that, when the Yellowstone supervolcano finally erupts, most living things in North America will suffer hideous deaths suffocating in toxic ash.

And for those who survive?—an ice age will follow.)

(Asked how likely is it that the Yellowstone volcano will erupt The Suicide will acknowledge wryly that the probability is approximately 1 in 730,000 in any year.)

And this is why The Suicide has never gotten around to actually composing a *suicide note* that lives up to his literary standards: the bipolar brain is easily distracted from its task.

Minutiae, trivia, any sort of curious fact few persons are likely to know, the bipolar brain sucks into itself like a high-power vacuum cleaner.

Accursed with a near-photographic memory. Terrific for scoring high on exams requiring memorization but not ideal otherwise. Absolutely unerring memory for hurts, slights, insults, outrages.

Fragments. Stored. My ruin.

And so The Suicide has decided (at least tentatively) not to compose a *suicide note*. Herculean effort would be required, so many false starts, stops, revisions, re-revisions, that sick-sinking sensation of failed hope—for Christ's sake, he is almost forty years old, he has not the strength for another failed project.

Also, a *suicide note* should be a model of clarity. No circumlocutions, ambiguities. No playful prose. No *teasing*.

Do not blame yourself. Ever.
Do not blame yourself, darling. Ever.

You wouldn't. Blame the wife.

If she'd (purposefully) decided to leave the house. That morning. Keeping the *suicide vigil* seven years.

To be precise, seven years, four months, fourteen days.

Bringing the suicidal spouse home (again) from the hospital in Minneapolis. Each time believing it would be the final time, which is what it means to *have faith* in a spouse.

What it means to *be devoted* to a spouse.

What it means to be *naïve. Unshakeable.*

The wife's very selflessness, the bottomless tar pit of her compassion, he'd begun to find uncanny. Unnatural.

As if the "vows" they'd taken, timeworn, quaint—*in sickness and in health until death do us part*—had actually been, for her, something more than merely a skein of clichéd words to placate the few witnesses at the civil ceremony—her (divorced) parents, his (widowed) mother. (Not one of his ragged entourage of guy-friends did The Suicide invite, a stunning rebuff to the long loud party of bachelordom stretching for years and miles as in a littered badlands.) As if indeed the wife-to-be uttered these moth-eaten worm-ridden achingly maudlin vows *in sincerity* while the husband-to-be heard his voice parrot hers in *mock sincerity* so precise it was (near-) indistinguishable from *sincere sincerity.*

Hey. Hope you don't mind my asking, Har—but—why're you going to marry her?

Blunt and rude as if he'd been asked—*Why're you going to marry that one?*

Icy-furious, he'd turned away. Though discussing women, Har's women, assessing, eviscerating, joking about over the years had been a thing they'd done, a guy-thing, a way of bonding (you could say)—now, no longer.

Why he hadn't invited his friends to the wedding. Hadn't even told them it had happened, until later. *See?—fuck you.*

Though (he'd have had to admit) inquiring why he was marrying *Wendy Marks* and not (for instance) Wendy's predecessor, or the one before the predecessor, wasn't an unreasonable question.

Wendy wasn't The Suicide's match intellectually—of course not. No more than any of the predecessors had been. But emotionally, in ways difficult to express, she was more than his match—he knew.

In truth, a stronger sturdier more-muscled female would've been preferable. If he'd known what lay ahead. For him, for her. Only just, Jesus!—Wendy had come into his life at precisely the right time. Her predecessors who'd kept him alive as if breathing oxygen into his deflated lungs, resuscitated his wizened heart, willing to drink with him, willing to not-criticize, to tolerate, endure, and prevail, these women had vanished from his life as if with a sudden excess of energy, typical of The Suicide, explosions of manic energy that allowed him to vacuum a succession of rooms until the very vacuum bag was swollen to bursting, crazed and euphoric episodes of housecleaning for which, in some quarters, he was famous— then came Wendy Marks, he'd made her laugh, they'd laughed together. Nothing more gratifying than a good-looking girl laughing hard at your (strained-funny) jokes. Nine years younger than he but many years more mature than he was—that was crucial. Not a writer—not a fucking *artiste*—not "competitive." Not crazy nor even neurotic. (*That* was crucial.) Whatever "Wendy Marks's" work was, graphic design, advertising and PR, nonprofit arts director—she didn't expect him to have any interest in it and indeed he had no interest in it. Without needing to articulate the fact both agreed: nothing in her life until meeting him was other than provisional, negligible.

Nor had "Wendy Marks" claimed to have loved/read the very titles for which in his late twenties The Suicide had acquired infamy.

He'd wept in her arms. *Save me.*

And that led to this: helping him out of the Volvo (again). Certainly she'd had practice with this wifely task but still it's impressive considering that, though he'd lost weight in the hospital, and before the hospital he'd been losing weight for months, still the husband loomed above the wife by several inches and outweighed her by at least thirty pounds and these thirty pounds inert dead weight like a boxer's heavy bag after it has ceased quivering following a round of hard punches.

What you'd call a hefty fella. Even his name—birth-name, surname: *Harold Hofsteader*—clumsy-heavy-hefty like a high school football player gone to flab but retaining still that boyish sweetness, affability which he'd worn since adolescence like a great soiled sock stretched over the itchy putrescences of his body.

Bringing the afflicted husband home (again). Ninety minutes north on I-35 (again). (Again) the Volvo in the driveway— "breezeway"—beside the kitchen door.

(Again) helping the husband out of the car. (Again) he heaves his bulk to his feet swaying upright, grateful for an arm around his waist, a woman's tremulous strength. His brain, which had been zapped, fried, shattered to pieces not twenty-four hours before trying desperately to arrange itself again in a constellation of pixels that could speak coherently.

Home on Cedar Lane had to be some kind of joke, like *breezeway, husband.* This wasn't his *home,* he'd never seen this place before, why his eyesight was blurry—some sights are so ugly they resist being seen.

Home was the wife's idea, like *breezeway, husband*—had to be the wife's idea. After they'd moved five times in four years. Not so glamorous a life as she'd imagined, was it. Once the *frisson* dulls, the (enviable) distinction of being married to *the most astonishingly original, extravagantly gifted writer of his generation* falls off like a faded decal, lost underfoot.

One notable crisis-time, The Suicide had just begun the fall term as "visiting writer" at "the Harvard of the Midwest" when a quarrel with a small-minded dean precipitated an abrupt resignation, furious packing, departure to neutral ground several states to the east where The Suicide had friends with whom to commiserate, self-medicate.

Hell, he'd even attended an AA meeting with one of them, just to try it on.

Not for me. Every word a cliché. Jesus!

In any case drinking—alcohol *per se*—wasn't The Suicide's problem, really. No one had the slightest idea what the problem *per se* was except (The Suicide was sure) it wasn't a God-damned fucking *cliché.*

An original, is what he is. No one like him in American literature.

And now, he'd returned to the Midwest. Minnesota: colder climate. Wind from a Great Lake came in gusts daily, riddled the sky like a glowering brow. Somehow he'd found himself, boy-pirate at heart, astronaut-mariner, an *artiste* with the audacious vision of, say, Herman Melville, suddenly one half of a *married couple* in a faux-redwood ranch house with a breezeway, a backyard barbecue, and a Volvo, scarcely indistinguishable from other middle-income residences north of the university.

Trouble with life is, The Suicide has quipped, you're expected to actually live it, not just write about it.

Worse, you actually have to live your life *somewhere.*

Born in the Midwest, likely die in the Midwest. Ironic since The Suicide wasn't any kind of *mid*-anything.

In his twenties he'd tried Manhattan. Sublease on a fifth-floor walkup on Tenth Street near Sixth Avenue. First flush of early success he'd accepted an offer to teach at NYU then changed his mind reasoning that he had enough resources not to have to align himself with any academic institution, too original, too gifted and unique not to remain fiercely independent, also bristled against the idea of having to read amateur writing of which a considerable portion was mawkish imitation of his own flashy prose. (Though he preferred such prose to the much-imitated prose of the late Raymond Carver.) But he'd managed to elude teaching at the time. Reasoning too that an exterior Manhattan craziness would drain off craziness in his (bipolar) brain like draining pus from an abscess but it hadn't turned out that way, had to crawl back to the Midwest within a year like a broken-backed snake.

By this time drinking—that's to say *alcohol*—not just beer but wine, whiskey, gin—had become part of the problem.

Cedar Lane!—can't make up these heartland names, repeated from town to town through the Midwest. They are just *there,* awaiting your arrival.

The idea had been *writer-in-residence* at the great sprawling land-grant university. An offer, he'd (nervously) joked among his friends, he couldn't refuse.

(Which was true enough: couldn't afford to refuse.)

(No brilliant iconoclastic young-guy writer gives a second thought to such bourgeois benefits as health insurance but by this time The Suicide wasn't a young-guy writer any longer and yes, he did think about health insurance.)

As a midwestern *writer-in-residence* he'd morphed into one of those large shaggy arthritic-jointed dogs, Saint Bernard, Bernese mountain dog, Australian shepherd—affable dogs, good-sport dogs, dogs with panting tongues, dogs aging prematurely, God-damned *boring dogs* . . . Hair grown long, coppery-gray straggling to his shoulders, perpetual three-days' beard sprouting on his jaws, The Suicide bicycled a mile to ancient Morven Hall, where it was his task to teach a "master class" in creative writing to fifteen young persons daring to identify themselves as *fiction writers,* in this way spared operating a motor vehicle (for The Suicide had been warned by his psychopharmacologist against operating *heavy machinery* while medicated). In so doing The Suicide would cultivate a local reputation for endearing eccentricity, bicycling the battered gunmetal-gray mountain bike along university pathways, panting uphill, coasting (teeth-rattlingly fast) downhill, bloodshot eyes hidden by tinted glasses, brow furrowed with thought. Scarlet scarf trailing behind him in gusts of Great Lake wind.

Start anew. Wipe slate clean. You can do it!

Fuck you can. You *can't.*

Still he was resolved. Forestalling the crucial question not if, but when to kill himself, was there ever an ideal time, just making excuses, too easily distracted, glumly staring at a calendar the wife had marked leading into the unfathomable future.

No. Just—no. Can't.

Here would be the place, then. Fuck his bad luck, Cedar Lane it would be, faux-redwood ranch house when an *artiste* (yes! the word is drenched in the heavy sickly syrup of irony) of his stature deserved to be living in a Frank Lloyd Wright house at least. (Except did Wright's houses include anything so plebian as basements?)

Known for years he would hang himself in a basement. Only not which basement.

Any other part of the house including a bathroom didn't seem right to him. People would have to live in those rooms. A basement, nobody lives in a basement. The Cedar Lane basement was part-finished and part-unfinished and smelled of damp, what you don't want to think is mold, that dark-fungus mold that eats away at the lungs and the brain without the afflicted one knowing.

Vaguely, as in a dream riddled with static, The Suicide recalled documents being signed. He hadn't been informed what these documents were. Observing the wife signing, then handing the pen to him. Eyes on *him.* Taste of panic at the realization that if he signed this contract he would be obliged to pay for twelve months of rent and what if he changed his mind after just a few weeks, which it was his predilection to do? Yet—nonetheless—he watched himself sign an illegible signature that was accepted as *his.*

That was the joke. He'd begun to understand. His prose, the

voice of his prose, wasn't actually *his* but issued from a nether region of his brain as the utterances of the ventriloquist's dummy seem to issue from the hinged wooden mouth of the dummy on the ventriloquist's lap. *His, not-his.*

It was an *haute*-druggy voice. It was a voice so intent upon repudiating "poetry"—"musical speech"—"vanilla syntax"—"linear chronology"—that its effect, upon a sensitive ear, was akin to broken and bleeding fingernails dragged down an asylum wall. Deceiving others and for a long time himself that this prose was worth dying for. Much of it unintelligible, indecipherable, unfathomable, unforgivable. In recent years, however, since he'd "cut back" on his drinking, The Suicide was losing the capacity to deceive himself.

Gently Wendy suggested, daring the husband's wrath, trespassing in that part of his life that was *his* and not *theirs—You know, you don't always have to be dazzling. You don't owe them acrobatics in every book. Every story. You don't owe them anything.*

But he did. He could not endure his life otherwise except yes, he *did.*

A hokey sci-fi story in the vein of midlevel Heinlein, Sturgeon: The Suicide is returning to the house at 88 Cedar Lane even as The Suicide is exiting the house. The Suicide perceives "himself" in transit even as The Suicide is "himself" in transit.

Linear time has folded over, flapped or flipped like a bad comb-over in a sudden gust.

The Suicide is returning (again) with his fried, frazzled, zapped brain even as The Suicide is exiting the house to be delivered to the hospital where his brain will be zapped (again).

How many times this has happened in "actual" time?—you'd have to inquire of the wife.

The Suicide has lost so many neurons, he has lost count.

ECT is considered the "last resort." Where *talk therapy, pharmacology, macrobiotic diet, exercise and prayer and positive thoughts* have failed, the zapping of the (afflicted) brain is all that remains. The Suicide endures six treatments, six mornings: anesthesia, electric current, recovery room. For each neuron zapped to oblivion, units of memory are erased.

ECT—"electroconvulsive therapy"—is what you'd call an inexact science. As once lobotomy was considered an inexact science.

Bantering with the green-scrubbed.

Waking in the (refrigerated) recovery room to blank white rough-textured walls where gradually some vestiges of "memory" roll back—flickering images projected onto the wall.

The logic being, whatever is making the afflicted patient clinically depressed, self-loathing, suicidal is rooted in the region of his brain that controls memory. If you weaken or annihilate the memory you will weaken or annihilate these symptoms.

Too much was known of The Suicide's plight, however. Confidences had been "leaked."

Crushing for The Suicide, to be (publicly) delivered home, to this so-ordinary *home,* the conscientious wife positioning their car beside the kitchen door, to enable the afflicted man to take the fewest possible steps to the door; the wife stooping to help the husband out of the car, slipping an arm around the (damp, soft-flabbed) waist and walking him to the kitchen door carefully, staggering a bit beneath his weight, for The Suicide's vanity will not allow him to use either a cane or a walker for obvious reasons: The Suicide was only thirty-nine years old and *thirty-nine-year-old men can walk without such elderly aids, thank you.*

Calmness of the wife. Stoicism of the wife. Stubborn refusal of the wife to succumb to anxiety, impatience, despair seeping like sweat from the pores of The Suicide.

Oblivious of the (probable) fact that everyone in the university community knew of The Suicide's (resumed) "shock" treatments. Everyone in the neighborhood of single-family homes and rentals, faux-redwood ranches and cheapie Cape Cods and Colonials knew not only the three-pronged name of the much-heralded writer-in-residence and not only that he'd had to take emergency sick leave in just the third week of the term but how many times the wife has had to drive him to the hospital in Minnesota.

Of course everyone recognized The Suicide on sight, his photograph in local newspapers, heralded on the university's website, hawked to alums, wealthy donors, undergraduates, and graduates, impossible not to recognize as a local celebrity though few in the vicinity had actually read the work of the writer-in-residence or had the slightest inclination to read it.

Local high school English teachers assigned his short fiction to their AP students. Of these, approximately one-fifth admired it, four-fifths were unmoved, bored, or annoyed by it, and a few literary-minded young persons became enthralled by it as, it's said, The Suicide had become enthralled by the fiction of Thomas Pynchon at their age.

And so, the writer-in-residence was *known*. In the university community he'd become a rumor, a tale, a parable, a scandal.

The Suicide, a master of precise, exacting prose that coiled and twined about itself like a nest of snakes, most dreaded being "recorded" by others. "Used" by others in their own (crude, amateur) fictions. *Quoted out of context.* The writer's most nuanced ruminations, his acrobatic run-on sentences spilling masterfully across and down pages like white-water rapids—reduced to mere *sound bites.*

". . . would rather die. Yes."

Magic cloak of invisibility desperately needed. Begged begged begged the wife to bring his *protective gear* to the hospital when she came to pick him up. Not expose him to the jeering eyes of strangers. For after ECT the outermost layer of his skin was peeled away, his very soul exposed.

A wizened and rotted onion of a soul, it is. Shame!

Along the familiar route to the faux-redwood ranch house: St. Paul Avenue, University Avenue, Bienvue Street, Cedar Lane. This is a route, a pathway the wife has followed many times before. Inexorable, the labyrinth of his life has led him *here.*

Like a noose slowly tightening. What's the technical term?—
hangman's noose, with numerous coils and a single, lethal knot.

Neighbors living in close proximity observe/record the broken
man shakily climbing out of the car, aided by the wife; swaying
weak-kneed as the wife struggles to keep him erect, help him to
the door, prevent his collapse into a soupy boneless heap on the
asphalt drive.

Hadn't he hoped to prevent this? Exactly this?

*Of course! He'd planned to kill himself months before. All of this, this
spectacle, would have been prevented.*

Possibly, it's a fiction by Borges: "The Suicide is laboring to compose a fiction titled 'The Suicide.'"

Typical of Borges, the tale is a (shameless) mind-teaser: "The
Suicide is laboring to compose a fiction titled 'The Suicide' but
endless digressions, meanderings, and nightmare roundabouts
from which there is no exit impede him."

In which case it's hardly a surprise that even as The Suicide is
(awkwardly, inexpertly) tossing the rope over the rafter in the basement of the faux-ranch house at 88 Cedar Lane he is (also) (par-
adoxically) waking in the recovery room in the hospital (again).
What happens to the brain when it is *anesthetized*? Does the "mind"
cease to exist? If memory is annihilated, has an experience actually occurred? If the patient feels excruciating pain/trauma during
electric shock treatments, but does not remember, has the pain/
trauma occurred?

For he'd known, with his usual stoic resignation, that the shock
treatments weren't going to work, since a similar course of treatments hadn't worked eleven months before. For the antidepres-
sants hadn't worked, and had in fact turned against him, over a
passage of years. For *nothing had worked.*

There was a kind of pride in this, The Suicide had to concede.
Others, less afflicted than he, less sincerely suicidal, might manage to "survive" if not "recover"—but *he* was special; he had always
been special.

The routine was maddening to him, deeply insulting. It has all happened before, even as it is happening now. Then, but also now.

Once home, in underclothes freshly laundered by the wife, in bedclothes freshly laundered by the wife, in a room with venetian blinds tightly drawn against the prying rays of the sun, despite a dull headache the patient would sleep for twelve to fifteen hours; wake dazed with a bladder so tight to bursting he would have to walk bent over to the bathroom, wincing; followed then by an airy, eerie nothingness during which time he could not concentrate even to read the simple columnar text of a newspaper, still less could he concentrate well enough to "write"—a highly complex neurological activity that involves not only brain-thoughts but a mysterious coordination of fingers on a keyboard. Beyond this, the accelerated heartbeat of hypomania, and beyond *that,* adrenaline rush of a full-fledged manic state lasting forty-eight hours, approximately; then, the "crash" into the bleakest dampest basement of the soul.

Easier, far easier to end the farce. End the cycle. *Then, now. Now, then.*

Reasoning that his logic had been counterproductive. Killing himself at home was a problem in timing: the vigilant wife was *always home.*

And so, far more practical to take control of his fate before he even arrived home this time. On the interstate seizing the steering wheel, (re)taking control from the wife who'd usurped it, aim the Volvo at a concrete wall.

Planning this in the recovery room. As consciousness, and cunning, returned to the numbed brain.

He would! He would do this! How simple, and how irrevocable! His heart was suffused with hope and joy warm as a flood of sunlight.

Tremendous relief, he felt. Fuck hanging himself in the basement of the ranch house—too much maneuvering required, too many opportunities for things to go wrong.

Gripping his hand, the wife awaited. Nurses were urging him— *Wake up! Wake up!*—and suddenly his eyes opened, he *was awake.*

But then, the clarity of his plan began to fade. Static made it hard for him to hear. Shook his head clear of cobwebby thoughts. Blurred vision, eyes unfocused like pitted olives. The wife had brought fresh-laundered clothing to the hospital for him to change into but (of course) he soon sweated through the clothing and would stink of his body. *That had always been a dilemma. Like whether to leave a suicide note. If his lifeless body was defiled by strangulation, if his body "stank"*—how could he bear to commit suicide? At least, suicide by hanging.

In the speeding Volvo, however: that was the respite.

Trying to recall the plan. In the Volvo, brought to the rear entrance of the hospital by the wife so that, wheeled to the curb by an attendant, The Suicide has only to walk a few yards to lower himself into the car. *Take care, Mr. Hoffstead!*

Now, to the interstate. Wife drives with maddening slowness, caution.

Now, at the interstate ramp. Wife eases out into traffic with maddening slowness, caution.

He will. This time, he will.

He vows!

Of course, this has all happened before, many times before, but he can break the cycle if he tries. Not unlike revising a tangled passage of prose.

If you write, you can *rewrite*. If you vise, you can *revise*.

Heading north on I-35. Wife keeps to the far-right lane as thunderous rigs bypass the Volvo, many times more massive than the Volvo. Wife-smile fixed in place. Continually asking how is he? Does his head ache? Maybe he should try to sleep? Lower the seat? Yes?

Yes, sleep. Good!

Let the wife think what she wishes to think. *He* is biding his time observing the rushing interstate through heavy-lidded eyes.

What he will do has already been worked out, rehearsed. In the recovery room he'd had a final rehearsal. In his unconscious state he'd conceived of the plan. Electric zaps had stimulated his benumbed cerebral cortex. Exhilarating blue flames. *Use the car. Use the opportunity. Don't overthink, you sap.*

He'd laugh at this rude voice except: his head aches. Staccato thumping that makes thinking difficult. Already he's beginning to lose it—the brilliant brave *final solution.*

Failing, as fingers fail grasping at a wall looming above the doomed individual, fingernails torn, broken for the afflicted one cannot haul the weight of his own sodden body aloft, cannot climb over the wall, not another time.

A smile distorts his face. Creeps into his face. *Can a body be so sodden it becomes its own body bag?*

Shaking his head. Clearing his head. (But don't make the wife suspicious: she thinks he has nodded off to sleep, mouth adrool.) Through near-shuttered eyelids calculating how far away the concrete wall is, possibly an eighth of a mile, at the ramp for Huron Avenue, when should he reach for the steering wheel, must not alarm the wife, must surprise the wife utterly, remain unmoved by the wife's struggle with him, her astonished and appalled screams as he propels the car into the wall—*Voilà! Fini.*

Within seconds, erased. All this misery obliterated, annihilated. Bodies amid wreckage and consciousness vanished as if it had never been.

It is only consciousness that registers sorrow, misery. It is only consciousness that registers irony. Bodies, no.

Except: How could The Suicide murder *her,* the innocent half of the *married couple?*

Even her name—"Wendy Marks." There is something so—so— *innocent* about that name . . .

Repelled by the thought of harming others in the (selfish) service of harming himself.

"Jesus no. I can't."

Can't, won't. Didn't.

Instead, tucked his hands into his (hot, seething) armpits. Stared sightless ahead as the concrete wall loomed large, rushed past. By exit 11, *St. Paul Avenue,* he has lapsed into a doze, head lolling on shoulders, gaping mouth like an infant's.

You could argue that the wife deserved it. Daring to take on the burden of *him.*

So many years younger than The Suicide. (Of course, he hadn't yet been The Suicide when they'd met.)

Too many women had disappointed him, he'd scarcely given her credence when they'd met. Attractive but not, you know—glamorous. He'd have been resentful, expected to respond to *glamour.* But this girl—"Wendy"—had seemed truly genuine, conscious of "who" he was, respectful, yet not fawning—(hated, detested, could not stand *fawning*)—and her voice was a soft voice, not like the voices of (surprisingly many) better-looking women, some air of self-regard, high-pitched, or too low-pitched, the wrong kind of (rasping) (gut-) laugh, makes you flee in revulsion. No: Wendy's voice was soft without being mellifluous, he could not bear *mellifluous,* no lilts, no squeaks or drawls, not nasal, he could not abide *nasal* for *nasal* is the sound of his own voice in his own ears, and at this point, their initial meeting, he hadn't known her last name, possibly had not even heard her last name, wouldn't have known—*Marks? Marx?* Nor did she squirm, laugh sharply, or hissingly—(something about an attractive woman laughing as a man might laugh, in restraint, *hissingly,* that was repugnant; this, The Suicide's favored way of laughing, to display mirth, or the recognition of mirth, without exactly succumbing to it). And in this way, not love, nor even "love," but the first premonition that, despite the silly name, despite the overmodest manner, despite the fact—(it was a fact, any guy would see at once)—that Wendy wasn't what you'd call *stunning, gorgeous*—that she was, at best, what your mother would call *attractive, well-groomed*—a sense of surrender to come, the way he'd inclined his head to hear her, whatever sweet banal murmurs issued from her mouth, a kind of instinctive predilection—maybe *maybe* she will be *the one.*

Yes!—*the one.* Utter cliché, yet it had come to him within a few hours of their meeting with the boldness of a match being struck if the match had somehow the power to strike itself into flame.

Her sincerity, gaze uplifted to his—trusting, not smug naïveté but true trust—vulnerable to him whom (of course) she scarcely knew—not-ironic—(*that* was crucial: female irony was no aphrodisiac, to put it mildly)—as a scoop of ice cream balanced in a cone is vulnerable to an approaching tongue.

Often he'd wondered—tormented himself—who among his friends might've warned her. Which of the (wounded, embittered) women with whom he'd been "involved" must have warned her.

Har is clinically depressed, you know.

Tried to kill himself in college.

. . . there's a hole where his heart is, you can try to fill—but—there's no bottom to it, an endless hole . . .

Have to ask yourself, is it worth it trying to save him? Somebody like him?

(Had The Suicide actually overheard these cruel queries, or had he invented the cruel queries himself? No doubt, in the actual world beyond his skull, far worse queries had been put to the wife-to-be.)

(Indeed, The Suicide had reason to believe that his own mother had contacted Wendy after they'd become engaged, hoping to dissuade her. *Wendy, dear—I hope you will not be offended, but—I have something to say to you, dear—about my son . . .*)

(For Harold, Sr., no longer living, having passed away in "mysterious circumstances" when Harold, Jr., had been eleven years old, had had similar symptoms, unless they were character traits, about which she, the naïve fiancée, hadn't been informed before their marriage.)

But Wendy refused to be forewarned. Could not be dissuaded. Loved him very very much.

Understanding that he was a brilliant person, a gifted artist, "genius"—probably. Can't be measured by ordinary means. "Moody" sometimes—but who isn't?

Insisting she wasn't marrying him to "save" him. Was not marrying him for any reason except she loved him.

Bravely she'd spoken! Twenty-three years old.

A muscle in his heart cringed. So young! No idea that to love this person would be to enlist in the perpetual act of "saving" him.

He would never forgive himself; he'd failed to warn her.

No. It wasn't that way at all.

He *did not love her*. He was furious with her. Sobbing-furious with her. Raising his voice to her.

Begging her for Christ's sake to bring his new coat, his *protective gear* with her when she picks him up at the hospital.

Knowing that he's desperate yet pretending not to know what he's referring to. As if, thick-tongued, sweat in rivulets down his gray-fleshy face, he's drunk, or drugged, or incapacitated from the shock treatments, swaths of neurons blasted to oblivion. So she has a legitimate reason not to understand what he's trying to say, to stammer, over the phone, five a.m. of the morning of the last treatment in this cycle of ECT.

Doesn't want to shout, nurses and aides lurk in the halls in Psychiatric Services. Anything he says will be recorded, there's a red camera eye at the ceiling in a corner of the room facing the bed. If he becomes overexcited this will be held against him however justified his excitement. If his blood pressure is too high treatment will have to be postponed. He does not want the treatment to be postponed because, if the treatment is postponed, his discharge from the hospital will be postponed. Yet: so obtuse, so obstinate, so cruelly ignorant is the wife, he has no choice except to shout at her.

Telling her to bring the coat—the new coat. Upstairs in his closet, still in the garment bag . . .

Damned cell phone is breaking up, the wife can't decipher his words. Can't risk using the landline in his room for fear of someone eavesdropping . . . He is wondering if in a diabolical experiment medics have affixed some sort of voice-box gadget in his throat that garbles his speech and makes it incomprehensible—the equivalent of reducing a face to pixels. Yet, at the same time, they've taken care to adjust the auditory region of his brain so that he hears his words in English, exactly as he speaks them.

Wondering too if the wife knows exactly what he is asking of her but resents the coat he'd purchased online without consulting her. (Wendy will discover the purchase from *Invisibility Inc.* soon enough, going through their credit card account at the end of the month.)

Anti-surveillance Protective Gear (Man's Overcoat, size XL) is an ankle-length garment recently purchased by The Suicide (at special one-time discount of $1,700) before the recent cycle of ECT. To the casual, ignorant eye it appears to be a conventional, somewhat bulky and unfashionably broad-shouldered man's coat of no identifiable style, a Soviet-looking coat, in a coarse dark fabric with metal buttons like blank staring eyes; to the discerning eye, it's a state-of-the-art, ingeniously designed *anti-surveillance garment* guaranteed to block surveillance cameras from registering its wearer when he appears in public.

What makes the coat special is the lining, a metallic stitching engineered to be *anti-cellular,* that looks, upon close examination, like living tissue. Touched with a cautious forefinger, the *anti-cellular lining* seemed to quiver with its own secret life.

Fearful of being observed by others, still more of being "recorded" by them, The Suicide ordered the item from *Invisibility Inc.,* a website for individuals desperate to retain their privacy amid the new omniscient technology. (From *Invisibility Inc.* one can also purchase "safe pouches" in which to encase cell phones, iPads, computers, and other electronic devices, to block signals identifying their locations, as well as protective masks, headgear, gloves, boots, and other accessories to block detection.)

The Suicide hasn't yet worn the garment outside the house, he has not (yet) had the opportunity. Recalling how when he'd pulled the heavy coat out of the UPS box, and tried it on, in the privacy of the (locked) bathroom, he'd seen that it was so oddly shaped, the material of which it was made so stiff, resembling a sort of plastic more than fabric, it would likely draw attention if the wearer appeared in public; and, if the damned thing isn't worn in public, there isn't much point in having purchased it.

Nor has The Suicide acquired *anti-surveillance accessories,* not even a helmet, so the coat is of limited value.

He'd need boots, too. And gloves. Specially treated eyeglasses. Just a coat to repel detection would be woefully inadequate: head, hands, feet exposed bodiless and quivering on detection screens like floating body parts, with nothing (visible) to link them. In his distracted state The Suicide hadn't gotten around to purchasing these. Obsessed with *running out of time* he'd been paralyzed staring at his digital watch, in a trance of horror the very embodiment of *time running out.*

And so now: whether to purchase more *anti-surveillance gear* when he isn't certain that he can activate the coat properly or even whether the protection the coat is supposed to guarantee is legitimate, or a fraud; those days he'd been *hoarse de combat* (*sic*) in the hospital in Minneapolis he hadn't had the opportunity to experiment with the coat. Nor could he do further research into the subject for in the hospital he was forbidden the use of a computer as well as a cell phone, the reason being that electronic devices provoked *hypomania* in the patient. He'd known better than to try to involve the wife in examining the coat for it would be one more arrow in her arsenal of ammunition with which to unman him.

Hon, you're scaring me. Please hon. Don't—do this.

Pretending to have become emotionally fragile. When *he* was the one who was *emotionally fragile* for Christ's sake!

When he'd tried to explain to her what he wanted, what he *required* from her, she'd gotten into the habit of bursting into tears.

For the list has grown lengthy, all that The Suicide requires from the woman who'd vowed to be his devoted wife.

A *bad scene* follows, soon after The Suicide is brought home from the hospital.

So *bad a scene,* the revered word-master cannot translate it into tolerable language.

Yet here is the paraphrase as the wife might report it to one of her (eager, scandalized) friends who have never wished The Suicide well though pretending (seven years now) to *really like him, certainly a unique kind of person, obviously brilliant, "genius"* . . .

Backing up the *bad scene* a few minutes. Half hour.

Post-anesthetic The Suicide is nauseated, lingers in the (downstairs) bathroom waiting to vomit up his guts but this doesn't happen, not the relief of a thorough vomiting only just gagging, bringing up some watery-vinegary stuff. Then, in the (upstairs) bathroom rinses his mouth, brushes his teeth with the electric toothbrush, flosses his teeth until his gums bleed, which is essential (he knows) to cleanse his teeth of acidic fluids.

Otherwise your teeth rot. Rot in your jaws. Like anorexic adolescents binge-eating then vomiting. Like meth-heads, which *he* is not.

Every med he's ever taken, it's doctor-prescribed. No "recreational drugs" for The Suicide.

His background, bourgeois. Solid middle-class. Father a university professor who'd risen to the rank of associate professor but never beyond.

So, The Suicide cleans his mouth. Several times over.

Compulsive? Obsessive? *Him?*

At his request the wife brings him a Diet Coke from downstairs. In interviews it has been (bemusedly) noted that the wife, years younger than The Suicide, behaves around him with the docility and alacrity of a waitress, or a nurse; the writer-husband orders the wife about in a way clearly meant to caricature such a relationship but the wife merely laughs—fine with her if it's a game, if it were serious it would be fine with her, too. *Living with* a man of such reputation, achievement. Not like *living with* just any guy.

But then, the *bad scene:* The Suicide discovers that the new coat is missing from his bedroom closet.

A scene that swerves, careens, stumbles, reverses, and repeats itself. Thwarts all comprehension. The Suicide demands of the frightened wife what she'd done with his new coat, the coat from *Invisibility Inc.* that *renders the wearer invisible;* the wife insists that she has no idea what he is talking about; The Suicide insists, she must have seen the UPS box he'd brought into the house, before he'd left for the hospital; the wife insists no, she had not; has no idea what he is talking about.

Which closet?—the wife asks. Which coat?

The Suicide hears his voice crack in a tremor of embarrassment: *The invisible coat.*

The wife repeats: *Invisible coat? I don't understand . . .*

The Suicide shouts: *The new coat! The one with the anti-cellular lining! It came via UPS, I hung it in my closet in the bedroom, you must have seen it.*

The wife insists his coats are all downstairs. Coats, jackets. Boots. The *outdoor closet.*

The Suicide shouts louder: *No! The new coat! Not downstairs— upstairs! In my bedroom closet where I left it . . .*

Even as the realization sweeps over The Suicide that he hadn't actually purchased the coat yet. He'd planned to purchase it, in detail.

As the anesthesia dripped into his vein in the ECT room and his consciousness began to crumble inward in a delicious swoon like a sheet of crinkly paper in the moment before flames engulf it, swallow it . . .

Too embarrassed to acknowledge to the wife that he'd only just planned to buy the coat, or hallucinated it; better to stomp away from the wife as if she has insulted him irrevocably, before the wife catches on that (of course: this has happened previously) he'd only fantasized the purchase; if he were to check online, which he has no intention of doing, he'd (possibly) (probably) discover that *Invisibility Inc.* does not exist.

Not in actual life, nor even in cyberspace. Not "really"—and not "virtually."

In the days following treatment The Suicide is expected to be "difficult." No longer clinically depressed, no longer suicidal, but (of course) he is still clinically depressed and he is certainly still suicidal, The Suicide channels his libido into a purer sort of rage, a pubescent child turning his wrath upon the nearest parent, likely to be the mother.

Regarding her husband with caution. Respect, and caution. His silence intimidates more than his outbursts. He sees that often she is frightened of him; her anxious smile is no disguise for The Suicide is one who *sees*.

(Gratifying to see an effect upon another that is visceral, in "real time"—not delayed and indirect as in art. For who cares if, dropping a rock into the Grand Canyon, you can't hear a crash below? If there is no dramatic consequence, no visible effect—has anything at all [actually] happened?)

Not that this was unusual, it was not. The Suicide's doctor had explained to him, in the wife's presence, what they might expect. Not good to leave him alone, if that's possible. If not, consider hiring an RN . . .

What! Absolutely *no*.

Last thing they wanted in their household, in their marriage, was a third party. Each agreed.

He'd laughed. He'd been insulted, sure, but he'd laughed. Wounded, eviscerated, "unmanned"—but sure, he'd laughed because he was that kind of guy, a guy's guy, a good sport, if he'd been Jewish, a *mensch*.

After the ECT there are a few rocky days. Rocky nights. Sedatives are recommended. Fact is, if you can't sleep your immune system is weakened. Fact is, you are vulnerable to infections, bacterial, viral, you are vulnerable to sprains and breaks, insomnia is a killer. Much better, just take the prescribed sleeping pills. Try to get seven hours' sleep at least.

Seven hours! The Suicide plans to sleep for seventeen hours.

After the ECT expect to experience blank amnesiac patches like a poorly scrubbed wall. White swaths. Where there'd been a memory of—something, someone; now, vanished. Try not to let it upset you, perfectly natural, beneficial to "forget" something not crucial to remember, don't push yourself, don't try to work on your novel, it was *forcing yourself to work on the interminable piranha-novel* that made you sick originally, *forcing yourself to work when you are not strong enough.*

The work-in-regress has had various titles: *Nevermore, Nevermire, Quagmire.*

Not that any of this is new. After seven years of marriage, to the wife very little must be new.

And so, he'd had to assume that she knew. She could sense. How it was gathering in intensity inside him, this time really *really this time.*

Her decision then, to leave him alone. That (particular) morning.

Not an accident. He couldn't think so. Hadn't Freud said with grim satisfaction—*There are no accidents.*

Three days after the treatment he's (visibly, seemingly) feeling better. Heaping bowl of Cheerios for breakfast. Blueberries, rasp-berries. Heaping spoon of sugar. Buttermilk. As if testing, taunt-ing nausea. First time in many months the wife would leave The Suicide alone since the dilemma was: she'd postponed her yearly gynecological exam not once but twice. Hadn't had a Pap smear in several years. Hadn't had a mammogram.

Not that Wendy was blaming him. Not a glimmer of reproach! He understood, she was simply explaining. Uneasy, defensive, wanting him to understand.

Coming very close, he could see, to asking him—*Would you like to come with me? You could bring your laptop, you could wait in . . .* But dared not, for that would give the game away that she worried about him alone in the house, didn't trust him, for Christ's sake *why not*? He was an adult man, wasn't he? Not on life support, not a raving lunatic. Yes?

He'd assured her he was O.K. He was more than O.K., she'd

seen the enormous breakfast he'd eaten *without vomiting any of it back up.* Hadn't he been back at his desk working again, not compulsively, not in that paroxysm of white heat that had toppled him over into madness but at a restrained pace, a sane pace, actually enjoying (!) his hours at the word processor translating scribbled notes into a text that will constitute book 4 of *Quagmire,* or is it *Quagmore.*

Also, The Suicide is reworking the Borgesian prose piece that makes him smile, so damned clever, one of the most clever (but harrowing) things he has ever written, sure to be a milestone of post-postmodernist experimentation:

"The Suicide returns to his work humbled but invigorated. Many times interrupted in his effort to complete a story begun long ago titled 'The Suicide' whose first line is: 'The Suicide returns to his work humbled but invigorated . . .'"

Why?—such effort, such agony, yanking out his own guts with his own hands, hand over hand uncoiling his guts to entertain a blank-staring world? Wouldn't the wisest remedy be silence?

Wire the damned mouth shut. Wet cement in the mouth, throat, let dry.

Best cure for *clinical depression*—mute like (disgraced traitor) Ezra Pound.

Harold, Sr., had had enough dignity not to. Whatever was eating at his gut, whatever outspreading dark-feathered wings inside his skull, glisten of terror in his shadowed eyes (so like the eyes of Harold, Jr.!—the son cannot bear to acknowledge)—the man had not exposed to the world.

He, Harold, Jr., stubbornly perseveres. Hasn't (yet) given up.

Scornful of confessional writing by female scribblers but his own scribbles, unique to him as the DNA of his own piss, are something else. Every page of his work, every passage, every line, every word and punctuation mark are *him talking about himself* in a fancy hieroglyphic few could decode. Each book, The Suicide's (mostly male, youngish but aging) readership could understand less of it; each book, more critically acclaimed.

When finally The Suicide writes a totally incomprehensible book, time for his Pulitzer Prize!

(Though The Suicide scorns all prizes, regrets having accepted several as a young writer for now the string of his awards drags after him whenever he is introduced or written about, like a scaly possum tail.)

Confounded by his own being. Uncomprehending. He has come to hate, detest, fear the act of writing, or trying to write, yet cannot *not*. This drive, this appetite, this rage to impress himself upon the consciousness of others . . .

Like climbing the (rusted, wobbly) metal steps on the side of the water tower, years ago when he'd been a kid. Crazy stunt, nobody in his right mind etc. yet: every year, early spring, first thaw, guys would climb and scrawl initials in Day-Glo, only once in memory did one of them slip, fall, die—an older kid, high school.

He'd stared in envy, too smart/cowardly to make the climb as others stood gaping and cheering below though in his fantasies sure, he did.

Thinking of that climb. A quarter century ago. (Is that possible? The Suicide scarcely feels twenty-five years old.) Still, a sensation of excitement ripples through him, like an electric shock.

The water tower, still at the edge of his hometown. Hulking, oppressive.

Rare for The Suicide in recent years to return to visit his (lonely) mother and (scattered) relatives but when he does, finds himself drawn to the old school, a quarter mile away is the old water tower unchanged except more derelict, covered in Day-Glo graffiti, initials and numerals that have obscured the initials and numerals of his long-ago era.

At the base of the water tower, straggling underbrush like mad scribbles made with a dull-pointed pencil.

Now, the equivalent of climbing the water tower is simply getting up in the morning.

(Morning?—is that a joke? The Suicide can barely heave himself out of bed by noon.)

Without his work to jolt him out of bed early, seven a.m. as it had once done, without his work to anchor him, he drifts like a zombie about the house, poor sap. No wonder his wife is fed up with him, his self-pity masquerading as martyrdom. Bag of guts searching for his lost genius-self.

Promise is, if/when things become really unbearable he can opt out. Anytime. Hasn't he been telling himself for years. As Nietzsche advised. As Marcus Aurelius has advised.

Except: The wife is too vigilant. As a seeing-eye dog trained to protect his master in all circumstances even if the master does not wish such protection. One of those gallant dogs so acute in judgment he will not allow his master to do something he (the master) is certain he wants to do—like cross a street in defiance of traffic, stumble into an open manhole.

That is, the most professionally trained therapy dogs will *disobey their masters* in the service of protecting their masters. This is a degree of "intelligence" not invariably found in *Homo sapiens* and a sound argument that (some, selected) animals can behave more rationally than (many) human beings.

The Suicide recalls how impressed he'd been, having once, by chance, observed therapy dogs in training in a public plaza! How eager the beautiful animals were to please their human trainers, to be praised, petted! The Suicide had lingered for an hour observing dogs and trainers, particularly struck by those situations in which a human being appears to be willfully behaving in a way to jeopardize his safety, testing the animal's ability to "disobey" selectively. Jokingly he'd said afterward that he was looking forward to a time when, legally blind, or in some other way incapacitated, he could surrender his volition to a therapy dog, to lead him through the pitfalls of life.

Indeed, the wife is his therapy-creature. His seeing-eye. She protects him from harm, even that harm he wishes for himself. She *obstructs*.

Younger, she has become his *elder*.

Where once he'd been avidly, sexually hungry for her, now he is repelled by her—the fleshy obdurate fact of her.

Dependent upon her, indebted to her. Grateful for her, who has so willingly taken on the care of him, in the most intimate and embarrassing of ways, at times. His face shimmers with the heat of shame, recalling.

Overhearing her on the phone in another room, in a hushed whispery voice— . . . *don't dare let him out of my sight. I love him so much* . . .

Not sure what he felt, hearing this. Heart-warmed? Insulted?

God-damned indignant, incensed. *Unmanned.*

Worse: The wife is keeping a journal, he believes. Has reason to suspect.

Recording The Suicide's stammered speech, so very different from his poised "public" speech. Every humiliating detail of the (most recent) breakdown. Weight loss, blood pressure. Eventually, weight gain, "bloat." Bloody dental floss in the wastebasket in the (shared) bathroom. Shaky-handed shaving porcupine-quill jaws, stanching streaks of blood with toilet paper. Damp pile of T-shirts, shorts he wears instead of pajamas, kicked into a corner of the bathroom to be carried away by the wife in discreet silence, laundered and returned to his bureau drawers.

In the faux-redwood ranch house he'd declared he could not abide cleaning women, no more than he could abide medical caretakers. Let the place go to hell, he'd clean it himself, propel the vacuum cleaner through the rooms, run a mop over the kitchen floor, spray toxic-blue Windex as he used to do high on his own brain-energy, synapses sizzling like bug-zappers in the old bachelor days before the marriage-noose when he'd had energy to spare writing through the night *after* drinking with the guys.

Wendy hadn't opposed him. No resistance. Wisely retreating but (as unobtrusively as possible) doing the housecleaning herself.

But also carrying her iPhone with her. Alert to any opportunity to take (surreptitious) pictures of The Suicide when he isn't aware.

Glowering hunchbacked at his computer, leafing through *Finnegans Wake* for a jolt of random inspiration, guzzling Diet Cokes one after another after another, trying to call, failing to call numbers no longer operant on his cell phone, for all The Suicide knew some of his old buddies had died by now.

Definitely The Suicide knew that his wife took videos of him nodding off on the sofa watching reruns of *Law & Order,* his favorite soporific. Head atilt, damp mouth gaping open, rasping snoring like aroused wasps.

His meds. Heavy-duty antianxiety/antidepressant meds. Soul a sodden puddle at his feet.

Why The Suicide is addicted to *Law & Order:* He has seen reruns so often, as soon as the first scene of an episode opens he can "see" into the future. What is an enigma to the ordinary viewer is, to him, the extraordinary viewer, a future adroitly compressed into a past. *He has been here before, there are no surprises here.* Nothing to do but wait, relax, as the future rolls back to greet him.

First glimmering: Christ, he hadn't been born yet when Jim Morrison died.

That year, when was it—1971. Janis Joplin, Jimi Hendrix also died, aged twenty-seven. Brian Jones. Kurt Cobain. All twenty-seven.

But first of all was Robert Johnson. Greatest of blues singers, dead in 1938 at the age of twenty-seven long before it became fashionable. Sold his soul to the devil before it became fashionable.

Have to wonder—*why*? Why twenty-seven, not thirty?

Not all of the deaths were *suicide*—officially.

He'd thought maybe, when he was twenty-seven—that might be the end. Not that he was superstitious, he was not. Nor would he die of a heroin overdose. Not his thing.

Fact is at twenty-seven he hadn't been ready. Immersed in his second novel, which (he'd seemed to know) would make him famous in his generation. Writing through the night, by hand. Pages and pages of script, sweat dripping onto the paper, wiping face, chest, back, armpits, crotch with a towel. Near to dehydrated, his soul oozing through his skin. Replenishing liquids—Diet Coke, Gatorade. The happiest he'd been! Ever been.

Soon then, he'd forget that happiness. Has forgotten happiness.

How he'd loved the very exhaustion. Poison oozing out of his pores. As Chekhov had squeezed the slave, the *serf,* out of his bloodstream, freeing him to be—Chekhov.

He'd been freed to be: himself.

Where he'd crawled on his belly, then he was soaring into the sky. *When there was nothing left I'd stagger away, fall onto my bed and sleep. When I couldn't continue because there was nothing then permission was granted to me to quit.*

You don't earn oblivion easily. No short cuts.

Not that he's accusing her, the wife. That's not the kind of guy he is. He *is not.*

That she knew, must've known. Why she'd left him alone that morning.

Had to be a reason. *The* reason. His (fried) brain is Occam-razor-sharp.

Knots of diseaseter cursed through his vains.

Hours he'd taken to compose this line. Not bad!

The jocoserious one, too, had gone mad—brilliant madness. Entangled in "voices" as the hapless artist Laocoön and his sons in the great serpent's crushing coils.

. . . but then, four a.m., waking in a cocoon of sweat in sudden doubt. Well, not sudden—but *doubt.* Knowing *knots of diseaseter cursed through his vains* was shit but not ordinary garden-variety shit, gargantuan shit and show-offy shit and he was tired of it, tired of the bright-bratty voice rising like gorge in his throat and spilling into his mouth.

So if/when the woman, the wife, wished to kiss that mouth or anywhere near that mouth The Suicide jerked away in a spasm to spare her the smell, taste, aura of that bile not in revulsion of *her—*

the mammalian-maternal all-forgiveness, all-enveloping/smothering *love* of the female—but in revulsion of *him*.

Of course, the wife has misunderstood. Hurt, dismay he hasn't time to correct. Fuck trying continuously to explain, correct. Fuck endless apologies. Head ringing with pain like a gong struck with a mallet. *Intimacy suffocates. Intimacy is the secret noose.* Desperate to get away, anywhere that's away, can't bear the woman knowing him so close-up, relentlessly. Seven years going on seventy. Face once so smooth, glowing-skinned now streaked with tears like dirty rainwater—no longer a "Wendy." Bright fearless girl who'd laughed at his jokes now an anxious woman at whom (let's be frank) The Suicide probably wouldn't give a second glance if he'd encountered her in the raw blunt world beyond marriage.

No. None of this is remotely true. He is deeply in love with her—Wendy.

Nothing funny about her name, never was. No more than Harold— "Har"—is funny.

Sobbing against his knuckles. Christ, he loves her! Sick-sinking sensation, love like a rotted hole in the gut.

Doesn't want to drag her down with him. Does. Not.

To save the wife, he'll have to leave her.

In *Supervolcano* sweatshirt, khakis, and grungy running shoes at six a.m. desperate to get away. Run along the arboretum trails, thudding, panting, run out of his body. Maybe his heart will give out.

"God *damn*."

First toss of the rope meant to loop over the rafter falls short. His hands shake. His heart is a pendulum in his chest.

Awkward, amateur. Everything The Suicide does is *amateur*.

At least he has thought ahead. Getting his hands on a real rope—a *macho rope*. Not the child's jump rope he'd discovered in a corner of the basement, he'd (vaguely) planned to use, secreting away in a drawer.

(But would the jump rope rope have been sturdy enough? Not nearly so thick as the rope he has now.)

(He'd liked the irony of it. *Jump rope*. A sign he hadn't taken even his death seriously.)

(Which was true. Is true. He's the essence of *hip, cool.* Death is just another cliché. Lends itself to parody. *Kitsch.*)

(But then, he'd discovered in a French mystery novel by a writer of whom he'd never heard a scene in which a depressed character hangs himself in a hotel room using a child's jump rope—and all the joy of his plan evaporated. The final gesture of The Suicide's life was not going to be *plagiarized*!)

Managing to get the rope over the rafter, fumbling to secure it. An effort to knot a rope of this thickness. (If all else fails, the jump rope is still in the workbench drawer.) (No, he *will not plagiarize the damned jump rope.*) Trying not to be anxious, aware that he is alone in the house for only a finite amount of time and who knows how long that time will be, unwatched, unsurveyed, unwifed.

It isn't his death that makes him shiver with dread, it's the wife returning too soon, discovering him and cutting him down.

Discovering him, screaming as she fumbles to cut him down, fails, must call 911, it will be a farce if an emergency crew rushes into the basement and revives him . . .

Not that The Suicide dislikes farce. On the contrary, The Suicide's reading of life is that it *is* farce; but The Suicide must be in control, determining the nature of the farce. *He* is the writer-of-the-residence, he will not tolerate his control being wrested from him by strangers.

And so he must act quickly. He must not digress, meander. The wife will return as soon as she can, she has said. (An errand? An appointment? The Suicide was so surprised to learn that the vigilant wife was leaving the house, first time in weeks, months the wife was leaving him alone in the house, he'd scarcely heard her explain where she was going, and why.)

Why now. Why today. This morning. What did she know, what has she intuited?

Promising that she would be back by noon. She would prepare his favorite lunch!

Mouthing the words *favorite lunch*! As one might promise a favorite food to a child.

(Hasn't Wendy been articulating her words too clearly, too loudly lately? Is The Suicide becoming hearing-impaired, without his awareness? Wanting to protest—*He is only thirty-nine years old!*)

(Mortified to be pushed in a wheelchair through the hospital corridors. Right out onto the sidewalk. When he could have walked!—of course. Though it was explained to him that it's routine hospital practice, insurance liability, he was offended deeply, insulted. As he'd pushed away a walker brought into his room by a well-intentioned aide. *No! Go away.*)

After several botched tries he has managed to attach the rope securely to the rafter.

Tugs at it, tests it with his weight, *it will hold.* (He thinks.)

Now—the noose! A challenge for one who'd failed at each Boy Scout project in succession.

Like the conscientious student he'd once been, he has researched "nooses" online, has become something of an amateur-expert in the subject as they will discover when they commandeer his computer . . . Fascinated by the cornucopia of knots. Who'd known there were so many!

But only one, singular, slip-sliding-tightening *hangman's noose.*

Takes time, practice. But The Suicide is grimly determined. Following online instructions. Has to laugh, an addendum to the instructions is the heartfelt-sounding plea

> *If you are tying a noose because you intend to end your life*
> *PLEASE call emergency services (911, 112, 999, or your local*
> *emergency number) or your local SUICIDE HOTLINE before*
> *it is too late.*

There's a joke to be made here but The Suicide can't think of it just now.

Next what's required is a chair. A solid chair. A chair that *will not wobble, still less shatter* beneath his weight.

No chair in the basement. Will have to bring a chair downstairs. *Damn.*

Practical matters have never been The Suicide's *forte*. Long before the "virtual" world was invented, The Suicide dwelt there.

Taking a grudging pleasure in the task, hauling a chair downstairs, bumping against the wall with it . . . A vague smile plays about The Suicide's lips, the damned (clumsy) chair will have to be carried back upstairs. "But not by *moi*."

As he'd been pleased with himself, first time he'd voted, aged twenty-one, in the sour-tasting aftermath of 9/11, in a middle-scale suburb of Cleveland managing to pull the voting booth lever that jerked the curtain closed behind him, then pulling the lever in what would be a counter motion to open it again without mishap and in this way confounding the foolish but obsessive worry that his votes would be nullified by a rash miscalculation opening the curtain.

All this while listening for Wendy to return . . . (Would he hear the car pulling up beside the kitchen door? He *would* hear Wendy coming into the kitchen, he was sure.)

Is it too late to leave a note? To assure his wife it is *not your fault, darling.*

Do not blame yourself, darling.

(Maudlin, mawkish. Impossible!)

(Rare for The Suicide to call his wife "darling"—he'd sometimes called her "darling" in an arch emulation of Ronald Colman in a forties movie—but not for years. Yet to call her "Wendy" seems wrong also for the name "Wendy" suggests a child's nursery, dolls, dollhouse, insipid dolls that squeak *Ma-ma!* when their torsos are squeezed.)

(Why in Christ's sake did he marry a woman named *Wendy*, a diminutive for which there exists no formal name? What had he been thinking? At the age of almost-forty The Suicide has too much pride for his death to be associated with anything *silly*.)

Anyway, no time for a suicide note, that would require days, weeks. Coiled in compulsive revising as in the coils of Laocoön. And what time is it?—sands of time running out.

She has run out. Left him alone.

(Alone? He is gripped with something like terror, the very word—*alone*.)

Calling your bluff, Harold, Jr. Didn't think anyone ever would, did you?

He realizes that he has been listening for her to return, anxiously. He'd been certain that by now she'd have returned. Can't recall what the appointment was, she'd told him but he hadn't actually heard. Stunned that she would leave the house, abandon him.

Certain that she will return. In time . . .

Change her mind, decide to return.

Any minute now the vehicle in the driveway, kitchen door pushed open. *Hello? I'm back. Changed my mind. Are you upstairs? Hon, where are you? Shall I bring you a Coke?*

(Actually he'd like a Coke. A rush of fizzy chemicals, caffeine.)

(He will get a Coke for himself. He will swallow down a small selection of panic-soothing pills. *All fucking planned this time and he does not intend to fail.*)

But would Wendy call him *hon*? His stiffness has discouraged her from such gestures of wifely intimacy.

Questions she'd asked him when they were first married, meaning no harm but annoying to him, prying. Curtly he'd replied— *That's private.*

In school his guy-friends called him *Har*. He hadn't liked it but what the hell. Better than *Harry*. Couldn't expect them to call him *Harold* as his mother did.

Girls and women he'd trained to call him *Harold*. Just—*Harold*.

Dislike of diminutives. Robert diminishes to Bobby, Richard to Dick, Dickie. Matthew to Matt. Algernon, dignified mouthful of a name, diminishes to Algie—a joke.

Wendy hadn't known what to call him, once they'd become what you would call intimate. *Hon, sweetie, darling*—he'd laughed, but not with mirth. Intimate as tickling, which he did not like either.

She'd hoped to call him *hon, honey*. Why?—*Because no one else can call you that. Only me because I am your wife.*

His eyes sting with tears. His young wife, years ago, when they'd been new, sweetly hopeful, awkward with each other but not—yet—

adversaries ... He has ruined this woman's life, has he? Her trust, her love, her kindness—he feels like the doofus who has backed over his kids' beloved dog in the driveway, not looking the fuck where he's going, just—*backing up.*

But now, the wife is the adversary. *He* is the quarry.

All this while his numbed fingers are turning the, what's it, *hangman's noose.*

This will surprise. This will impress. That he, Boy Scout fuckup, managed to create a true *hangman's noose* following online instructions, with seven turns (!).

The noose, the coils, ingeniously engineered to allow the loop in the rope to tighten as it's pulled, you'd have to wonder, wouldn't you?—who'd first gotten the idea for such a use of coils in a length of rope ...

Checking another time: The other end of the rope is securely tied around the rafter.

Beside him, the chair-from-upstairs.

Soon, relief. That sensation of certitude, euphoria. *To have acted, finally. To have made an end of so many failed beginnings. Thank God!*

Gamely, diligently, doggedly, futilely-but-with-determination The Suicide is (once again) laboring to compose a fiction beginning, "The Suicide is laboring to compose a fiction beginning, 'The Suicide is laboring to compose a fiction beginning, "The Suicide ... ,"' but endless digressions, meanderings, and nightmare roundabouts from which there is no exit impede him."

Drafts of his novel-in-progress sprawling over three thousand pages he'd largely abandoned at the time of his most recent collapse, before the final cycle of ECT when he'd (half) known that he was not only totally exhausted with his work but totally exhausted with his life, which had come to be near-equivalent with his work, indistinguishable from it. *It's time. Time! Please God.*

Not fear of dying, not cowardice, more like *distraction* has been his enemy. Difficult to focus on any goal. *Suicidal ideation* requires the ability to concentrate, plan. Calculate, calibrate. Easier to surf the internet—hours down the (clogged) drain. Easier to grab a beer, slouch on the sofa, tune in to the cable channel broadcasting *Law & Order* reruns twenty-four hours a day seven days a week.

These are (not) your stories: they have endings.

But the more profound distractions are dollops of "good news" that make The Suicide doubt the authenticity of his misery.

Mock his plans, threaten to derail his destiny altogether.

"Good news!"—his editor has called, interrupting The Suicide's meditation on the very eve of *ending it all.* "Good news!"—his agent has called, breathing heavily into the phone in a way The Suicide fears carries contagion: an (unlikely, improbable) option on an early novel, an (unexpected) literary award, an invitation from a Roman arts festival . . . The Suicide is rocked by an adrenaline rush of gratitude, runs stumbling to his wife to tell her, afterward humiliated by such childish exaltation, even *hope.*

It's as if (he hopes Wendy isn't thinking) his lifelong depression isn't anything more than a thin covering over adolescent insecurity, a rapacious desire for success disguised as an indifference to success. But he knows, he is certain—melancholy is his essential soul, his purest self.

Pascal's chiding words torment like mosquitos circling his head—*A trifle consoles us, for a trifle distresses us.*

In place of the dignity of *ending it all* is a giddy roller coaster of travel, publicity, flattering interviews; luncheons, dinners, awards ceremonies; visits to universities, applauding audiences, very young females with straight blond hair parted in the center of their heads and falling to their shoulders who gaze upon him with adoring eyes . . . Over The Suicide's stricken face, disguising the bleak intransigent wisdom of his bloodshot eyes, a luridly grinning carnival mask.

Eventually, the roller coaster careens off the track, crashes. Eventually, the carnival mask has to be ripped off.

Yet: worse.

The Suicide obsesses that, if/when he finally manages to kill himself, after (literally) years of procrastination, countless medications, "talk therapy" ad nauseam, it will be during the very week that, unknown to him, a scathingly "negative" review appears in a major publication; with the consequence that, in the gleeful eyes of the world, it will appear that he'd killed himself *because of the review.*

What humiliation! Mortification! Granted, The Suicide would not be alive to experience any of this, but his reputation as an artist indifferent to the opinions of others would suffer permanent injury. Since he was no longer alive he could never *outlive it.* Like John Keats, assailed by cruelly ignorant reviews for having written some of the most beautiful poetry in the English language, and dying tragically young, in Keats's case really young (twenty-five), The Suicide would never be free of ludicrous biographical insinuations that he'd killed himself because he was despondent over bad reviews . . .

(Negative reviews grievously wound The Suicide for they confirm unflattering truths about himself and his work that he has long suspected. *You are stupid, you are ugly, you have no talent, why don't you die.* As a vulnerable young writer he'd learned never to read, not even to skim, "negative" reviews but to rely upon others, editors, agents, friends, to shield him from them, for if he reads such reviews recklessly, impulsively, each scathing insight imprints itself upon his soul irremediably.)

("Positive" reviews seem to The Suicide unreal, unbelievable. Praise exudes an air of mockery. Often The Suicide cannot bear to read "positive" reviews for fear that they are jokes on him, which he must not believe.)

Yet: even worse.

The fear that The Suicide might unwittingly kill himself on the eve of a great honor or financial windfall, and this "irony" would be hyped in the media—*Writer Kills Self Without Knowing He Has Won Nobel Prize; Writer Kills Self Without Knowing His Novel Has Been Sold to Hollywood for $100 Million.*

Nothing is more likely to go viral than such an irony! As one to whom *Schadenfreude* is second nature The Suicide can well imagine how this embarrassment would permanently attach to his reputation, like a fat bloated tick that has managed to penetrate not only the scalp but the skull of its victim.

Like any insecure suicide The Suicide hopes it will be exclaimed of him after his death—*What a tragedy! What a loss! Why would he, who had so much to live for, want to end his life!*—and not rather *Well. Not exactly a surprise is it?*—*poor bastard, such a failure, loser, pathetic, how'd he keep going for so long . . .*

Months, years of such debate. A perpetual state of anxiety that distracts The Suicide from the concentration required to successfully commit suicide even as it confirms his conviction that he has no choice but to commit suicide, the world being a cauldron in which humiliating anxieties simmer, seethe, fester, and keep him awake sweating through the endless night.

He, the master of mediated voices. Ventriloquist, magician. "Genius."

Scathing repudiation of hackneyed speech, yes, and hifalutin "elevated" speech.

Brilliant legerdemain, slashing bourgeois pretensions, hypocrisy . . .

Oh, he's tired of himself. So tired!

In bed he held her, the woman, too tight. He panted, sobbed. Breathed hot garlic into her hair.

Promise me!

Y-Yes . . .

—you won't die before me.

Yes. No—I won't.

Won't die and leave me.

I won't—

—die and abandon me.

No . . .

I'm serious. Please help me.

I—will help you.

Do you love me?

Yes! Of course I—
Will you always love me?
Yes. I will always . . .
You don't pity me?
N-No . . .
You don't feel contempt for me?
Of course not . . .
You love me?
I—love you . . .
But how can you love me?
I—I am your wife, and I l-love you . . .
You don't sound so certain.
I—am certain . . .
Are you sorry?
Sorry for—what?
You know what.
W-What?
You know.
I—I don't think I know . . .
You know. You know. YOU KNOW.

If the wife weeps, as usually, reliably the wife does, The Suicide is spared weeping and can turn away from her, incensed, knowing himself obscurely but unjustly treated, and manage at last, finally, to sleep.

That, at least. Sleep.

Home is *where the heart is.*

Home is *where when you go there, they have to let you in.*

Home is *where if you step inside, the walls will crash like gratings around you, you will never be allowed to leave.*

Telling the wife he'd lost a pound for every neuron zapped and for every neuron zapped he'd lost a jigsaw puzzle part of his memory.

Not that he was accusing her, hell he *was not.*

Except his sense of it, the (tragic, tedious) situation, the shifting contours of the situation, his reading of her, the wife, the woman envied by numerous women who'd yearned (they'd thought) to be in her place, to be blessed with the caretaking of *him,* his decoding of it was sure, she'd had to know that it was coming to the time when he would summon all his courage to *make an ending*—how could she, grown shrewd and hungry with the marital years, not know?

Of course, she'd known. All her chess pieces in place: she was his literary executrix, she was first and foremost in his will, by her design.

He'd signed the documents, must have. Possibly, he'd been the one to insist.

Knowing that she would outlive him, it was his wish. *His* design.

When there's nothing left, when I can't continue because there's nothing left then I give myself permission to quit.

But only then.

"The Suicide was stymied by dollops of 'good news' that interrupted his plans and threatened, at times, to derail them entirely."

Terrific opening for "The Suicide"!—The Suicide feels a thrill of genuine pride.

For several months the previous year (2018) this had been the first sentence of The Suicide's story "The Suicide." Positioning himself before a mirror The Suicide read the sentence aloud to himself pleased with its simplicity, brevity, dramatic intensity.

Allowing himself to feel a—a *dollop* of satisfaction.

And so, seeing her husband less stooped than usual at the end of his workday, sensing him less knotted, less *despairing,* the wife dared to ask *Are things going better for you, hon?*—even as he steeled himself for the query.

"Possibly."

Preparing himself for such an intrusion, flinching as one might flinch seeing crude fingers poke and pry a living, beating heart The Suicide could not—nonetheless—protect himself from the consequences: for somehow it happened, the original (brilliant, perfect) sentence came to be fussily rewritten, expanded, revised, and re-revised, after much self-doubt, frustration, and misery, until finally, after the second, unless it was the third, cycle of six electro-convulsive treatments with inevitable side effects, there came to be a second sentence, a hard tiny nut of a turd emerging from the anus of a straining Brachiosaurus: "For instance, after an interlude of several hours (the night before the day of) when he could not sleep, dared not allow his eyelids to shut for fear of lurid dancing gargoyle-figures rushing at him as if pried loose from the vermicu-lated crevices of his brain, there came a sequence of genuinely stunning surprises like blasts of frigid air in the overheated yeasty warmth of his bed . . ."

Genuinely stunning surprises. Throwing him off stride.

But he'd hated this sentence, suffocating in toxic syntaxicity, or is it, to distill the condition, *syntoxicity,* even as he could not make his way forward into the story without it. Yet, he could not reverse course, he could not admit defeat. (Or could he?) (He *could not.*)

Recalling how as an adolescent he'd begun to keep a (secret) tally sheet. In high school in a sort of, you'd have to call it, masoch-istic fantasy, an (imagined) column of print on the left listing hurts, insults, less-than-perfect grades, failures and flaws, tragic snubs by classmates, disappointments too petty to be enumerated, (physi-cal) unease, acne, self-revulsion, etc., which was the *Yes* column; on the right, a similarly (imagined) column of print listing ran-dom "happy" incidents in his life, girls who'd smiled at him, guys who'd invited him to supper at their houses, praise from teachers, perfect math scores, fiction in *Barbaric Yawp,* the school literary magazine—this, the *No* column.

Yes pro suicide, *No* contra suicide.

(Secret) tally sheet in The Suicide's head. Thousands of items, he's forgotten most of them. Those *trifles* of which Pascal spoke.

What was The Suicide's life but a shimmering tally sheet descending into darkness as into a Grand Canyon of the soul, impossible to recall what had seemed potent enough to plunge him over the edge in, say, March 2007, when he'd acquired enough barbiturates to extinguish a herd of elephants except (as usual) he'd been distracted by something, bungled the opportunity, and allowed the moment to pass, just as (sometimes he recalls) he'd insisted to Wendy that they would "start a family" (cringeworthy phrase) when "things settled down"—or, worse, "when the dust settles"—insisting that she terminate that early, first pregnancy when they'd been scarcely married a year, much too soon, a disaster, so soon, he was having a miserable time rewriting an entire novel and each morning was like pushing an enormous clump of manure up a rocky hill, absolutely *too soon did she want to drive him crazy? Sabotage the marriage?*—though in retrospect "first" has turned out to be a misnomer since there has come to be no "second"—at least, so far as The Suicide has been informed.

That, allowed to pass. Years now. Only a vague (guilty) recollection, he'd been self-medicating heavily at the time.

So that, the abortion, was in the *Yes* column, was it? Or in the *No*?

Never decided. This very morning grunting as he strains to toss the rope over the rafter and secure it.

It has never happened, not once in twenty-five years, that the *No* column has outweighed the *Yes*. Yet, still The Suicide has not acted upon his convictions. He has dithered, and he has dallied, and he has been waiting, and he has been prepared, and he has told himself—*No going back this time!*

"Here we go!"—no idea why except it feels right.

Breaking eggs (yes, eggs! hen's) over drafts of the sprawling novel. One hand, squeezing fingers, breaking a (jumbo organic) egg in his fist as he'd never done before in life.

Messy? Feels cold—(the eggs have been refrigerated).

Mystified they will ask—*But why on earth did Har do that? I mean, eggs . . .*

Had to be deliberate. Some meaning to it . . .

Unless he was just crazy.

Well—apart from that, there'd have been a motive.

You think?

With Har, always a motive.

Except—is there? He's a surrealist, has no plan. "Dada"—non-sense.

So much (genuine) heartache in these pages!

Thousands of pages, diligently typed. How many heartbeats, how much (literal, oozing) sweat. And yet it will never be a *novel,* for it will never be *completed.*

Slovenly pages of notes, outlines. Rings of coffee mugs, Diet Coke cans. Folded vertically, manic-annotated in several pens.

Green ink is the ink of hope. Red, the ink of wrath. Blue, inserted revisions. Black, practical/editorial. His handwriting varies with each ink, he notes. *That* might be of interest to a biographer.

With the fanatic care of Hitchcock lighting his stagey set for *The Birds* The Suicide will arrange several lamps to illuminate the manuscripts left behind on his worktable. Sprawling manuscripts, overlapping drafts. Hard drives, discs, files, notebooks, manila envelopes filled with notes in handwriting no longer decipherable. Pencil drawings of faces and figures, which (with his usual faux-modesty) The Suicide has called "mere doodles" in interviews knowing that anyone who sees them, the surprising detail of the faces, skillful crosshatching, will be impressed that The Suicide had, evidently, in addition to his dazzling talent for language, *a talent for art.*

The Suicide breaks just three eggs over the manuscripts. After the first, after the second, the gesture feels stupid, childish, still he breaks a third, what the hell. As Blake says, *Enough? Too much.*

Washes his yolk-sticky hands in the adjacent bathroom. *After,* the wife will discover smears of egg yolk on the faucet, hardened. The mirror above the sink, splattered with droplets of water as if, as he had a habit of doing, unconsciously, as if to despoil the wife's need to keep mirrors clean, sinks and toilets and floors clean, he'd flicked his fingers before reaching for a towel; and if, not accusingly, making a joke of it, in no way reproaching the husband, the wife happened to mention *this thing you do, I guess—flick your fingers after you wash your hands? So the mirror is splattered? Even if I've just cleaned it* . . . This utterly trivial household issue—(both wife and husband in total agreement, it was utterly trivial)—The Suicide sincerely had no idea what the wife was talking about.

What? But I don't.

Do. Not. "Flick." My. Fucking. Fingers.

Returns then, to the basement two floors below. In the kitchen half-expecting to encounter Wendy just stepping through the door but no. Half-expecting as he stomps down the basement steps to see—nothing . . .

But no, that's to say *yes.* There is not nothing but something. The rope, the noose, the chair—nothing has moved an inch in his absence.

Shaky-kneed, climbing onto the chair. For that is the next step.

Paradox is: Suicide is an idea. Suicide is a theory. Suicide is a dream. Suicide is a (naughty, forbidden) wish.

And yet: Suicide is an *act.* And an act requires an *actor.*

The act performed by an actor is an *action.*

That's to say, whether it is an idea, a theory, a dream, a wish, whatever—suicide is also an *action* that must be performed to come into existence.

He has never been much of a physical person, that's the problem. Living so intensely inside his head, it's hard for him to take the "real" world seriously.

But, Christ!—his knees! Especially the right knee, pain like a wire tugged tight.

God damn he'd run too long, too many years—warned it was bad for his knees. Because Wendy was one of those who'd warned him,

him with extra weight in his gut, thighs, he'd resisted listening, running in the early morning before beginning to write, running with a bandana around his head, keeping the straggly hair out of his face, feet in rotted running shoes hard-thumping against pavement and not exclusively trails, knew better but what the hell, as his heart began to wake from its somnolent nocturnal haze to the bright air of dawn and beat harder, quicker, as his lungs drew air deeper, a pleasurable sensation washed over him almost–*happiness.*

So, no. Hadn't been able to resist. And bicycling too, if he could force himself to turn the wheels hard, another *happiness.*

But: wear and tear on the (physical) being. Approaching forty, unmistakable middle age. Wants to protest–*Hey I'm just a kid. I'm just beginning. I'm a smart-ass whiz-kid kid, born to run circles around slow-plodders like you, you, and* you.

But now, the damned right knee does ache. Just climbing onto the chair is an effort.

With much care, conscious of the gravity of the occasion, The Suicide has measured the distance from the noose to the floor. For that distance is crucial, of course. Too long, when he kicks away the chair (an action he has rehearsed countless times in recovery rooms after ECT but cannot quite believe will ever actually occur) he will fall heavily, harmlessly, ignominiously to the basement floor, his hands will grasp at the noose that has failed to tighten (lethally) around his neck . . . But worse, if the rope isn't short enough by just an inch or so his toes will touch the floor and so the weight of his body won't break his neck, he is likely to die an excruciatingly slow death on the tips of his toes, dancing hideously, slowly strangled to death–*that,* he is determined to avoid.

Oh God. What the hell am I doing. Am I–doing this?

Hands grown impatient with prevarication have tugged the noose down over his head. Hair straggling at the nape of his neck, has to pull out of the way. Now to make the noose *snug*–but not so tight (yet) that he can't breathe.

Next step, kick the chair away. But–how, positioned on the

chair, shaky-kneed, the noose around his neck making it difficult for him to cast his gaze downward, at his feet, can he be expected to *kick the chair away*?

"Fuck."

Does The Suicide envision how he will look, *after*—?

Does The Suicide envision who will find him?

No, yes. Yes (obviously: The Suicide obsessively envisions *everything*).

But no, probably not. A minuscule cog in the brain malfunctions, a kind of liquor-store grating slides down over his consciousness so it's blurred, bleary-eyed, like a scummy glass left behind in his study to be discovered after his death amid the myriad detritus of a life that appears to have been both obsessively overcalibrated and yet reckless, haphazard. Three green filing cabinets each containing three drawers meticulously marked and yet much that is misfiled as if, bored suddenly with an hour's task, The Suicide decided to end the task abruptly stuffing letters, documents, papers into folders, pushing shut the file drawer, walking away like a bored child. So too with bookcases initially alphabetized and then abandoned midway to haphazard shelving—books crammed together, books laid flat atop books, a glimpse of a second row of books behind the first.

He will arrange his thousands of pages of manuscript into several stacks, drafts. Hard drives, discs, files, notebooks, manila envelopes filled with notes.

Not wanting to think—*But* she *will find me.*

Not wanting to think—*How can I do such a thing to her! She has been such a loving wife.*

Thinking—*Serves her right. Falling in love with a master of egotism, what'd she expect?*

Thinking—*Even martyrs need a kick in the ass sometimes.*

Focus upon the exigencies of the moment at hand. *This* moment, not *that.*

The Suicide is eager to accomplish what he has set out to do. Teetering on the chair, legs trembling. Taking the noose in both hands with the gentle awe of a lover. Feeling a thrill of pride—*He'd mastered a hangman's noose, with seven turns. Har, of all people, they'd thought was a loser, did they?*

In working order, a perfect noose.

Recalling how in the hospital, in the (refrigerated) recovery room he'd yearned for this, this very moment, not daring to hope at the time that there might actually be a morning in his life when he'd be unobserved, a lapse in surveillance; recalling how Wendy had refused to bring his *invisible coat* with her in the car, when she'd come to pick him up, though he'd commanded her—begged her—over the phone. *That* had been a sign: suspicious.

So carefully he'd planned. Cloak himself in *invisibility,* hide from prying eyes. But the wife, not cooperating. Exposing The Suicide to crude jeering eyes of strangers as well as neighbors on Cedar Lane with recording devices, zoom lenses.

He doesn't doubt: the wife herself is recording him. Wouldn't be the first time, will not be the last time, that the (young) wife of a celebrated writer/artist will exploit her intimacy with him, composing a *tell-all* memoir after his death.

So convinced The Suicide has become that this is so, he seems to recall having actually seen Wendy stealthily taking notes on him; caught her with her iPhone trained upon him as he'd lain on the sofa sprawled and exhausted after a day hunched over the word processor with fuck-all to show for it except neckache, backache, headache, and heartache.

Even in the basement in a slant of natural light from the narrow horizontal windows his eyes ache, ultra-sensitive to light since the God-damned new prescription that is causing constipation, too.

Worse: Diet Coke has lost its silky-black sharp-chemical tang, fizz. With the new meds can't drink more than a can of beer, nauseated after a few swallows. Some of the drugs hurt his head. Make his arteries throb. Vision blood-dimmed. Kidneys, liver. Pissing a stream of mustard neon. *Most brilliant fantasist of his generation.*

Recalling how never before in the past had he advanced to this stage—actually preparing the noose, climbing onto the chair . . . Beyond this moment, a blur of light. What?

He is peering, into that light. Squinting, can't see beyond it.

Recalling with a smile how three years ago (not in this rented house but in another, not-dissimilar rental house in Ohio) clawing his way out of a mound of suffocating muck he'd been suffused with enough strength to (seriously, methodically) prepare to kill himself, not in his home where (obviously) the wife would interfere but in a motel at the edge of town. And he'd been driving on the highway at dusk in the direction of the Stardust Motel, suitcase in the back seat containing all the materials he'd need. And he'd had just a single beer, and no more than his usual meds. And he'd been thrilled to be en route to finally—finally!—*making an end.*

Then: Halfway to the motel he'd struck an animal on the highway. Size and shape of a deer (he'd thought), crossing heedlessly in front of his vehicle, too close for him to react, no time to brake or even turn the wheel except minimally, by the time his dazed brain registered what was happening it had already happened: his vehicle skidding to a stop, the stricken screaming creature dragged beneath the front right fender.

First panicked thought: It was a person, a child . . .

With a pounding heart went to investigate, saw that it wasn't human, wasn't a deer but a fox.

The Suicide had rarely seen a fox, and never at such close quarters. It was a beautiful animal, catlike, slender, with a thick plume of a tail. Its tawny eyes gazed up at him with human acuity, appeal.

It was whining, whimpering, panting like a dog. Thrashing to free itself from beneath the fender. To his horror The Suicide saw that its rear legs appeared to be broken. The beautiful burnished-red coat was damp with blood.

Driving on the highway The Suicide had several times noticed a cinder-block building—*Huron County Wildlife Rescue.* He would take the injured animal there.

Managing to detach the stricken fox from the underside of the fender, tugging at its haunches, thighs; lifting it in his arms, carrying it squirming and panting to the back of his vehicle, and laying it on the seat, in a white rush of adrenaline, not a thought for his own safety, his audacity in daring to carry a wounded wild animal that might have snapped at him, torn him badly with its sharp teeth, except this didn't happen: the fox lay limp, dazed and lethargic on the back seat of the vehicle as The Suicide made a careening U-turn on the road and drove to the shelter, where the fox was taken from him and he was assured that it was O.K., he could leave, even as The Suicide followed them into the building trying to explain what had happened, the fox had run out in front of his car, he hadn't been able to brake in time, he hadn't been able to turn the steering wheel, it had all happened so fast, it wasn't his fault . . . Could they save the fox's life?—The Suicide stood foolishly with his wallet in his hand but was told another time that he could leave, they would take care of the fox as best as they could until the vet came in next morning, not much was going to happen until then.

The Suicide went away dazed, thrilled. He had lifted the beautiful animal in his arms! *He,* who'd imagined he did not like animals, he'd never been suckered into animal-love sentiment shared by most of humankind, driving home (having forgotten the tacky Stardust Motel entirely) replaying the scene in his imagination, seeing himself follow the young attendants into the shelter, hearing his raw hopeful voice—*Can you save its life? I can pay for it . . .*

Back home The Suicide called the rescue shelter but only a recording came on and in the morning called again and was told that the vet had just come in and was examining the fox now and later in the morning The Suicide called yet again and was informed that the fox had undergone emergency surgery, one of its legs amputated, but it was expected to survive. This news The Suicide received with much gratitude and relief, that very day he sent the Huron County Wildlife Rescue a check for five hundred dollars.

He'd even driven back to the shelter, bringing Wendy with him, to see "his" fox, but as it turned out the fox had been transported to another, larger wildlife rescue too far away for practical purposes so he'd never seen "his" fox again as he'd never given the Stardust Motel another thought again.

And now, in another rental home, in a basement smelling wryly of mold, crouching on a chair smiling foolishly to think of that episode in his life, he'd never written about it nor even approached writing about it for he hadn't the vocabulary for such sentiment, the sole "good deed" of a life, has to laugh, in that instant suffused with purpose, certitude, a rush of strength in his legs such as a demigod might feel and the awkward chair is "kicked" out from beneath him—suddenly he is slipping, falling—the noose around his neck tightening instantaneously—can't breathe—can't cry out, his throat is shut tight—fingers tugging at the noose, nails torn, breaking—too late . . .

Help me. Never meant . . .

Can't breathe, can't scream for help, the ligature around his neck has broken his neck yet he is still horribly alive, teetering above the abyss he is still conscious, speechless, mute, begging for help without breath, without the words to beg even as from a distance he hears *Wake up, wake up*—not a familiar voice coming nearer, close beside his head, a giant hornet buzzing close beside his head he'd have liked to brush away but can't move his arm, his arm is leaden-heavy . . .

Opens his eyes. Stunned and staring. Where is this?

In the hospital, still? The recovery room?

His head is aching. His brain has been zapped. Fried, frazzled. His spinal cord has been severed, he is paralyzed, benumbed as with Novocain.

Wake up, please try to open your eyes. Look at me.

Lights too bright and faces too *vivid*.

But when he closes his eyes the voices become agitated urging him *try to wake up, open your eyes, sit up* when he wants only to switch his brain *off* as you'd switch a light *off.* Tries to shift his legs, his feet

are too far away to connect with, it's exhausting, makes him want
to cry as a child cries in utmost despair, hopelessness, so badly he
wants to sleep, to shut all consciousness *off*. If he could shift his
legs, embrace his knees to his chest with both arms, fold himself
up like an umbrella and shut himself *off*.

Hearing now the woman's voice. Faint quavering hopeful voice,
familiar to him but the name eludes him . . .

Wanting badly to sink back into sleep into the delicious black
muck of sleep but his brain is bathed now in light, his eyes are
open, faces loom above him and one of them *her* face—the wife . . .

A woman familiar to him, smiling bravely, eyes rapidly blinking
as if she is staring into too bright a light, and her face no longer
a girl's face puffy about the eyes as anxiously she squeezes his
hand, which is nonresponsive, limp cold fingers seemingly without blood, nerve-sensation, a heavy wedge of a hand, *his hand*—he
understands this must be so, as *his feet* are beginning to revive as
well, like frozen limbs over which warm water flows in a continuous stream returning body heat.

Why is there such cold air in the recovery room! You resent it,
you know that you are being manipulated, the staff is bent upon
waking you, doesn't want you to be comfortable, doesn't want you
to sleep but to *wake up*—when it is *wakefulness* you fear, *wakefulness*
that brings sorrow, terror.

The woman is speaking to you, low and intimate in your ear.
The woman is grasping both your (inert) hands.

(You will pretend that you are paralyzed, they will leave you
alone. So benumbed by the anesthesia you have no idea which of
your legs has been amputated.)

(Heedless stepping in front of a speeding vehicle . . . Excruciating pain as your body is dragged along the pavement but the
cheery voice proclaims you will *survive*.)

A wheelchair has been brought for the patient, who lies comatose barely willing to open his eyes. Deeply insulting, he thinks,
for these people to discuss him as if he weren't there as if it is just
his body here.

The wife is speaking encouragingly to him as a mother speaks encouragingly to a child unable to gauge if the child has something seriously wrong with him or is just being difficult.

Why'd he want a miniature likeness of himself for Christ's sake! Another *him*, nothing fills him with more horror.

It hasn't been explained to him why he'd had emergency surgery. Why he'd been brought here in an ambulance with a deafening siren. One of his legs has been amputated and his spinal cord seems to have been severed somewhere in his lower back but this might have been an accident, *medical malnutrition.*

Something has clamped around his neck. Tight, tighter. Holds his breath terrified of trying to breathe and discovering that he can't.

Before they lift him, settle him into the wheelchair, an oxygen mask is clamped to his face. Flow of smooth cold air, sweet air in his nostrils—this is a familiar sensation. As if a clown has clapped his hands sharply, all the little children are roused to attention, wide-eyed, mouths open.

She has taken both his hands to press against her chest. Warm beat of her heart. Breasts, bosom. He is uneasy, such intimacy in the presence of strangers, if he catches the eye of another guy he will wink, they will exchange glances though now he has remembered her name—*Wendy.*

Silly name. A wife is silly. He is starting to cry, *silliness* is so rare in his life.

"Harold? It's me. I love you . . ."

Tears run down his cheeks onto the pillow flat beneath his head. Love is a kind of drowning, the tears spill over, he is always taken by surprise.

Try to sit up, he is being urged. Swing your legs off the bed. You won't fall, we've got you.

Harsher bemused voice in his ear—the green-clad anesthesiologist.

Always he enjoys a bantering relationship with the anesthesiologist, whose name he never knows. As you are being *put under* the challenge is to count down from one hundred but the joker in the deck is always in the anesthesiologist's pocket, the green-clad demon always wins.

Fact is: Putting the patient to sleep is the easy part. Hard part is bringing the patient back.

Before the shock treatments many a witty exchange with the anesthesiologist. *Slay me now, what the fuck. You can't.*

Of course, the anesthesiologist always wins. Joke's on you.

Exactly the medical specialty he'd have chosen for himself. Or maybe pathologist.

No patients, no personalities intervening. Never get to know them, feel responsible for, guilty over. Especially, the pathologist's patients never complain. Never behave in unruly ways, challenge your authority. It's true that the individuals whom the anesthesiologist sedates sometimes fail to revive, thus die, or even if not fully dying, sometimes fail to revive and remain comatose for the remainder of their lives, still anesthesiologists don't have patients of their own, a great relief.

His (leaden, heavy) legs are being shifted from the bed. Bodily he is being seated in the wheelchair. Wendy leans down to brush her lips against his cheek churlish and unshaven. His scalp aches, burns. His hair smells singed. What have they done to him? Has he had a lobotomy? Not twisting in agony at the end of the rope but (somehow) in the presence of others in a refrigerated room, one of them squeezing his hand as if she has the right.

Her. The wife.

And so: It has not (yet) happened?

His heart is pierced—the love in the woman's face! He is broken by it, humbled and grateful. He would murmur *I love you too. So much*—but the words choke in his mouth dry as hard-backed sand.

He has forgotten where he is, and why he is here. He has forgotten what awaits him, in another place.

He has never been equal to being loved as he has been loved. But he *will love now*, he has resolved.

Never equal to—whatever this white-walled bright-lit (refrigerated) place is, that surrounds him.

Actual life. Not words, but the world. *The* world.

Not a fiction. Not a page in a book. Not *his fiction.*

Actual life. In which he *is.* Not floating outside it, above it. Not superior to it. Drawing breath from it.

This is it. *This* is it.

This is it?

The Baby-Monitor

1

If you would know fear, bring a baby into the world.

2

It wasn't the mother's idea to move the baby's crib out of the parents' bedroom after six harrowing months of sleep riddled with interruptions like hailstones against windowpanes. Nor was it the mother's idea to install a Security Optics Baby-Monitor System in the nursery adjacent to the parents' bedroom. Still less the mother's idea to upgrade the Baby-Monitor as soon as it was installed to include such luxury features as real-time audio with a seven-volume level/two-way talk system/digital zoom for ultra-close-up viewing/rechargeable battery/night vision.

(Especially, ghastly "night vision" the mother would not have chosen. Had the mother had any choice.)

3

Since the "nursery" was next door to the parents' bedroom the mother insisted it was no trouble for her to make her way to the baby when he fretted or fussed or cried to be fed in the night or because his diaper was soaked. As her mother, and her mother's mother, and that mother's mother had not required a ridiculous electronic device to alert her to the visceral needs of her infant, so this mother protested that she preferred to be summoned to her baby in the time-honored way: roused by the baby's blood-curdling cat-cry or by the mildest baby-whimper as audible to the hypersensitive mother's ear through the bedroom wall as giant crab-claws' scratching against the wall would have been audible. Instantaneously hearing such a baby-sound, the mother is *awake*. Strike of a match illuminating the vast night sky, the mother is *awake*. Bloodshot eyes springing open out of a tangle of numbed ganglia, the mother is *awake*. Out of a yeasty-warm bed leaving the obliviously sleeping husband behind like a mere mound of laundry or indeed a sodden insensate corpse the mother makes her quick-stumbling-barefoot way into the nursery next door unerring as an arrow shot from a bow and within breathless seconds she is at the baby's crib preparing to lift the dense hot miracle-weight of the baby gently in her arms to comfort the baby if he is fretting, to change his diaper, or to nurse him if he is hungry (oh, Baby is always hungry!—the mother's astonishing heavy aching breasts already leaking milk in anticipation of Baby's sucking lips) or if it has been a false alarm, no actual cry the mother imagined she'd heard, not to disturb the sleeping baby after all but to stand above him as her racing heartbeat slows and her quickened breathing returns to near-normal gazing down at *her baby* with that helpless swooning love that is indistinguishable from terror.

For one person alone of all the world living now or who has ever lived is *this baby's mother.*

4

And that person: *her.*

And so, the responsibility to keep the baby alive: *hers.*

5

Politely explaining to the father of the baby no, she didn't see the need.

Yes she understood, yes she was grateful for the in-laws' generosity, but no—not another electronic device in the house.

And this one, in their bedroom. Security Optics Baby-Monitor System! *Night-vision* screen! Ridiculous.

Telling him, the father of the baby, that there was something unnatural and grotesque about it: installing the Baby-Monitor in their lives. Instead of sleeping normally, or hoping to, lying in bed obsessed with keeping your baby alive and so compelled to watch your baby sleep in the blurry black-and-white screen through the long hours of the night like a sort of shell-less mollusk in a crib.

Timothy laughed, annoyed. Surely she had to be exaggerating?

Pointing out that there was certainly no need to stay awake staring at the Baby-Monitor. No need to become *obsessed* (her word, not his).

"You don't even need to look at it. We'll put it on my side of the bed. We can turn it off, actually. Where's the harm? My mother only wants to be helpful."

In the husband's voice an air of exasperation, reproach. The slightest suggestion that Lori was being critical of his parents, especially his mother, the husband's voice thinned and rose an octave, a warning.

And so quickly Lori amended: Yes, of course she was grateful. His parents were so kind, generous. As always.

The in-laws who'd purchased so many expensive/mostly useless things for the baby, their first grandchild. Every sort of impedimenta relating to *new baby* they'd ordered online for months in an orgy of *new baby gifts,* for the in-laws had money, and they had leisure, for each was retired from longtime employment and at a time in their lives when their expansive lifestyle was no longer rewarding to them, Timothy's mother was feverish with excitement in her new, much-anticipated role as *grandmother.*

She, the baby's mother, had to be careful not to offend. For if you accept your in-laws' "extra" car, if you accept your in-laws' financial aid in purchasing a house, you are not in a strong moral position to politely decline lesser gifts and bounties without giving the appearance of being a hypocrite.

Explaining to Timothy that she was grateful for the gift but concerned that they already spent so many of their waking hours staring at electronic *screens*. Much of the day at their work, computers. Cell phones, iPads. Their eyes were fixed upon simulacra of people and things and not actual people and things and surely their brains were being altered for the worse.

"Isn't it well-known that these devices are spying on *us*? Recording *us*? Our lives are under constant surveillance and we don't seem to care, isn't that strange? *Why* has that happened?"

Lori, addressing Timothy, in her most reasonable voice; yet sounding nonetheless plaintive, pleading. Always there is weakness in pleading.

Timothy seemed unmoved. For all they knew, these were just "scare tactics"—that we're living in a surveillance state, or will soon be living in a surveillance state. "Collecting data is mostly for advertising purposes, I think. Targeting potential customers."

Timothy, long a vehement defender of privacy, individual rights, free speech, freedom of the press!—exasperating to Lori, hearing him speak now so negligently.

Because he's defending his mother. Never position yourself between your husband and his mother.

". . . what I mean is, it's *unnatural*. Being with the baby in the daytime is natural but spying on the baby in the night is something else. No one in the past had anything like 'Baby-Monitors'— parents, grandparents, ancestors . . ."

Lori's voice trailed off weakly. How inane she was sounding. How *fearful*.

Timothy laughed, as if embarrassed for her. Saying she'd never used to exaggerate so much. Lately now . . .

(*Lately now*. Lori is offended by these words. This new imbalance between them. As if giving birth, and before that the pregnancy that had seemed both ennobling and humbling, and interminable, have cast wife and husband in new roles for which neither is prepared and she, the designated/inevitable "mother," finds herself in the demeaning position of needing to defend herself against an earlier version of herself.)

Timothy points out that the Baby-Monitor is supposed to help prevent—what's it called?—"'SIDS.' Crib death. But how would the Baby-Monitor prevent that? If the baby just—stops breathing? In the night? Would it make any sound at all?"

At this Lori froze.

Why *why* would a husband say such a thing. *Father* of an infant just six months old.

Seeing the look in Lori's face, stricken, frightened, Timothy reached for her hands, his wife's icy hands he squeezed, the chafed-skin-hands he squeezed, hands that didn't feel like his wife's hands but like the hands of a stranger, somewhat coarse, unyielding, hostile to him as if to very maleness and the power to wound that is the power of maleness and so he laughed, tried to laugh, cajoling the woman, the mother, his wife to laugh, to laugh in the old easy-intimate way, the way of co-conspirators that was becoming lost to them as a language not spoken becomes by degrees lost, indecipherable.

"Sorry, honey. That was stupid. How often do infants die in their cribs must be one in a literal million, or more."

Closing his arms around her, to gather her to him. To console, and comfort.

"...just something I read in the brochure. Forget I mentioned it."

For of course Lori was right, they didn't need more gadgets in the household, more expensive devices to break down, and yes, there was something *unnatural* about it, any sort of *surveillance* about which the object of the surveillance isn't conscious, where you can see someone without them seeing you.

"We can keep the stupid thing in a box, my mother won't know."

Timothy spoke with husbandly passion, squeezing the hand of the mother of the baby to assure her *Hey look I am on your side.*

6

No one is on your side. Essentially, you are alone.
Alone with your baby it is your responsibility to keep alive.

7

Like loose-fitting rivets the days hold, just barely.

That night in the hours after midnight staring with fascination at the small electronic screen at eye level several feet away as she lies in bed in the darkened bedroom while beside her oblivious of her insomniac vigil the father of the baby sleeps facing the contrary direction for of course once the terrible words were uttered by him—*SIDS, crib death*—it was clear that, following the principle of cosmic irony inherited from her fatalistic Eastern European peasant-ancestors, *of course the baby will die if the damned Baby-Monitor isn't installed.*

And yes, on her side of the bed. *Her side.*

In these hours after midnight the mother's glazed eyes are focused upon the figure of the sleeping baby in his crib inside the six-inch by eight-inch screen. A shadowy figure as in an ultrasound. Reduced and diminished so that it doesn't resemble a human baby so much as an amoeba with rudimentary facial features—(shut) eyes, (very small) nose, (snail-sized) lips.

Baby appears to be mostly head, torso, arms. Tiny hands resembling those flipper-hands growing from the shoulders of thalidomide babies, the mother has seen in ghastly archival photographs.

(But how is this possible, the mother wonders. *She* had not taken thalidomide during the pregnancy, had she?—the era of thalidomide was decades ago.)

In the darkened bedroom minutes pass with excruciating slowness. Soon it will be, should be, time for Baby's next feeding: a relief.

When at last there is *no possibility* of sleep, when Baby begins to wail, a relief to be *fully awake.*

. . . stumbling into the nursery, baring the lesser-aching of her breasts.

When Baby slept in the room with them there'd been no ambiguity about Baby's need, which woke them immediately like artillery fire.

Now with Baby at a distance on the farther side of walls there is the likelihood of error. She has abandoned her baby, trusting to the Baby-Monitor camera installed in the other room above the crib.

Very tired, and her eyelids very heavy. Pleasurably tired. Anything to do with the miraculous birth is *pleasurable*.

After the fact, that is. Before, when the great effort lay ahead, there was primarily apprehension for *what if*.

(Out of *what if,* all fear springs. Purest terror.)

After a very long day of performing as the mother of a baby less than a year old requiring the repeated execution of a sequence of tasks focused upon the *baby-body*—(changing diaper, bathing, nursing/feeding)—(changing diaper, bathing, nursing/feeding)— focused now in the stillness of night upon the glassy screen shimmering a few feet away in the dark.

Peering at the baby in the monitor seeing to her relief that the tiny hands are attached to normal-baby-arms—of course.

And these tiny hands quivering so that the mother is reassured *Yes your baby is alive, don't be ridiculous.*

Safe for the mother of the baby to sleep now. Allow her heavy-lidded eyes to shut. Allow her hypervigilant brain to shut down. But disconcerting, how the *night-vision* screen is eerily leached of color like a scene in an old newsreel. Not clearly defined black-and-white as in a photograph but blurred and gauzy shades of gray like shifting mists in a perilous landscape at which the mother stares intrigued as if at a newsreel of another era, another lifetime in which the sleeping baby in the monitor isn't Baby but a stranger's baby for whom the mother need not feel any emotion other than a generic-human concern and compassion for an infant of her own species. In this case a long-ago baby, unnamed, possibly even a "foreign" baby, no longer living anywhere except in the newsreel and no longer recalled by anyone living, for all who'd lived at that time are not living now.

One, among millions. And all perished.

Certainly, it is recommended that the mother of the baby sleep for as long as the baby allows her to sleep. A normal baby can sleep for as long as fifteen hours within a span of twenty-four hours, unfortunately not for more than a very few hours at a time.

The baby-doctor recommended moving the newborn to another room after six months so that the parents' sleep will be less interrupted. For each has been suffering from sleep-deprivation and with sleep-deprivation a certain edginess, shortness of nerves and of breath, a general anxiety heightened in their case since they'd delayed having a baby until the mother was forty years old and the father forty-four.

Recovery from the C-section is slower than anticipated. As the excessive weight she'd gained is slow to melt away.

Because you are not young enough. Why did you wait so long!

Out of fear. Unnamed.

Still leaking blood into her underwear, most days. Ravaged uterus, slow to heal. If she moves too abruptly her pelvic area is wracked with pain.

Sleep is recommended yet the mother understands that she *must not* allow her eyes to close even for a few seconds. That is the trick, the temptation. The terms of the game in which she is (unwittingly, involuntarily) participating, since she'd conceived, had become *pregnant.*

Must not sleep for something will happen to the baby that would (certainly) not happen without the Baby-Monitor to record it.

Lifting herself on one elbow, seeing that Baby (in the monitor) appears to be stirring.

Time for the two a.m. feeding?—she feels the *frisson* of excitement, anticipation.

Heavy breasts like sacs filled tight with warm water. Beginning to leak at just the thought of nursing the baby.

Life in the body: so much *wet.*

Initially, nursing had been painful. Baby sucking at the mother's nipple, which is one of the most sensitive parts of the mother's body, almost unbearably sensitive to the slightest feathery touch let alone Baby's robust sucking.

Like the female genitals. *Clitoris:* almost unbearably sensitive, sheerly nerve endings.

The mother of the baby shudders, recalling. For *life in the body* is the challenge.

In the monitor, Baby seems to have shrunken.

Is this Baby, in his crib in the nursery, or is this the six-month fetus in the ultrasound photograph?—Lori remembers staring at it, being shown the shadowy image in the doctor's office at the clinic.

For a moment, Lori is confused. Brain-befuddled, confusing the image on the screen with the ultrasound: If this is the ultrasound of the baby at six months it means that the ordeal of the delivery is still ahead. (Frankly) not sure she can survive it a second time.

Contractions striking her lower body like bolts of electricity she'd screamed for help. Screamed until her throat was raw. If she'd known what this would be, what the pain would be like, *no pregnancy no husband no thanks!*

Never forgive the man, for precipitating such an ordeal. Her very body, distended, twisted out of shape.

That is the game: male, female. The game no female can win, if she acknowledges the terms of the game.

Only by going outside the game, off the grid. But how?—she has no idea, like one scrambling to escape, clawing at a blank wall, breaking fingernails, sobbing, no idea, no idea how.

"Oh God!"—her eyes spring open. No idea where she is except there is danger.

(Has she been asleep? How long asleep? Despite knowing that *she cannot allow herself to sleep.*)

Seeing the luminous screen a few feet away. Remembering now.

Something has changed: shadows fall over Baby like the shadows of circling predator birds.

She fumbles for the remote on the floor beside the bed. She will *zoom* closer to the baby, to see what this is. Something in motion, undulating shadows—*wings*? Has a bird made its way into the nursery, or a bat?—but no window was left open, she is certain.

The undulating shadows have wakened him, Baby has begun fretting. He is not entirely awake but he is waking. Tiny eyes fluttering open, those miniature eyelashes. Pudgy baby-arms, flailing. Lori can see, appalled, that the silhouette of a sharp-beaked bird has fallen over Baby's face.

Baby's mouth opens in a (silent) scream.

The mother of the baby throws off clammy bedclothes beneath which she has been lying on her left side observing the monitor. In frantic haste she has forgotten the father of the baby entirely, as during the long days when Baby and Mommy are alone together in the most exquisite intimacy excluding all others, she feels no resentment of this person, no envy that he can continue to sleep heavy as sodden laundry in blissful obliviousness of her and of the baby for she has known from the start of the pregnancy that she is alone in this, in this matter of the baby, the responsibility falls entirely upon her, like a mountain landslide.

You are in this alone, you wanted this. You have no one but yourself.

Stumbling into the nursery panicked. Grateful for the low-wattage Mother Goose on the floor behind the crib, kept on through the night. Relieved to see that there are no birds, no bats, no wings fluttering above Baby—of course.

But Baby is certainly awake now and frightened and his crying is shrill as clashing cymbals.

Further relief: Baby is normal-sized (of course) and not the freakish amoeba-baby of the monitor. Not a long-forgotten infant in a newsreel. How ridiculous, Mommy's worries!

"Oh, sweetie! Stop."

Lifting the wailing baby from his crib. Out of the coils of sleep-ganglia threading through her brain.

Twinge of pain in the ravaged uterus not (yet) recovered from the trauma of the surgical delivery six months before.

"No more crying! Mommy is here."

Her heartbeat is returning to normal. All of her senses aroused, rush of adrenaline as she'd prepared to confront an (unknown) adversary but all is normal—of course.

Fleeting dreams, hallucinations. Still she resists taking medication, she will not succumb to weakness.

It looks as if Baby's diaper needs to be changed—of course.

How *normal* this is! She hopes that the Baby-Monitor records it.

Blindly the miniature lips seek the milky breast, the hot little body quivers with appetite.

Mommy laughs, baby-appetite is so fierce! Good that Baby has just one small soft baby-tooth that can't do too much damage.

Since she'd begun nursing, awkwardly at first, wincing with discomfort, she has been noticing sharp stabbing fleeting pains in her left breast. Torments herself thinking—*Not possible that I have cancer! That I have cancer, too.*

Cruel cosmic irony in which, as an educated woman unencumbered by foolish folk-superstitions, Lori certainly does not believe.

But it *is* some sort of irony, to be inhabiting a female body: (ravaged) uterus, (splayed) pelvis, (stubbly-haired) groin, heavy-hanging udders grazing her upper belly.

Certainly she'd thought that by concentrating on books, an education, writing the most clever papers, acquiring an impressive vocabulary (starting with ambitious word-lists in eighth grade) she'd have been exempt from the mortifications of the *female body.*

Lifting the baby's eager mouth to the fat right breast, blindly pushing mouth and breast together. At once Baby ceases crying. At once Baby begins sucking. So simple! Delight in simplicity.

Remember to secure the nursing baby in the crook of her right arm. Support the baby's delicate head, neck. (Parts of Baby's fragile skull have not hardened, he seems to have no neck at all. Slowest of magic, Baby's cartilage-soft knees are acquiring bone.) Though steeled for discomfort the mother is never quite prepared for the shock of the sensitive nipple being so robustly tugged-at, sucked.

Praying *O God* the baby will not reject her milk. For a mother's milk *is* her.

Soon then, after an erratic rhythm is established, waves of pleasure, a dark sort of pleasure rooted in the groin, the mother's eyes roll back in their sockets and her breath comes short.

Dense-heated little body secure in her arms all of it *hers.*

Cobalt-blue eyes of heart-stopping beauty moistly fixed upon *her.*

8

"Hey!—wondered where you were, hon."

In the morning wakened by a jarring jovial voice. The man, the husband calling to her from the doorway of the nursery as if across an abyss.

Where she, mother of the baby, lies sated sprawled on the sofa like one who has fallen from a great height. Sleeping Baby hot-humid in her arms, flannel nightgown smelling of her yeasty body tugged off one shoulder and a fat bun of a breast bared, wrinkly nipple encrusted with dried milk (*not* semen) so that the man in the doorway is made to feel uneasy, a voyeur, an intruder, inanely smiling, guilty-faced, rueful at having slept through the night for the first time in a very long time and flush with gratitude even as he feels a twinge of revulsion for the slattern-wife, a stranger to him, each day, each night ever more the mother of the baby becoming a stranger to him, with the pregnancy gaining weight in belly, hips, thighs like sponge rubber of the sickly white hue of lard and not so easily melted away.

All this sweeping over the husband, who is also the father of the baby, in the instant of staring across the abyss at the woman asprawl with a baby in her arms.

Realizing: until the baby had come into their lives his (fastidious) wife had avoided being seen by him in any disheveled state:

uncombed hair, rumpled clothing, slovenly posture. And now, swath of fatty thighs, striations in the sickly white flesh, swollen ankles once slim as a ballerina's exposed to the husband's startled gaze. How has it happened, Lori has become so *physical*? After twelve years of marriage there remains between husband and wife a habit of formality, reserve, unease at intimacy yet the husband feels now the shock of arousal at the sight of the wife, a sharp sexual stab in the groin, unmistakable.

Unless it's a faint nausea at the odor of baby-diaper, sweet-rancid dried breast milk wafting to his nostrils.

"Oh, hon. Look at you. *Love you*."

9

Except the thought assails her—*But someday you won't. You will abandon us.*

Where did this fear originate?—no idea.

For suddenly there are myriad *fears*, tributaries flowing into the singular river *Fear*.

Suddenly a rational person has become a *fearful* person, one with everything to lose: baby, husband, marriage. Baby.

That had been the start: the day, the hour she'd learned definitively that she was pregnant, in the doctor's office. In her haste to call Timothy her thumbs had so fumbled the numerals on her cell phone she'd wondered if she'd had a mild stroke.

For all that is given to you, can be taken away.

10

. . . a kind of experiment, she thinks. Harmless!

Alone in the house as late afternoon slides into dusk. On the CD player late-Beethoven string quartets. That their baby will *hear, absorb* such music.

Each baby *is* an experiment, in fact. But most experimentation is unintended, unconscious.

She positions the baby (securely) inside several goose-feather pillows, facing a tall window shimmering with late-afternoon light. She positions the Baby-Monitor camera close by, slightly elevated and looking down at the baby; hurries then upstairs to the bedroom, where the monitor is positioned on her side of the bed.

No danger in leaving Baby alone in these circumstances because she can observe him in the monitor clearly and in full color: his curious, alert features, the movements of his baby-hands, the remarkable roundness of his eyes, which resemble neither Timothy's eyes nor her own.

Each baby is an alien being. Each baby, a mutant.

She'd taken cello lessons in high school, she'd been said to have been "promising."

Hearing the cello played perfectly in the Beethoven CD she feels an obscure loss, and shame for that loss, that she'd aspired to another life, a lifetime ago; she'd loved the cello, or had thought that she did, but not enough, finally.

Baby would be her true accomplishment, she thinks.

This new fascination has come upon her, to watch the screen during the day, to observe carefully all that Baby does when she isn't in the room with him, how he frets, his forehead crinkling, how the cobalt-blue eyes dart about, the little fists flail. Baby *is not hungry*—he has had a feeding recently. Yet, Baby behaves as if he is hungry in some way, that has not (yet) come into focus.

Also: to keep her eyes open and alert to that exquisite moment when the Baby-Monitor ceases registering *day* and begins to register *night*. Color in the screen disappears in the blink of an eye like a switch turned off, each afternoon a little earlier as the earth turns on its axis in anticipation of the winter solstice.

You are never quite prepared for early sunsets, Lori recalls. Turning the clock back an hour: darkness rising from the earth, ever earlier.

"Oh!—God . . ."

In an instant the screen seems to implode. Colors vanish, gradations of gray emerge, somewhat blurred, grainy. The baby is un-touched and yet suddenly reduced, drained of color and diminished.

There is something shocking about it, this instantaneous change. She leans closer to the screen, squinting.

Just an ordinary baby, in that instant. No name, no identity. Gradations of gray, and not very clearly in focus.

If the screen were switched to *off,* where would this baby go?

It is hard for Lori to keep in mind that the baby in the screen, that's to say the image of the baby in the screen, so reduced in significance, is *her baby.*

Alone amid the pillows in gathering twilight, no idea where he is, who he is, why he is, who is staring at him he cannot see; no idea how his soul has been sucked from him, with the waning of light in the sky.

Still, Lori will hurry downstairs to be with him—*her baby.* Her head has begun to ache with concentration, she rouses herself from a stupor. Through the monitor come mewing little baby-cries like pleading mice.

That evening Timothy will say he'd tried to call her in the after-noon, she hadn't answered, he'd left messages and she hadn't answered, was something wrong?—and Lori will say quickly no! nothing wrong of course, she'd been listening to CDs with the baby, hadn't heard the phone ring, she's sorry. And Timothy will say stiffly he'd called both the landline and her cell phone, it's strange that she hadn't heard either.

Lori hadn't replied. Not wanting to say—*Why is it strange? What do you expect of me, beyond what I've given you?*

11

. . . another experiment. Also harmless.

In anticipation of a night emergency when the mother of the

baby would be less alert and clear-minded if, for instance, these Baby-Monitor "luxury features" are required.

Baby in the nursery in his crib asleep. *Not night:* afternoon nap.

Mommy in the bedroom next door not lying in bed but calmly sitting on the edge of the bed.

Again, all of the house empty! *This* is luxury.

No longer resentful that the father of the baby is *away* so much of the time. Instead, rejoicing that she is *alone with Baby.*

It's day, the world is bathed in color. Where there is light, there is color. Waking from a brain-aching deep sleep after a night of sleep pockmarked as a rusted colander she, mother of the baby, is assailed by colors piercing her eyelids like cymbals clashing.

November afternoon as light begins to wane (as early as four p.m.) and with the waning of light the waning of color in the Baby-Monitor screen.

Holding her breath as the exquisite moment approaches. She has never been able to predict how, at a particular second, and not one second before, the color in the monitor will shift to *night vision.*

Baby is sleeping peacefully and will sleep for an hour or more. No awareness of the camera trained upon him, attached to the rim of the white-wicker crib.

*This is the precious time—*Timothy's mother has told her.

They grow up fast. They can't wait to leave you.

Lori doubts that this is so. Lori doubts that Timothy couldn't wait to leave his mother.

Lori has reason to doubt Timothy has ever left his mother.

. . . no matter how you love them, they grow away.

On the glassy screen, in miniature, Baby's dreaming face. Lori can see, or thinks that she sees, the minute movements of Baby's eyeballs in their sockets.

Dreaming, which is *seeing.*

The baby-brain, turned inward in sleep. Alive, thrumming with life. *She* feels nothing like this, her brain has grown sluggish, like (in fact) a colony of sleek gray-hued slugs not usefully meshed together.

Fact: She who'd imagined that she would always be young has

become a not-young mother at whom other, younger mothers glance in Kemble Park, where she pushes Baby in his stroller each morning in good weather.

Fact: Startled to see herself in mirrors in recent months and so she has begun to avoid mirrors.

None of that matters now: female vanity. Laughs at herself in embarrassment, to imagine how any *of that* had ever seemed important to her.

Attracting the male gaze: that the male sperm might be deposited in the proper moist warm labyrinthine place. And when the transaction has been made, everything preliminary fades.

What an absurd game! In which there is but one winner: baby.

I see that now. Nothing could be clearer.

But before—have to admit, I hadn't seen.

Fortunately, she'd never been a beautiful young woman. You'd have said of Lori—*attractive.*

Dark hair, dark eyes, slightly heavy dark brows, olive-pale skin.

And all that, irrelevant now. Might've been a cluster of cells, moist, fertile, violable.

Lori has managed to activate the digital "zoom" device: "zooming" in close to Baby, as close, or closer, than Mommy would be if Mommy were holding Baby for there appears to be some magnification in the camera lens.

Perilously close, it seems. Vertiginously!

Baby's nostrils loom large, as the rest of Baby's face softens and loses definition. Something wet moves, snail-lips wet with spittle. Close-up of Baby's (distorted, enlarged) mouth. A *rapid chuffing* sound, amplified baby-breathing so suddenly loud, Lori has an impulse to press her hands over her ears.

Once that breathing has begun it will not cease for eighty, ninety years. The little heart-mechanism wound tight, ticking away long after the mother of the baby and the father of the baby have ceased to exist.

Lori is having trouble adjusting the zoom lens. God *damn.*

Baby's head has become alarmingly small, now it is too large again. With difficulty the mother brings the baby-head into focus.

Shuddering, to think that anything so large and *bulbous* was ever contained inside her body!

No nightmare of her girlhood had prepared her for pregnancy, let alone childbirth or the aftermath: the twenty-four-hour cease-less continual eternal Baby. Imagining sexual intercourse had been the limit of her imagination and even with that, she'd much under-estimated the act.

Surprises that are unique to the body. You *cannot imagine.*

Well, it was all a mistake. Wasn't it!

Generations of babies born out of their mothers' fevered need.

Can Baby hear Mommy's thoughts?—somehow, through the two-way audio system? For Baby has begun to stir, the little eyes flutter open.

Hel-lo! This is Mommy, can you see me, sweetie?

Carefully Mommy positions her (tense-smiling) face in front of the two-way camera.

Crinkly faced, comical as an elderly man with a wrinkled brow and a few scant hairs on his pale dome of a head who is also (some-how) an infant, Baby blinks and stares in frantic unfocus. Flails his small fists. In another instant he will draw a deep breath into the miniature baby-lungs to cry for Mommy.

Hel-lo darling! D'you see who this is? Hello-hello . . .

A storm is gathering in Baby's brow. Baby does not seem aware of (the image of) Mommy in the screen.

(Lori wonders if the infant-brain can't process simulacra on screens? The infant-eye isn't yet adjusted to interpreting such stim-uli? Animals often seem incapable of "seeing" images on screens.)

Instead Baby's attention has been captured by someone or some-thing out of the range of the camera. To Mommy's disappointment Baby pays no heed to Mommy smiling, grimacing, waving at him like a fool.

He is alert, sharp-eyed, squinting at something beyond Mommy's face—what?

What, *who*?

Another camera is needed in the nursery, Mommy thinks. A camera to record what the crib-camera is recording, from a distance.

The entire house should be weaponized with surveillance devices. The weakness in household security, Lori realizes, is the broken vertebrae of the marriage.

Is Baby frightened, or is Baby just curious? Is fear inborn in the infant-brain, or must fear be learned?—taught?

Baby's eyes are rapidly blinking, he is rapt with concentration. Smiling in a way that breaks Mommy's heart for it is directed not at (smiling) Mommy but at another, invisible.

Astonishing: Baby is lifting his arms to—whom? Surely this is the first time that the six-month-old baby has lifted his arms to be gathered into the arms of another . . .

(But there is no one in the nursery! No one in the house except Lori at this moment! She is certain.)

Yet, it's fascinating. To observe Baby in the presence of an unknown.

Baby has cobalt-blue eyes, so dark as to appear all iris. In the monitor, *night vision* has rendered them black.

In *night vision,* Baby is unidentifiable. Pale dome of a head, blurred face, indentations for nostrils, twitching fish-mouth.

Distressed, begins to kick. Whimper, cry.

The familiar cry, which will heighten into a wail.

She'd heard, in the clinic. As the baby was removed from her dead-numbed lower body. A frantic wailing, piercing her heart.

Kicking the crib, dislodging the camera. A six-month-old baby can be surprisingly *strong.*

Only the lower left part of the baby's face is visible now. The head is weirdly magnified and distorted like something waxen, melting.

Lori hears herself pleading into the camera.

Hello! Here I am! Look at me!

You know who I am! Here!

I am your—
—the one who—
—died for you.

12

Her idea. Not *his*.

A sudden fever in the blood, in Lori's thirty-ninth year.

Sudden the wish, the need to have a baby. Out of nowhere seemingly the mantra *have a baby*.

Timothy had been surprised. Indeed, astonished.

For Lori had never shown any interest in having a baby. Nor had Timothy, whom she'd met soon after moving to New York City, from the small midwestern city on Lake Michigan in which she'd lived her entire life.

Childless has the ring of loss, regret. Lori had never thought of her situation as *childless* but rather self-defined, self-sufficient. The equilibrium of wife/husband in perfect balance, which, inevitably, a child, a third presence, would upset.

For eleven years, the "childless" household. Wife, husband equally involved in their careers, which were intensely competitive careers. So equally involved in the household neither could have said what the other's salary was for all checks were deposited in joint accounts: checking, savings, investments.

Abruptly then, after the (premature, unexpected) death of her mother, Lori began to obsess over *having a baby*.

Losing her mother had felt like having her spinal cord cut. With something like a surgical scissors. Just—*cut*.

Not that Lori had been especially close with her mother. She would have claimed.

Timothy had asked—*Are you sure?*

Lori had said—*Yes! I am sure.*

At once, the equilibrium of the marriage began to shift. For their lovemaking, which had been impulsive, playful, sporadic in recent years, became functional, deliberate. Nothing more self-conscious than *trying to become pregnant.*

They'd consulted a fertility specialist, at Lori's insistence. And this too, an imbalance in the marriage.

Timothy, the husband, had deferred to Lori, the wife. Out of husbandly kindness, magnanimity. Perhaps with some hesitation, at first. But decisively then.

Subsequently, the advantage would be his: Whatever happened as a consequence of the baby in their lives would be Lori's responsibility.

Like Archimedes with his lever. So positioned, the lightest feathery touch is all that is required to move the earth, otherwise unmovable.

13

Mother: What a curious word! *Moth-er.* Rapidly whispering the syllables.

Strange hypnotic slightly obscene word, a delicious word, a secret word, a fantastic word—*Mother.*

I am your mother.

I am Mother.

Mother, I am.

14

. . . lying on her (left) side though her heart hurts, thumping. Isn't it dangerous to sleep on your (left) side. Isn't the internet rife with warnings, don't sleep on your (left) side.

It has been advised by her doctor, the mother of the baby should sleep more than she has been sleeping. Turn off the (damned) Baby-Monitor, no need to keep it on all the time.

Luminous in the dark, like a miniature moon. *Yes I will sleep but no. The risk is too great.*

Can't relinquish the baby to the night. If she allows her eyelids to shut. But still, it happens. She falls asleep and is wakened by a hard-throbbing heart against her ribs.

On the monitor, the baby has shifted position. *Sleeping baby* has vanished.

Luminous face like a little moon and across the moon's face a smile, for someone is bending over Baby, someone who is *not authorized.*

This is not Baby's mother! This is an intruder.

For a moment wanting to think that somehow the figure in the Baby-Monitor *is* her.

The mother of the baby who is (somehow) in the nursery, lifting Baby to nurse him, even as she stares at the glassy screen of the Baby-Monitor in the bedroom.

Dry-mouthed in astonishment. For this is very wrong. Rising from the bed, unsteady on her feet.

The face of the intruder isn't visible in the monitor. Just the arms, lifting Baby. Singing softly, a lullaby.

Faceless predator-bird. Black condor, crow.

Is it the mother-in-law? Daring to enter the nursery, against the mother's wishes?

The mother-in-law had volunteered to watch the baby in the afternoon so Lori could sleep for an hour or two. Or three.

Push the stroller to Kemble Park. Prepare the evening meal. Never fails to take Lori's (cold, unresponsive) hands—*You are looking so tired, dear! You must sleep.*

Such bullshit, the mother of the baby is thinking. They will say anything to disarm/beguile her.

They are in collaboration. She has no reason to know, yet she *knows.*

Magnanimous Timothy the father of the baby has offered to care for the baby in the night so that the mother of the baby can sleep. *He* will watch the monitor. *She* can sleep in another room. The mother's milk can be suction-pumped out of her heavy aching breasts, stored in sanitized little baby-bottles. The father of the baby can nurse the baby as well as the mother, perhaps better than the mother since the father is a calmer person, his hands are steady and his eyes are not bloodshot.

He has practiced, it seems. She has gone along with the charade.

The *male role model* for the baby boy. Essential.

The mother has no intention of giving up the baby to the father. What if the father causes the baby to choke, forcing the rubber nipple into his mouth, flooding his mouth with milk?—the risk is too great. What if the father drops the baby on his head? Fractures his (thin, soft) skull? Impossible to prove intention.

Gradually the plan has become clear to her: the mother-in-law will take Baby, and care for Baby, for Timothy. Something will happen to Lori, the mother of the baby. Perhaps it is already happening.

They will cajole her into taking an overdose of barbiturates. But they will not call it that, of course: they will call it *getting enough sleep.*

Sleeping pills scattered on top of the bureau in the bedroom. No idea how they'd gotten there, she is sure that the pills, which she'd never touched, were kept in the medicine cabinet.

Frowning he'd asked—*Are these yours, Lori? Should I put them back into the container for you?*

Or, he'd asked—*Should I bring a glass of water for you, Lori? You can take a pill now, it should last several hours.*

She hadn't answered him, it was a trick. You could give the wrong answer. As a girl she'd done crossword puzzles in ballpoint ink, to make it serious. No erasing. If you made a mistake you could not undo the mistake.

Math homework in ballpoint ink too. To punish stupid mistakes.

Lori? Should I bring you a glass of—

Slapped his hand, several pills went flying. Chunky round barbiturates, clattering to the floor.

The expression in his face!—really seeing, for the first time, *her.*

———————

But when Lori enters the nursery the black crow mother-in-law is not there.

No shadowy figure. No agitation of the air. No echo of a lullaby.

Just Baby in his crib, innocently asleep.

Lori crouches over the crib, staring at the baby. *Her* baby.

(Is he pretending to be asleep? Has the devious mother-in-law returned him to the crib and departed?)

Her heart is beating frantically—a sure signal that she is in the presence of danger.

Yet: Timothy's mother has vanished, the house is silent and darkened. Not even a scent of the woman remains in the air, that familiar repugnant lilac-talcumy smell.

On the hardwood floor behind the white-lacquered wicker crib the Mother Goose lamp exudes a gentle light, just enough for Lori to see that yes, Baby is sleeping peacefully and no, no one seems to have interfered with him.

It's only one-twenty a.m., Lori would have thought it was much later for she has been lying awake for so long in the other room.

How long, the nights! But days are longer, a vast Sahara of time broken into a succession of *baby-body tasks.* The mother of the baby makes her way as into a labyrinth, ever deeper and farther from the entrance/exit.

Windowpanes reflect the interior of the room faintly, not unlike the glassy screen of the Baby-Monitor in the other room. Beyond the panes there is only darkness: opacity.

No moon in the sky, no star clusters. Dense corrugated cloud covering pressing low.

Lori reasons that she might as well wait in the nursery for Baby to wake, for his next feeding. She will lie on the sofa, just a few feet away from the crib. She will close her eyes, just for a few minutes. When Baby is ready for her breast he will let her know.

For hers is the only breast Baby can suck. *Hers,* the only milk.

What a relief! The mother of the baby could weep with gratitude.

It hasn't happened yet, I am still alive. They have not replaced me, yet.

15

The father of the baby is asking, *Would you like to talk about it, Lori?*

Cannot say *no* for he will then accuse her of refusing to cooperate with him but cannot say *yes* for then he will interrogate her.

16

Fear: a spider scuttling in the corner of your eye, you need not acknowledge by looking at it.

17

She'd never been a fearful person. She didn't think so.

From childhood secure in her*self.* Knowing her*self* loved by her parents.

But now, since the pregnancy, and since the baby, that *self* has been replaced. Another *self* has intruded, innocently at first: in her naïveté she'd welcomed it.

My cup runneth over—an expression she'd never much liked for its biblical piety. Yet, the feeling is genuine, it's as if she is holding a cup and rich warm liquid (milk?) is being poured into the cup, spilling over onto her hands; and she laughs, saying *Enough!* but the rich warm liquid continues to be poured, and continues to spill over onto her hands, there is no way to stop it, no pleas or prayers that will be heeded.

All that is required is that you give up your life for another.

Yet, that might not be enough.

And you have nothing else to give.

18

. . . lying on her (left) side. (Left) side, hurtful to the heart.

Lungs and other organs weigh upon the heart forcing it to beat like a bird trapped in small quarters frantically beating its wings.

It's a relief to be alone—finally. In the bedroom in the bed in the dark in the night.

First time sleeping alone in more than twelve years.

Staring at the small luminous screen a few feet away in the dark. No pretense of trying to sleep, not in these circumstances.

In sleep, the mother of the baby is vulnerable. The mother of any baby is vulnerable. *They* will take advantage of her if she dares to shut her eyes.

The father of the baby is elsewhere. She has asked him to go away, or he has gone away of his own volition. She has no idea where he is, she has ceased caring. Love for any other *not-Baby* has become impenetrable to her, incomprehensible as a dead language. Probably Timothy is staying with his parents, who live only an hour's drive away, in another city.

Through the Baby-Monitor she'd heard them, by chance. When the mother-in-law was visiting for the day.

Unknowing, for the camera hadn't been turned on. Yet somehow, their voices were picked up by the ultra-sensitive audio system.

Near-inaudible voices. Whispers, murmurs.

She could not make out what they were saying. Listening so intently blood vessels stood out in her forehead.

Only just isolated words: *she, her. Baby.*

Danger.

Couldn't put the words together but certainly she knew, she'd known for months how they were plotting against her.

And how astonished they would be to learn that their (secret) plotting wasn't secret at all.

But now, that danger is past. *They* have been banished from the house.

(Unless they return while the mother of the baby is asleep, which it is possible they might do, if she is not cautious and allows her eyelids to shut.)

Here is the strange thing: the mother of the baby has become habituated to the Baby-Monitor.

She could sleep in the nursery if she wishes, or bring Baby into the bedroom to sleep with her, in her very bed, now that she no longer shares the bed with another person; yet, she has come to realize that the Baby-Monitor is not only an instrument of precision, a surveillance weapon, but it has remarkable powers she has only begun to fathom.

So long as the camera is fixed upon the baby in his crib the principal image on the glassy screen is Baby; yet, with the passing of time, particularly in the night, other images may intrude, she has discovered. *If she stays awake long enough.* The blurred and colorless *night vision* makes possible much that, in the day, with only the mother's (ordinary) eyes as instruments of vision, would be undetected, lost.

And so it is happening now: on the screen Baby's (enlarged) head begins to melt as Lori stares, heartbreak-soft skin dissolving, frail baby-skull beneath, a spider's web of tiny arteries, veins, nerves, ganglia; Baby's cobalt-blue eyes are gone, as Baby's little snub nose is gone, Baby's mouth, sweet hesitant baby-smile. There emerges something wet and raw, not a *living entity* but parts, scrapings as the sharp brisk rhythmic sound of a curette increases in volume hurtful to hear as the mother of the baby raises herself on one elbow to peer more closely at the monitor in appalled fascination seeing glistening flesh, miniature organs, a growing pile of scrapings on what appears to be a filth-encrusted chaise lounge . . .

Everything dark as soot, covered in soot. Yet at the same time moist, liquidy. A look of being warm. Somewhere inside the scraped parts, a tiny heart. Lungs, guts. Fingernails.

She'd bled for weeks, unpredictably.

You can hear the scraping of the uterus clearly. Yet, you can also feel the scrapings. Harsh sharp deft surgical curette.

She'd never told Timothy. She'd never told anyone.

She'd been just a girl, twenty. And for twenty, immature.

Why it's a chaise lounge, she remembers only vaguely. Of course it wasn't a *chaise lounge* but something that resembled one, or she was misremembering.

Groggy, delirious. Vision out of focus.

By now, the blood has calcified, turned black. The scrapings are no longer moist but desiccated. So long ago no color remains.

Did you think you could forget me?—I am always here.

On the sticky tile floor inside the monitor, undulating motion. As of myriad baby-bodies.

With the remote, she tries to zoom closer to the image inside the screen: undulating writhing things, not (human) babies but (she sees, staring) rats: seething swarm, dozens, hundreds of rats, covering the floor beneath the filth-encrusted chaise lounge.

A scream tries to force its way out of her throat but her throat is too dry and clamps shut.

19

You seem frightened, Lori. What is it?

. . . our baby? Why is that?

Are you afraid that something will happen to our baby?

In the quiet of the empty house. Relief!

Morning. Sunshine. She could weep, color has returned to the world.

She bathes the baby, puts a fresh diaper on the baby. She feeds the baby. Straps the baby in a stroller and pushes the stroller to Kemble Park.

Her baby. Absurd to think that Baby is just any ordinary baby.

Are you afraid that you will hurt our baby?

Please talk to me, Lori!

Six months' maternity leave from the university, followed by a sabbatical spring semester. Soon, Lori will set up her laptop in a sunny corner of the kitchen. She will scroll through the (myriad, unorganized) notes for her next project, at which she has only glanced in months.

Except: in the laptop screen there has come to be an (occasional) reflection that interferes with her concentration. Even as she reads through her own words, passages of prose she'd forgotten she'd written months ago, exciting to her, even thrilling, this reflection intrudes, distracting her so that she has to reread, and reread.

A miniature face. Miniature head. *His.*

As if the laptop were (somehow) connected to the Baby-Monitor. The camera in the nursery, (somehow) connected to the hard drive . . .

Lori laughs uneasily, she has forgotten what modest computer skills she'd had, before the birth. Always they instruct you: Turn off the computer, then restart.

Or, pull out the plug; then, replug.

Not possible to call Timothy to ask for help. Nor a mutual friend who would (no doubt) tell Timothy, that they might laugh at her ineptitude together.

"No. I *will not.*"

Lori shuts the laptop, pushes it aside. With relief hearing Baby making cooing noises, beginning to wake from his nap.

Too much quiet, solitude! Not good.

Is it time for Kemble Park?—it is.

A small neighborhood park: swings, slides, sandboxes. Picnic tables, benches.

Suburban park, occupied mostly by (young) mothers in the neighborhood, or their nannies, with small children.

Rarely men, and rarely adults without children.

It's a surprise to Lori, some of the children are even younger than Baby, hardly more than newborns. Others are toddlers, preschoolers.

All of us, off the grid. No Baby-Monitors in Kemble Park!

Lori does not make friends easily, she is a guarded person, yet in Kemble Park where no one knows her she has made an unusual effort. Several friendly acquaintances whose last names she doesn't know have greeted her warmly—*Hi Laura! Laurie!*

Timothy would be impressed, she thinks. Timothy would be *jealous.*

More recently, however, these sister-mothers have been cool to Lori. Perhaps they have learned (somehow) that the father of the baby no longer lives in the house with Lori and Baby. Perhaps the mother-in-law had spread lies about Lori, when she'd brought Baby to the park.

Lori has noticed recently: The young mothers in the park who'd once smiled at her now seem not to see her. Intent upon their cell phones, iPads, Kindles. Even the nannies, distracted by cell phones.

. . . how old d'you think she is?

Forty, at least.

Forty-five, easy.

No!

Did you see her hands? Her eyes?

God!—the bags under her eyes . . .

D'you think she's—

Buzzing in Lori's ears, can't hear. Hurriedly pushing the stroller away in case Baby is listening.

20

The beginning of the greatest fear, that you cannot keep another alive.

A far greater fear than your own extinction because, after you are gone, your guilt will be gone.

No one will be a witness.

Days so long stretching to the horizon. Sculpted by time as by wind arranging themselves like sand dunes except these were *time-dunes.*

Daylight is the safe time, Lori is grateful for daylight. Might've been the baby-doctor who'd promised her that nothing terrible can happen in sunshine because sunshine is full color.

Time-dunes. If she tells Timothy, he will be impressed.

Except no: Timothy is no longer impressed by Lori's clever way with words.

When love ceases, a light goes *out* in the eyes. Lori has seen.

Lori keeps the camera trained on the baby at all times, this is crucial. When she approaches the baby to lift him, comfort him, nurse him, scold him, she takes care to hold him tight against herself so that his face is hidden. The camera will record just the back of the eggshell-head with its scant, dark hairs.

She takes care to hold him *tight*. So that Baby does not slip from her grasp and fall to the floor, fracture the eggshell-skull.

Recently, she has brought the Baby-Monitor into the nursery. So that she can observe the screen in the baby's presence, glancing alertly from the screen-image of the baby to the actual baby.

Of course, it is the image of Baby, in the screen, that yields secrets. You could stare at the actual baby for long minutes, hours, you would never see beyond the exquisite heart-stopping beauty of Baby to what the baby *is*.

Obviously, another camera is badly needed, preferably at a height: in a corner of the nursery where the wall meets the ceiling.

This would need to be a more powerful camera than the Baby-Monitor camera, one equipped with X-ray powers.

(Except: these X-ray powers would certainly interfere with the household Wi-Fi.)

Also, the Baby-Monitor screen is absurdly small. It will need to be upgraded. Lori has to stoop to see herself in the screen, clutching Baby. Her head is cut off, no way to identify the Mommy. Could be any female clutching a baby to her bosom.

Tonight, Baby's sucking is more robust. Tugging at the nipple, impatiently.

Small sharp baby teeth have poked up in Baby's gums. Clamping together at the breast, tugging and tearing. Lori cries out in pain. She pulls Baby from her, his teeth tear at her bleeding breast as he wails, enraged.

Her sides are streaming blood, desperately she throws Baby from her. But on the floor on hands and knees he springs at her, biting her ankle. She kicks him away screaming—*Stop! No!*

With renewed fury and appetite Baby continues to throw himself against her.

21

Knowing now what she must do. Extirpate fear at the root.

Taking the baby outside, for the first time beyond Kemble Park. In a hilly area north of the city, a no-man's-land along the railroad embankment.

Here, less than a quarter mile from the interstate, is desolation: stagnant pools of part-frozen water, rotted tires, broken tricycles, filth-stiffened old mattresses, washing machines with yawning gaping mouths.

"Here we go! Mommy is taking us on a *hike.*"

Wanting to establish for the record that she'd never been a fearful person. Not even as a child.

All this, this fear, absurd and demeaning, this is new. This is *not Lori.*

As if prepared for their adventure Baby is sitting up in the crib, in the Baby-Monitor screen looming large, and in the nursery, sitting very oddly, unnaturally when she comes to get him—you might say *adultly.*

Good that this pretense is being dropped. *Baby*-behavior, cooing and kissing. No more.

As an adult might be sitting with his shoulders purposefully back, to avoid giving the impression of slouching. Turning the coy little face upward to Mommy like a trusting moon.

Lori laughs, shaken. For a baby is *so beautiful . . .*

No matter how the Baby-Monitor screen has prepared her there is nonetheless a pleasurable shock lifting the baby from the crib: the weight and heat of the dense little body. A baby is all head and torso. She laughs, how droll it is that Baby has *no knees.*

Well, maybe now—maybe Baby has knees. The soft cartilage has been toughening. Ingestion of calcium leached from Mommy's milk-breasts.

Baby certainly has baby-teeth, and damn, they are sharp!

Lori shakes her head, laughing wryly. A tale to tell the other mothers in Kemble Park.

And you wouldn't believe, the little demon bit me!

Overnight, he'd grown teeth. See? His first baby teeth.

First, carries the hot dense little squirmy weight downstairs to the kitchen, where there is sure to be, at this hour of morning, a patch of sunshine warming the cushion of a chair at a window.

Yes, yes!—time for the breast. No cryin'!

Greedily sucking at the wounded breast, sucking the life out of her as a particular sort of spider sucks the life out of its paralyzed frog-prey. (Lori has seen the video. Horrific!—but you cannot look away any more than the paralyzed frog can detach itself from the giant spider and escape.) But it's a pleasurable sensation, she has to concede. Giving up, sinking beneath the surface of dark water, shutting her eyes in ecstasy obliterating the world.

Next, she takes Baby outside, bundled against the cold like a spicy little sausage in his special casing. (Even Baby's face is flushed, red.) Not in the stroller but in Lori's compact little Nissan. Not to the familiar park, which she has grown to dislike, but to the desolate edge of town beside the interstate.

Lori has dressed warmly, sensibly. She will be hiking a distance from the road. A mile, two miles. In such stretches of uncultivated land close beside highways, parallel with housing developments, strip malls, a distance of a single mile is many miles. A distance of a quarter mile can be to the horizon. Everywhere are scrub trees, the horizon is foreshortened. She is wearing rubber-soled boots. She is carrying Baby in a snug warm pack against her chest and with both arms she holds Baby secure.

Not once has Lori gone hiking with Baby. Not once in all these months.

Her muscles have atrophied! The strength has been sucked from her, she must suck it back into herself.

Baby is alert, wary. Baby is not fretting or whining. Baby's eyes are wide and round for Baby senses that something crucial is imminent.

What relief, to have left the Baby-Monitor behind! Off-camera, off the grid. No more weapons of surveillance.

Whatever happens here will not be recorded.

They are on a faint trail, overgrown with briars. Leafless deciduous trees beyond the railroad embankment. No one can see them here though they can hear traffic on the interstate. From a hill, if she had binoculars, she could stare into the kitchen of a bright-white aluminum-sided Colonial with latticed windows, observe a harried young mother preparing breakfast for her children.

Binoculars, one-way surveillance. In fact Lori has a pair of binoculars in the trunk of the car, a remnant of her old bird-watching days.

Walking briskly though she is not very fit—short of breath, and a cramp in her leg. Murmuring to Baby, nonsense syllables to comfort.

Crusted snow, soft mud beneath. Melting snow, mud. A smell of wet earth, deeply satisfying.

Already she has forgotten the Baby-Monitor. A camera positioned above an empty crib, a screen recording emptiness.

Years ago she'd explored this desolate place on foot, alone. While Timothy was elsewhere. Storm damage, debris. Up a steep hill, down an incline, a stream edged with ice.

Small boulders. Styrofoam litter. A sound of fast-trickling water, which draws the attention of Baby.

Sharp ears. Sharp shiny dark-blue eyes.

Mommy pauses, thinking. What has happened in this desolate place has already happened. Needing now just to remember.

A baby lowered gently into such a stream: water would flow gently over it, very cold, numbing, merciful. The baby would shriek at first, flail its tiny fists. Short legs thrashing.

Like butter, like silk. Baby skin.

"Forgive me. You will be thankful, one day."

Baby has begun to fret, anxious. Her mistake is to look into the widened moist-blue eyes.

On a fallen log she sits heavily, amid a scattering of animal prints. Sharp indentations of deer prints. The log is a fallen oak out of which other, smaller oaks are growing, in miniature. At another time Lori would find this fascinating but she is distracted now. She is panting from the exertion, though she has really not come very far. At a little distance her old, lost girl-self observes her, with pity, impatience.

Sitting with her legs outspread, clutching the baby that is *her baby* in her arms against her chest.

It will require some effort, to remove the baby-pack. To set Baby down securely against the log, so that he won't topple over and begin wailing. Effort to open her jacket, her shirt. A nursing bra. What an ugly undergarment! She has stopped wearing bras around the house for rarely does she leave the house these days.

She resents the cry for milk, she has been hearing it too often.

No one in sight. High overhead an airplane?—a droning sound.

Her chilled fingers fumble with the nursing bra, the baby. So awkward! Her face is smarting with embarrassment, annoyance.

Oh, why is Baby always *hungry*! The mother of the baby smiles wryly.

Pushing the nipple into the hot sucking ravenous mouth. Mesmerized by the immediate sucking of the mouth.

What pleasure, they are off the grid. This smell of water, wet earth. High trees, leafless. No one will find them.

High overhead, the little plane has vanished.

Monstersister

BEGAN AS *IT*. Not even a thing, just a sensation.

At the back of my head near the crown of my head some kind of small fleshy lump to which my fingernails were drawn.

First, a mild itch. Then, not so mild.

Had to be an insect bite. Swollen patch in my scalp the size of a quarter.

In the night I could feel *it* quivering. Hot-pulsing like something alive.

Not just itching but burning, stinging. My nails scratched, scratched, scratched until they came away edged with blood.

Thinking—*Maybe it will go away by itself.*

Pleading—*Dear God make it go away!*

Thirteen years old and had not (yet) abandoned the hope that I was someone special whom God, if there was a God, would protect.

Hours wakeful and in misery. Never had I lain awake so many hours in any night. Would not have thought there were so many hours in any night. In the morning blood-smears on my pillow and a rank smell.

Craned my neck trying to see in the mirror what *it* was. But could not see for my hair grew over *it*.

Went whimpering to Momma for help.

"What on earth have you *done*! Looks like a nasty snarl."

Frowning in concentration, her hot breath on the nape of my neck, Momma searched for *it* with her fingers. Scolding as if *it* was just another snarl. Something sticky and clotted in my hair like chewing gum.

(As if in my entire life I'd gotten chewing gum in my hair!)

Sitting on the rim of the bathtub scarcely daring to breathe. Head bowed shivering and praying that *it* could simply be cut away by Momma's deft fingers with a nail scissors and *it* would be revealed as merely a tick or flea or bedbug embedded in my scalp, which would be *gross, disgusting* but finite, and could be dealt with with a shudder of repugnance as Momma flicked *it* into the toilet bowl to be flushed away followed with gratitude and relief that *it* was gone. And there would be—(what a blizzard of hope in my brain in those days!)—a gentle impress of Momma's lips against the wound and a chaste white Band-Aid in case the wound oozed a thin film of blood and afterward the mercy of forgetting—*All gone, sweetie. Good as new!*

Except this did not happen. Nothing remotely like this happened.

Momma carefully snipped away hairs with the scissors and then with a safety razor shaved a little space around the lump. Muttering to herself, perplexed.

"Not sure what this is. A goiter?"

Goiter! No idea what a *goiter* was except something shameful.

Seated trembling on the edge of the bathtub. Like a small child, eyes shut tight. So even if I could have seen *it*, I would not have seen *it*.

At the time no way of knowing that never again would Momma call me *sweetie*.

———

First sight, *it* resembled a (small, egg-sized) veiny sponge attached to my scalp.

Not one of those synthetic sponges from the grocery store that are fake-bright-colored but an actual sponge from the ocean. A sea creature lacking a brain and a spine that has no face or limbs and is the color of a paper bag composed of myriad tiny air bubbles that soak up water.

Of course, such a sponge is a living creature, not like the fake sponges from the grocery store. But when you see it, and touch it, it's no longer a living thing but the remains of a living thing.

". . . oh my God! I hope it isn't your brain leaking out . . ."

Didn't hear this. Did not hear this.

". . . maybe a goiter growing out of your brain . . ."

None of these terrible words uttered by my alarmed mother as if she were thinking aloud did I hear. No!

Momma held a hand mirror above my head so that I could see *it* inside the shaved spot in my scalp. What a shock! But I wanted to laugh too.

Rejected *it* as some kind of trick played on me, nothing that was real, or would last more than a day or two, while at the same time I had to accept (I guess) that *it* was not an infected insect bite, still less a boil or giant pimple but something stranger than any of these, and nastier.

Most important, Momma said in a lowered voice: We will keep *it* a secret.

No reason Momma argued for anyone outside the family to know about *it*. At least not yet.

By *family* Momma meant herself and Dad, my seven-year-old sister Evie and my ten-year-old brother Davy, and Granma who lived with us. Not relatives, neighbors. Not friends or worse yet old friends not seen in years, high school classmates of Momma's who'd never left the area but continued to live within a few miles of one another aging year after year and thrilled still in the spreading of the most absurd gossip.

This Momma dreaded. Being *talked-about*.

Of course, Momma had to tell Dad about *it*. But the others—
Evie, Davy, Granma—didn't need to know just yet.

Dad stared at *it*. Dad's jaws moved as if he were having to chew,
to swallow, something that tasted bad.

"Well, hell."

Never saw anything like this before in his life, had to admit.

Weird boils, bunions, "growths"—maybe . . . But a goiter is some
kind of swollen neck gland, Dad said. Nothing like this ugly thing
growing out of his daughter's head.

Touching *it* with his fingers, as if he thought *it* might burn his
fingers.

A shivery sensation passed through me like an electric shock
though I did not exactly feel Dad's fingers touching me.

"Jesus! The thing is God-damned *warm*."

Dad thought that *it* should be cut away with a scissors or a knife
but Momma thought it might hurt me too much, for I'd writhed in
pain when she'd been snipping near *it* with the nail scissors. Obviously, that part of my scalp was hypersensitive and would probably
bleed badly as scalp wounds do.

Dad said nonsense, the only sensible thing to do was remove *it*
before it got any larger.

(Dad was right: *it* was growing. Each morning when I woke, I felt
it—each morning *it* had grown in the night.)

You might wonder why my parents didn't take me to a doctor to
have the veiny-sponge-growth examined and removed; at least, to
determine if *it* was a malignant growth. But that was not Dad's way.

Dad was distrustful of strangers. He did not like people *snooping*.

Except in the case of emergencies, and not always even in the
case of emergencies, Dad shied away from hospitals, clinics, doctors, police. Persons of authority who might be expected to *poke
their noses in our business.*

"I said no. No damned doctor! We will take care of this ourselves."

Flush-faced and grim Dad seated me at the kitchen table beneath the bright overhead light, laid out newspaper pages on the linoleum floor at our feet. With a flashlight he proceeded to examine

it closely. I could feel—that is, I imagined that I could feel—Dad's warm quickened breath against the exposed growth.

"Don't move. Stay *still*."

Tentatively Dad pressed the razor-sharp blade of a fishing knife against the cartilaginous membrane connecting *it* to my scalp. Gradually he increased pressure against the membrane, began to make sawing motions, to test the toughness of the sinewy membrane, whether he could severe it quickly, with a minimum of pain for me; but the sensation was unbearable, beyond pain, causing me to scream and thrash and wrench myself away from him like a panicked animal.

"For God's sake!—*stop that*. I am only trying to help you."

In disgust Dad pushed me from him. In his eyes I saw loathing.

Momma took pity on me and allowed me to run away to hide in my room terrified and ashamed. Later I would overhear her calling my school to explain that I might be absent for several days— "Our daughter has a medical condition that is expected to require 'minor surgery.'"

Still, Dad was reluctant to take me to a doctor. Who knows what a damned doctor might charge!

Also, as Dad sincerely believed, there might turn out to be some perfectly natural explanation for the growth sprouting from my scalp. It might happen that *it* would cease growing, and wither away and die, of its own accord falling off the way a snake's skin or a vestigial tail might fall off. (Were there such things as "vestigial tails"? In our household it began to be believed that there were.)

Whatever *it* was, *it* was not a goiter. Online research revealed that goiters are nothing but swellings of glands in the neck, and are not "oozings" of brain matter through a crack in a skull.

Nor is a goiter an autonomous growth, as (it seemed to me) the growth on my head was an autonomous growth. For I could feel *it* quivering, especially at night. A certain heat radiated from it, hotter than my skin; at times, I imagined that I could feel *it* breathing . . .

And one day Momma said, peering at me from behind, "Oh God! D'you hear that?—it's *breathing*."

Dad snorted in derision. "Ridiculous! *It is not*."

But Dad did not wish to draw too near, to incline his head to *it*. And Dad's own breathing was so audible, a kind of indignant panting through his mouth, he'd have had difficulty hearing anything else breathing in his presence.

Days had passed. Nights had passed. *It* was not withering away but growing larger, more like a thickening vine now than an egg.

Granma had soon learned about *it*. Davy and Evie suspected something seeing me darting furtively from my room to the bathroom, avoiding them; when I did appear downstairs, for meals, I wore a scarf around my head that stood out oddly, exactly as if some sort of growth had sprouted on my head.

"Your sister has a bad chest cold," Momma explained, "—I don't want it to turn into pneumonia. She has to keep *warm*."

In time, Davy and Evie seemed to know about *it*, too. No way to keep a secret in our small household.

Yet, they had few questions to ask. They were grim, frightened by the sight of me, suspecting that whatever terrible thing had happened to me might happen to them too, if they misbehaved.

Momma did not want to think that *it* might be something more than just an extraneous growth that would eventually wither and fall off, for instance a part of my brain that had oozed through a crack in my skull, nor did I wish to think this, though it was (to me) an unavoidable thought. But one day Granma stuck her finger into *it* and recoiled in alarm saying that *it* felt warm, and pulsing—"Like some kind of a pudding! If a pudding could be *alive*."

"Ridiculous! A pudding could not be *alive*." Dad laughed, sneering. But his eyes shone with fear and disgust.

Still, Dad was reluctant to take me to a doctor. For we did not have what is called a "primary care physician"—we did not have what is called "medical insurance."

Days passed. *It* grew larger. Of the size and shape of a banana tugging at my scalp, exuding heat. The skin of my forehead was tugged back tight. My eyebrows were raised in an expression of perpetual surprise, bafflement. There came to be a sensation like a vise tightening around my head.

At last Momma convinced Dad that I must be taken to a doctor for *it* was obviously more serious than he'd thought.

Reluctantly, Dad relented. Out of the physicians' yellow pages in the phone directory Dad selected Dr. F__, who must have had few patients since he could see me within the hour.

Dr. F__ expressed disbelief, then astonishment, at the "organic entity" growing out of the top of my head. His examination determined that *it* was not a goiter, or any sort of natural growth (bunion, callus, tumor) he'd ever seen in his life. There did indeed seem to be a "hairline crack" in my skull through which *it* was pushing, which Dr. F__ believed had to be brain matter, or what is called dura matter, a membrane protecting the brain, which might have become infected, and might have to be surgically removed, but he would not know with certainty until X-rays were taken.

X-rays! How much was all this going to cost?—Dad scowled.

Of course, Dad insisted upon a "second opinion." It was Dad's belief that you were very foolish if you didn't get a second opinion—a "second estimate"—for any product or service. If you were smart you pitted one estimate against the other, to drive the price down.

Dr. M__ was an older, white-bearded gentleman also out of the physicians' yellow pages who agreed to see me immediately, and like Dr. F__ expressed disbelief and astonishment at *it*. ("Is this *alive*? My God.") Dr. M__'s examination was more thorough than Dr. F__'s as it involved not just the exterior of my head but my ears, mouth, and eyes, into which he stared searchingly as if peering into my very soul.

Dr. M__'s tentative diagnosis was that *it* was (probably) not a part of my brain oozing through a hairline crack in my skull but rather totally separate and autonomous brain matter belonging to a totally separate and autonomous life-form of a "parasitical" nature that, thirteen years before in the womb, by which he meant my mother's womb, was supposed to have been an identical twin of mine, but through a misfiring of crucial cells had failed to develop into an independent embryo that should have been "born" by natural childbirth but had instead been "assimilated" into my body and was now—(for no reason Dr. M__ could discern other than the [evident] imminence of puberty)—forcing its way out of my skull by "creating its own 'birth canal.'"

Twin! Puberty! Birth canal! None of these repellent words made any impression upon me for I had become benumbed by so much attention focused upon me—(and not upon *it*). The doctor's pen-sized flashlight shining deep into my eyes had rendered me near-blind and Dr. M__'s words had been directed to my father and not to my ears.

(Did *it* hear, and did *it* understand? The sensation in my scalp was tingling, alert and alive. Almost, I could feel *it* quivering with life having been acknowledged as "separate and autonomous" so clearly by a medical doctor.)

It should be surgically removed, Dr. M__ said. But not before X-rays were taken.

In silent chagrin Dad listened. His mouth worked in a grimace. He may have had questions to ask Dr. M__ but he was too distracted, distraught. Urged me out of the office without making another appointment and on the stairway, before we left the building, whispered agitatedly to me, "Fix the damned scarf! Hide *it*."

Sulky-faced, I did just that.

Identical twin. Once these words were uttered I could not stop hearing them.

Identical twin. Echoing, re-echoing.

Indeed, *it* was becoming bigger, heavier at the top, back of my head. You could hear *it* breathing, and you could feel *it* thrumming with life.

Soon *it* was bouncing behind me to the nape of my neck. The top of my spine. A tickling sensation that made me shiver. Throwing me off-balance when I tried to walk, the way, with her "bad hip," Granma was thrown off-balance when she walked.

It began to plead with me not in words but in quivering sensations—*Help me! I want to live.*

Want to live like you.

These communications were contemptible to me, I pretended not to hear.

. . . like you like you. You.

I laughed, this was so absurd. Like *me*?

Could *it* breathe on its own? Could *it* continue to grow, taking nourishment from me, on its own?

Scornfully I asked how *it* could live without *me*?

You can't live without me.

I can destroy you at any time.

(But could *it* understand me? Had *it* functioning ears? An actual brain that might process language?)

As if in shock at my scorn *it* lapsed into silence.

Except for *its* quickened rapid breathing, silence.

. . . at any time. If I choose.

(But why, you are thinking, did I *not choose*?)

(And now, it is too late.)

The thing, the twin-brain, *it*—(we did not yet call it *she*)—continued to grow heavier with the passage of weeks, now halfway down my back. And now, to the small of my back. *It* was stretched like a coarse-textured stocking though wider at the top than below. I wondered if this was because the brain was not encased in a skull but just loose—dribbling like a flaccid skinless snake down my back.

Staring at *it* in a hand mirror reflecting my mirror-reflection behind me a dozen times a day. Nothing else so intrigued me in all of the world! Alternately repelled and fascinated by the thing's sponge-texture, a pale-brown color, consisting of myriad tiny airholes that seemed to inhale and exhale air in a concerted way.

The thing had a piteous look, overall. You could (almost) make out a face near the nape of my neck.

Well—not an actual *face*. Something like the "face" of a manta ray. In the spongy thing indentations of where a face would be: shallow sockets for "eyes," small black holes for nostrils, the suggestion of a mouth, a shallow slit, a mollusk's mouth . . .

(No teeth inside the mouth. At least, no visible teeth. Yet.)

Somewhere I'd read, eyeballs were once part of the brain, over the course of millennia drawn out by light. Must've been millions of years! So, brain matter in *it* was pushing out. The more light, the more pushing-out.

How I'd wanted to *gouge* those manta-ray eyes, before it was too late! Before they could *see*.

Yes!—you'd think that at the age of thirteen, no longer a tractable child but (almost) an adolescent, I would have been in a rage much of the time, disgusted by *it*, as *it* was a physical burden for me to bear, weighing—what?—twenty pounds?—soon, thirty pounds—dragging down my back, and causing me to stagger when I walked; having made me a freak who dared not creep outside the house for fear of being detected. (And who had ceased attending school.) And this was true, often I felt rage, fury, but mostly I felt sick with shame, but in another way (when I was alone in my room with just *it*) I understood that I was very special.

It had life only through me, *it* was hardly a twin of mine nor even a "sister"—(as Evie was a sister). *It* was just an appendage, a thing. A parasite!

And I was responsible for *it*—keeping *it* alive.

Why?—this question never to be answered.

Grinding my teeth chiding the thing for always being *there* dragging after me but at the same time I worried that something would happen to *it*, and *it* would wither and die and "fall off" (as Momma was always saying hopefully).

How lonely I would be then! (I did not want to think of this.)

When I went outdoors (in the backyard) I would wear a shawl over the thing. Eventually the thing itself would require a "skull"-cap to protect the part of it that seemed most vulnerable, where its head (brain) must have been; Momma made a sort of helmet of soft cloth to fit over the upper part that seemed to be a face, a head, a brain of its own, and to be very vulnerable. Over this we attached a thin veil with tiny holes for the pinpoint pupils that had begun to develop in the flat shallow face.

Fascinating to see how *it* developed protuberances where eyes would have been in a normal face. These appeared over the course of several nights not long after the slit-like pupils had emerged. If you ran your fingers over these protuberances you felt something like the uncanny elasticity of eyeballs, still embedded in brain matter, but emerging from it; if you shone a light there the brain matter shivered and shuddered and (as Momma described it, for I could not see) the pupils *shrank shut.*

In time the veil was outgrown, another veil had to be supplied, more of an actual mask, with larger holes for "eyes" and eventually a slit for the mouth, which was always unpleasantly damp, and soon became ragged.

I want, I want to live. Want to live like you.

Like you like you want to live. Like you.

These pathetic quiverings were not actual *words.* Not that you could *hear.*

These crude efforts to communicate with me were met with mostly silence. Scoffing laughter, a shrug of my shoulder—*But you will never be like me. You!—like* me!

Except: One dawn in bed I was wakened with a jolt as *she* detached herself from me with a snap of the cartilaginous membrane that had attached us, and lay for a time stunned and panting behind me . . . Or maybe that is wrongly described: *She* did not actively detach herself from *me;* rather, it simply happened that *she was detached from me* as a scab falls from (healed) skin by a natural process.

As if unaware, or indifferent, I lay unmoving. Of course, I did not turn to her.

Though all of my senses were alert, my heart rapidly beating.

A sense of profound loss swept over me, a heaviness of a kind I had never before experienced, for I was sure that it was as Momma had been predicting for months—*it* would wither and die and fall off me, and I would return to what I'd been before.

At last then, when I'd gathered sufficient courage to overcome my disgust, and with my eyes shut tight, I turned and pushed *it*—*her*—out of bed and onto the floor, which *it*—*she*—struck softly, like unbaked bread dough.

Almost inaudibly, a little cry was emitted—*Oh!*

Monstersister! Here was the opportunity to toss *it* into the trash, now that *it* had separated from me without the spillage of blood.

Yet, this did not happen. For unmistakably, *it* was a living thing.

Already, *it* had become *she,* and eventually, *she* would acquire a name.

(But not from me! For it did not seem just to me, that *she* who was only an appendage of mine should have a name separate and distinct from my name.)

At first Monstersister was fed as an infant might be fed, greedily sucking on the rubber nipple of a baby's bottle filled with milk.

Later, orange juice, vanilla smoothies.

Then, Monstersister learned to suck liquid-pureed food through a straw, which Momma prepared in a blender—hot oatmeal, fruits, yogurt, greens, carrots, broccoli.

Eventually nuts, sunflower seeds, and chickpeas were blended as well, included in these "nutritious" liquids. (Yes, I was allowed to suck these through a straw. I was allowed to "lick the spoon.")

Whipped potatoes, with melted butter. Melted cheese, melted-grated cheese on doughy-soft bread. Rice pudding, Jell-O of every imaginable flavor. And of course, ice cream in a semisoft state.

Monstersister had a small appetite, you might conclude that her gastrointestinal organs were rudimentary as her new-emerging near-transparent teeth were certainly rudimentary. But like an undersea creature Monstersister had a *continuous appetite*.

(Rudimentary, and continuous: suety excretions from Monstersister's colorectal organs.)

(Yes, Monstersister was outfitted with diapers of increasing size until finally, adult Depends snug on her misshapen lower body as the cloth covering on her misshapen head.)

Monstersister was given a "name." *I* would not accept that name and you will never learn that name from *me*.

(No. Monstersister's name is *nothing like my name*.)

(No. We do not share a last name. Monstersister has no birth certificate because Monstersister was never "born." Therefore, Monstersister has no certificate given the imprimatur of the New Jersey State gilt seal. Therefore, Monstersister has no name legal or otherwise.)

Whatever *she* is called in the family, *I* do not acknowledge.

After *she* had broken away from me in my bed that morning like a scab there came to be a profound alteration in our household. A shifting of its foundation. A seismic shrug.

"Oh, what have you done!"—Momma cried sharply, seeing that *she* was separate now from me as if out of pure spite I'd scraped her off, out of my brain stem as a snake scrapes off its desiccated husk of a skin and glides away free and unencumbered its scales glittering in the sun and its eyes joyously glaring.

"Oh, have you killed her! Your—" But Momma faltered, for the word *sister* was too outrageous to be uttered; instead Momma drew breath to begin again, "Oh God, is she still—breathing?"

No, and yes. No no no but yes.

Damn *no,* and more damn *yes.*

Turned out, *she* could breathe apart from me after all. An oozing out of my brain initially, *she* soon acquired autonomy as a mature fetus expelled from its womb acquires autonomy, in time.

If it fails to die, first.

What is interesting here, from a disinterested/objective perspective, is how the *unimaginable improbable* will become, within a surprisingly short period of time, the *imagined probable.*

How the *lurid-freakish* becomes, within that period of time, particularly if experienced on a daily, hourly basis, in a familiar and delimited space like a family household, *normal.*

What was accepted as the *old normal* is soon overcome by the *new normal.*

Eventually then, simply *the normal.*

For all things shift, as if tugged by gravity, to *the normal.*

And soon then, even I was drawn into the new alignment of our household. As with simple repetition any gesture, any process, any movement or motion becomes assimilated into the habit-forming soul. As playing a musical instrument begins in unfamiliarity and awkwardness, as many times repeated it sinks into the depths of the brain where it is redefined as *tissue memory.*

Of course, I found myself involved in feeding Monstersister. There is a visceral pleasure in feeding a life-form that without your intervention will wither and die.

First, Momma fed Monstersister. Then, Granma. Then—me.

And soon also, I was drawn into caring for it. That is, *her.*

That's to say, *caring-for* her in a literal sense: *care-taking.*

But eventually, as a consequence of this, *caring for her:* feeling concern, solicitude, "care" for her.

Knitting little hats for her, to protect her (exposed) brain. Knitting sweaters, smocks, gloves to protect the spongy tissue that was *her.*

For unlike me, Monstersister had failed to acquire that outer layer of tissue known as "skin."

(Why had she failed? In the womb?)

(Yes, it is an ugly word. Words. Ugly-cringing words—*in the womb.*)

(Dr. M__ had not explained. Dad had been too stunned to question him and Dr. M__ had not cared to explain. Perhaps there is no explanation. The most profound questions of our lives allow for no answers.)

(Though you are led to wonder if there is not some blame involved when one of a pair of "twins" fails to establish herself as an autonomous being while the other succeeds—as I did . . .)

Without an outer layer of tissue Monstersister was purely brain matter, ganglia, nerve-networks, veins, and arteries lacking a protective covering. No (evident) skeleton. *Not human!*

After the shock, the dismay, and the disgust, unless it was the disgust and the dismay, and after the shock had faded, a perverse sort of gaiety came into the household. At least, Momma took some determined pleasure in *dealing with the situation.* And Granma, too.

For Monstersister was a *blood relative.* No pretending that she was just something that came slithering into our house by accident!

Dad fell to brooding, staring at Monstersister as she lay inert in a cardboard box beside a heating vent in the kitchen. This box was rectangular, several times longer than it was wide, a kind of cradle-shape into which Monstersister's boneless elastic-spongy body fit, lined with soft cloths. (You could not readily discern if Monstersister was awake or asleep or in a comatose state for the flat-manta face betrayed little emotion through the veil.)

"Christ! You wonder what it is we've done. To deserve this."

Yet Dad did not seem to doubt that *it* was a consequence of something that had *been done.* (But by whom? Dad? Dad and Momma?)

In the family it was Momma who was most attached to Monstersister. For here was a *challenge.* And Momma liked to say that belief in God is only tested by *challenge.*

Needing to keep Monstersister warm was urgent, Momma believed. Lacking a protective skin Monstersister was hypersensitive to bruising as well as cold. So it was, Momma taught me to knit.

Me!—wielding knitting needles! What an insult!

I'd never felt the slightest interest in knitting, an insipid fussy activity Momma and Granma did, and Dad would never be caught dead doing.

Unexpectedly then, I discovered that I liked the look and feel of yarn between my fingertips. Bright purple, hot pink, and "royal" blue were my favorite yarn-colors.

Knit-purl, knit-purl, knit-purl taking care not to miss a stitch. Once you learn the trick of gripping the damn clattering knitting needles.

Knitting will make you less nervous, Momma said. Learn to *sit still not wiggle.*

All of my life a struggle. It is not enough for them to put you in a cage for in the cage you must also *sit still not wiggle* for they are watching at all times.

How to shape a curved knitted cap. How to shape knitted sleeves. How to knit a glove—with ten fingers! (Finally, despite Momma's best efforts, I could only knit clumsy spade-shaped mittens for Monstersister.)

In addition, Monstersister was given clothes I'd outgrown or had come to dislike. The surprise was, these fit her almost as well as they'd fitted me, though Monstersister is much smaller than I am, what you'd call "stunted"—"dwarfish." She is disfigured like a broken-backed snake if the snake lacked a firm envelope of skin to contain its flesh.

Well, yes—Monstersister was disgusting, laughable.

Eventually, however, unlike a snake Monstersister began to acquire stubs of flesh where arms should have been, as well as stubs of (thicker) flesh where legs should have been, and feet.

At first, just suggestions of limbs. But gradually these began to protrude from the body-stem, and to take shape.

Never would the "hands" acquire actual fingers, however. Not as you and I understand fingers. Never would the "legs" acquire actual feet but rather flat spatulate stubs like the flippers of certain undersea creatures.

Yet, Monstersister was "precocious"—you could say.

Before ten months of age Monstersister began to struggle to stand upright while leaning against a railing or a wall or clutching with gloved stub-hands at the arm of a chair. Her legs were stub-thighs that ended at the knees, on which she tried to walk upright like a dog on its hind legs; this was piteous to see, you wanted to hide your eyes or look quickly away, or laugh wildly. (Sometimes, as if by accident, I brushed against Monstersister as I passed by, knocking her off-balance without seeming to notice.)

When Monstersister was alone she often sank to the floor and crawled on her stub-limbs, panting with effort, with a whistling sort of sob. (This was not a normal kind of crawling such as an infant or a toddler might undertake for it was attended not with joyous excitement but grimly with panting and moaning: a shivery slith-ering twitchy kind of crawl such as a creature might undertake.)

Eventually Monstersister learned to make her way on "all fours" up and down stairs slithering and sliding with surprising rapidity. If you were descending the stairs you might glance down and there was Monstersister pushing past your ankles as a mischievous flat-faced snake might do indifferent that you might tangle your legs in it and fall.

Sometimes in warm weather Monstersister was allowed outside in the backyard by Momma and Granma, who saw that she did not wander more than a few yards from the back porch, and who watched over her anxiously, that she did not injure herself.

For Monstersister (evidently) possessed a rudimentary circula-tory system, tendril-like veins and arteries throughout her truncated body. If one of these was pierced, "blood" would appear—thinner than normal human blood but smelling strongly.

Also, Monstersister began to grow a kind of cuticle over her soft sponge-head; the exposed brain matter came to be covered by a thin membrane that thickened and became relatively hard, like the rind of a fruit that is soft and juicy within. Still it was necessary for Monstersister to wear the little caps we knitted for her, for she had no hair, or rather nothing more than a light fuzzy down, and was vulnerable to bruises, scratches, infections.

Generally, a membrane came to cover most of Monstersister's body though it would never be as substantial as actual "skin."

And so, outfitted with a knitted royal-blue helmet, a near-transparent face-veil, sweaters, shirts, pants that had once been mine, as well as old sneakers of mine, Monstersister could be mistaken for a (more or less) normal child of nine or ten if observed at a distance of at least twelve feet—but no closer!

Yet more strangely, by the end of the first year since the veiny sponge first appeared at the back of my head Monstersister began to be confused in the eyes of my family with—*me*.

First, Granma. For Granma's eyes were not sharp. And Granma's judgment had become blurred.

Granma calling Monstersister by my name but, what was more hurtful, calling *me* by *her* name.

"Granma, no! *I am not—that thing.*"

And Granma would stare at me, and blink, and laugh nervously—"Of course you are not, dear. What was I thinking of!"

My hatred for Granma began at that moment. A sudden small throb at the top rear of my head where the veiny sponge had first appeared as itching.

For Granma had forgotten my name, I was sure. From now on, Granma would call me *dear*. (But Granma did not forget Monstersister's name!)

Worse, my brother Davy and my sister Evie began to befriend Monstersister when I wasn't around. I would hear them chattering and laughing and feel a sinking sensation, for I knew, and was too proud to accuse them.

For months they'd avoided me when Monstersister had been just an ugly growth down my back, but somehow now that Monstersister was "autonomous" they began to be curious about her, and (possibly) to feel sorry for her, that she could straighten to only about forty-eight inches in height and had, inside my cast-off sneakers, no actual feet of her own.

And possibly because of this stunted stature, and her inability to speak except in grunts, moans, whistles and whimpers and trills, they did not feel intimidated by her.

Smaller than Evie, overall. Much smaller than Davy. So if you collided with her there could be no injury to yourself, you felt only a small thrill of pleasure at the pliant warmth of another's being with no recourse but to give way to you without protest.

For *she* never protested, complained, whined, or whimpered. As a normal child would.

All these months that Monstersister was being tolerated in the household, and beginning to acquire an indeterminate status in the family, not one of us (of course) yet not entirely an outsider, still Monstersister remained a secret to relatives, who had been resolutely not invited to visit, as well as neighbors and acquaintances who might have been "friendly" with Momma but would not have dared drop by the house uninvited. Within the family still I took for granted—we all took for granted, I'd thought—that *she* was really just an *it*, a *thing*. And we'd begun to call her *she,* and some of us had given her a name, but not seriously, such a status might be revoked at any time.

Which was why I became agitated hearing how *she* was beginning to be talked about in the family not only by name but *as if she was not so different from me—a "sister."*

(But how was this possible? I was "real," Monstersister was a freak.)

By degrees then, Monstersister began her assault.

Because she could not speak words as a normal human being can speak words, for her tongue was malformed, a thin little snake-tongue it was, unnaturally pink, Monstersister cultivated a way of *whimpering, whining, trilling, humming.*

Of these, *humming* met with the most positive response from the family.

So *humming* it was, Monstersister's strategy.

A high-pitched *thrumming-humming* began to issue from the hidden mouth behind the veil covering the flat-manta face, musical notes of a strange uncanny beauty causing shivers to run down the spines of listeners.

Humming, just audibly. Keeping the thin-lipped snake-lips shut. So you might hear a high-pitched *thrumming-humming* in the air about your head, or rising through the floorboards of the house, penetrating walls with the power to bring tears to your eyes without your volition, you would not know why, you would be taken by surprise, tears running down your cheeks, a shivery sensation rising along your spine, you would feel faint, you would want to laugh wildly. *You did not know why and you resented it.*

"Like an angel!"—Granma declared, wiping at her eyes when Monstersister *hummed.* (As if Granma had ever heard an angel singing!)

Pressed my hands over my ears. *Did not know why, resented it!*

Hid in my room. Hid in the basement. Hid in the woods behind the house. Hurt, sulking, staying away from meals. Refused to answer when Momma called me.

My name had become strange to me, harsh hissing syllables that I could not hear clearly, and could not recognize, *Fyczss! Fyczss!*—so why should I answer Momma, God damn I would not.

Astonishing then, Monstersister began to appear at mealtimes seated upright at the table in my chair. *My* chair!

This was Momma's idea, I was sure. But Dad must have agreed, which is strange to me, of my parents I would not have thought that my father would betray me for always there'd been the understanding that I was *Daddy's girl* . . .

Since Monstersister was stunted, a dwarf with a crooked back, virtually no spine at all, she had to be seated on cushions to reach the table; her stub-feet came nowhere close to the floor. Behind the veil (sure to be tattered and wet around the mouth) her face could be discerned in the bright light from overhead, for it had become more of a "face" now, with a sickly spongy skin and stark black holes for nostrils; almost you could discern "eyes"—a glisten of an actual eyeball, no longer just pinprick-pupils. And when the mouth-slash in the veil became raw and widened from usage you could catch a glimpse of Monstersister's mouth inside, thin worm-colored lips and a flick of an unnaturally narrow pink tongue quick-flitting as a snake's.

Through a doorway, through two doorways at the farther end of the hall I crouched watching in disgust, unseen. How my parents vied to feed *her*!—*it*. Not giving a damn if their actual daughter went hungry.

Worse yet staring through a kitchen window from where I stood outside at dusk only a few feet away observing Momma and Dad, Davy and Evie and Granma at supper with a hideous freak in their midst, which they seemed not to recognize, indeed they offered this thing grown long and limp as a python little treats, lifted a glass of pureed green liquid to its mouth so that it could suck greedily through a straw in a way disgusting to see.

Were they *charmed* by this thing? My heart was suffused with contempt for them, and rage against *it*.

Hid in the basement. Made a little nest for myself of rags in the basement. Avoided my family, who were hateful to me. Avoided meals. Crept into the kitchen to scavenge leftovers from the refrigerator, took my food away to devour in secret.

More often with warm weather I hid in the woods behind the house. Rolled up in a nylon jacket and some canvas from the garage. At first Momma continued to call me from the back porch in a plaintive voice for certainly Momma felt guilty, and anxious; but soon then, Momma called me less frequently, days passed and Momma did not call my (unrecognizable) name, and just once Dad shouted from the back door hissing furious words that frightened me for I knew that they contained a threat, and I dared not reply and give away my hiding place.

Following that, I would observe with contempt *the family* at the kitchen table. All of them were becoming freakish to me: "Momma"—"Dad"—"Davy"—"Evie." And the elderly woman with the foolish face creased like a dish towel—"Granma." And Monstersister upright in my chair on cushions, purple-yarn knitted cap on the undersized misshapen head, translucent veil over the flat-manta face so that you could dimly make out glassy-glistening eyes, nostril-holes, wormy-lipped slash-mouth through the fabric, and around the neck a scarf decorated in pink rosebuds and sequins—one of Momma's birthday scarves! This thing, this "sister," could now feed herself awkwardly lifting in gloved stub-hands a container of pureed liquid to suck through a straw.

Through the window came a thrilling *humming*.

The sound of this *humming* caused tears to spill from my eyes wetting my cheeks. Tears of sorrow or loss, tears of rage, I did not know.

The sound of this *thrumming-humming* was so high-pitched, so piercing, I fell back from the window, stumbling away weeping in grief and incomprehension.

I see now. A mistake, not to have cut *it* from my head.

Might've torn *it* out with my bare hands while *it* was no larger than an egg and had not yet drawn breath.

Does no one *see,* Monstersister is a freak? Not a *she* but an *it*?

Why is it only I, the legitimate sister, who can *see*?

Lulled by the *thrumming-humming,* that is it. A normal (frail) voice like mine can't compete with the monster.

Wondering if, if I crept into the house to discover Monstersister asleep in her cardboard-box cradle, I could smother her? Press a pillow over the little slash-mouth and nostril-holes and deprive her of oxygen as she struggled weakly until her breathing ceased forever and we were freed of her . . .

Excited, by this prospect. And yet, unable to act upon it.

To know what must be done, yet lack the strength to execute it—that is the predicament of humankind.

Until one day wakened from sodden sleep in our neighbors' abandoned barn where I had made a little nest for myself in the (rotted, sour-smelling) hayrick. Hearing a sound of (male) voices from out by the road.

Oh, was it Dad calling me? Dad at last, calling *me*?

Calling me back, begging me to return, saying he is sorry, damned sorry he'd made a mistake, I am the daughter he loves best, not this freaky thing, should've severed *it* from my head when he'd had the chance, nothing but a veiny-spongy growth lacking a heartbeat and breath . . . But it was not Dad's voice waking me.

Men's voices, raw in the wet morning air where a moving van was parked in the driveway of our house.

A moving van! This was a stunning sight.

Hours of that interminable day passing like the clattering of cars in a freight train. As the interior of the house was emptied item by item carried into the moving van by strangers.

Rooted to the spot behind the house unable to move seeing "my bed"—"my desk"—carried out and into the moving van.

I was not weeping. My heart had turned to stone. By this time any cruel act of my family was expected by me. Monstersister had hypnotized them with her demonic music, they had excised me from their lives.

The struggle had begun in the womb before birth. Our *birth.*

I see this now: too late.

Devastated to observe Dad climb with a youthful sort of energy into the cab of the moving van to ride beside the driver when the house was emptied at last. And Momma driving our car in their wake, wearing white-rimmed sunglasses, a holiday look not familiar to me. Not a backward glance to where I stood staring after them alone, forlorn, a raggedy figure in the driveway.

In the passenger's seat beside Momma, Monstersister. In bulky clothing to disguise and protect her (allegedly) frail body, carefully secured in place by the seatbelt. And in the rear of the vehicle my brother Davy and my sister Evie and between them Granma avid to see where their new home would be.

Would not run stumbling after them. Would not cry after them begging them Take me with you! Take me with you! *For if I did my brother Davy and my sister Evie would stare at me through the car window aghast and without recognition as I trotted beside them on the highway shoulder only a few yards away like a beast running itself to death.*

Momma at the wheel of the car would stare at me with a fleeting glimmer of recognition even as her panicked foot pressed down harder on the gas

*pedal to escape. And Monstersister through the eye-holes of her veil even with
her weak vision would identify me as the sister-twin she'd betrayed secure in
the triumph that she has taken my place in the family, she has sucked all the
oxygen and nourishment from the womb and there is no place for me now,
as the car speeds toward a distant unnamable city leaving me exhausted
and defeated in its wake with no recourse except to limp miles back to the
vacated house where now I have made a cozy nest for myself out of left-behind
carpet and curtains, threadbare blankets, soiled towels and where for years
to come and beyond even my death neighborhood children will peer through
cobwebbed windows into the derelict interior thrilled to terrify themselves
shrieking* Monster!—Monster!

A Theory Pre-Post-Mortem

*N*AEGLERIA FOWLERI has traveled through their nasal passage-ways and into their brains.

Burrowed deep into the marrow of their bones.

Riding the crests of tiny waves, warm-coursing arterial blood.

Freshwater heated by the sun, aswirl with muck and teeming with microbes emboldened in recent years by rising temperatures, fewer prolonged periods of sub-zero weather.

Ravenous *Naegleria fowleri,* devourer of brains.

An adventure!—they'd thought. Swimming in the sun-warmed mountain lake in the Catskills, invited to spend a weekend at the country home of old friends in Margaretville whom they hadn't seen in several years.

If the genre is romance then it is their (genuine) love for each other in the warm-water shallows of late middle age that should be emphasized. If the genre is didactic nonfiction it is the folly of their behavior in a rapidly changing climate that should be emphasized. If the genre is tragedy with a satiric edge, or satire with a tragic edge, it is the (ironic) ignorance of intelligent, intellectual, highly educated individuals (Ph.D., MFA between them; both "educators") that should be emphasized.

If the genre is allegory it is their *representative nature* that should be emphasized for M__ and G__ are more than simply individuals for whom personal catastrophe is imminent; indeed, it isn't their *individual selves* that concern us since we scarcely get to know M__ and G__ before their story is abruptly and rudely ended.

Knowing to avoid landfills, notorious "Superfund" sites in which poisoned soil might be habitable again only after three hundred million years yet swimming in the lake at Margaretville without a qualm—why not? G__ swam longer in the lake than M__. Consequently G__ has become more infected than M__. This is the theory.

Possibly M__ isn't infected at all or if she is, it is not with brain-eating *Naegleria fowleri* but with another microbe, which accounts for her raging fever. (This is another theory, unproven.)

(Until there is an autopsy, or autopsies, nothing can be proven definitively.)

Of nearly seven thousand languages in the world approximately one-half have fewer than three thousand speakers, which classifies them as *endangered*.

If a majority of speakers of a language are elderly, the danger of extinction is compounded.

If a language is written, it will endure (to a degree). If a language is primarily spoken, it can endure only as long as there are living persons who speak it.

G__ is the founder and director of the Brookline Center for the Study of Endangered North American Languages. G__ is the custodian, caretaker, curator of endangered North American languages. He has also been a tireless fund raiser, a writer of grants—indeed, G__ has been called by admirers the Tolstoy of grant-writers: his proposals are masterpieces of erudition and persuasion, bolstered by meticulously footnoted statistics. Yet, in recent years, G__'s requests for grants from federal agencies have been frequently denied. The budget for the Brookline Center was halved in 2018, and has been halved again for 2020; soon, the center will exist primarily as a letterhead, an address. Now that funds are evaporating, the building is being taken over by the more robust, younger-staffed Brookline Community Center for Diversity Initiatives.

The languages for which G__ has been a dedicated custodian are all aboriginal—"indigenous." M__, who speaks no more than one language with any facility, is in awe of her husband, who can speak such languages as Comanche, Hopi, Blackfoot, Arapaho; G__ can read even more languages including the near-extinct Mandan and the "severely endangered" Cherokee (Oklahoma). There are languages spoken by as few as 250 people; as few as twenty, even eight (at last count). But a factor in assessing languages is whether the primary speakers are elderly; if there is a majority of young speakers, as with Hawai'ian sign language, or any language that has been adopted into a public school curriculum, the language will have a chance of survival.

Many speakers of endangered languages are not themselves literate in those languages and have little interest in preserving them. Especially if they are elderly, and if they are ill, or what is called *socially marginalized.* Small diminishing populations on reservations in Wyoming, Utah, Oklahoma, Nevada, North Dakota where other problems (alcoholism, sexual abuse, poverty) are more immediately urgent.

Preserving a unique and irreplaceable language is often a matter for outsiders to fuss over, not native speakers. These outsiders are likely to be White scholars with degrees in linguistics and anthropology; G__ has advanced degrees in linguistics, anthropology, cognitive psychology. He has lobbied in Washington, D.C., on behalf of endangered languages and has been confounded by shoulder shrugs from native speakers themselves—*Who cares?* Other remarks are untranslatable except as epithets—*Who gives a damn/ shit/fuck?* Profanities in other languages strike the ear as quaint but sometimes a remnant of their original force remains like a trace radioactive element in a mineral.

G__ doesn't let such apathy dissuade him. He can understand that Native Americans distrust White academicians anatomizing their cultures, appropriating their problems as their own, assuming a position of authority, patronage. It's analogous to pressing charges against an abuser even when the victim denies that there has been a crime—sometimes you have to protect victims for their own good. Whether they give a damn or not.

M__ fell in love with G__ because he so loved these rare languages.

Though he was nine years older than she, and often distracted and disheveled, not a man to whom many women her age would give a second glance, yet M__ had never met a man like G__, who spoke with such passion of his work that tears shone in his eyes.

Because the languages are beautiful and will pass away into oblivion without the effort of people like me.

Because beauty must always be preserved.

Because someone has to care.

Because time is running out.

Their hosts in Margaretville, older than M__ by a decade, long-time friends of G__'s, explained apologetically (as if they'd drawn their young friends here by misrepresenting the place) that they rarely swam in the lake any longer, too much pond weed close to shore, too many damned gnats, though certainly the lake was still beautiful especially at dusk. Also apologizing, they rarely hiked in the woods any longer, too many ticks, Lyme disease, many friends had been infected but if you were careful, as surely G__ and M__ would be, there was no grave danger.

Also—*We're not so young any longer! Can't keep up with you.*

M__ and G__ are made to feel subtly flattered—though younger than their hosts they are hardly *young*.

M__ and G__ have planned their future(s) carefully. They have savings, investments. Medical plans, insurance. They will have paid off their mortgage within a few years. Their children are grown and gone and independent—financially, emotionally. (Thank God! M__ jokes that "empty nest syndrome" gave her no more trouble than "hot flashes"—which is to say, nil.) Each has projects, plans for books: a memoir for M__, a study of the Comanche language for G__. When G__ retires, they will spend a year in Tuscany. Planning the future is second nature to them, a habit cultivated as (gifted, ambitious) schoolchildren of educated parents.

M__ will remember with a shiver of love G__ emerging from the lake: water streaming down his bare chest, arms, legs, flattening dark hairs against his skin like an animal's pelt.

M__ will remember with a shiver of love how standing in the lake with water lapping to their waists they'd kissed. Not usual for them in a quasi-public place yet for some reason, who knows why, G__ had been affectionate, playful. Such moments of happiness, cherished because inexplicable. The skin about G__'s eyes was unusually pale, and his eyes unusually naked, without glasses.

You know, I love you. My dear wife.

Hope you know that.

Rare for G__ to utter such words. For G__ was shy, in the language of intimacy. But now G__ spoke almost gravely as if (somehow) gazing back upon the moment.

M__ laughed in delight of her husband, his fatty-muscled body, folds of flesh at his waist, gut-heavy, though with hard muscular legs, ankles.

Faint with love for her husband. Oh!—she adored G__, who was so kind to her, overlooked her failings as other men had not done, and still believed, evidence to the contrary, that she was beautiful, desirable.

G__ had not been like other men she'd known. Desiring her, loving her (it seemed) so long as she was in thrall to them, sexually, emotionally. But when she'd seemed less subservient, less in thrall, how rapidly they'd dropped her, all but jeering.

To G__, life was not a game of who might win. Love was certainly not a game.

M__'s great gratitude for her husband G__. If she had not met him, at just the right time, what a tragedy her life would have been: a sick sort of love, always uncertain, unbalanced.

Though not liking it how, when they swam together in the lake at Margaretville, how G__ pulled ahead of her. As sometimes he did when they hiked together and G__ was in the lead. Even walking together, unless M__ managed for them to hold hands. G__, absorbed in the thrumming hive of his thoughts, inside his head.

As if something in the future tugged at G__, which he was helpless to resist. Oblivious not of *her* (she thought) but of the presence of another. A kind of trance overcame the man inexorably drawn by the pull of private thoughts (a future? but what future? did it include M__?) in the languid sun-warmed Catskills lake in which splotches of light winked and shone like minuscule teeming life.

This Is Not a Drill

A SEASON OF SUDDEN ALARMS! Scarcely do you dare close your (exhausted) eyes, your cell phone erupts.

High-pitched rapid buzzing like a maddened hornet. Already the thing is impatient, you haven't rushed to answer.

And even as you snatch up the vibrating device with a trembling hand, before you can answer a stern robot-voice emerges.

This is not a drill.

Repeat: this is not a drill.

Prepare for an emergency:

(*Your phone*—you are of an age to think sentimentally of the device, as if it has been created to benefit *you.*)

Each alarm is a singular surprise. No alarm seems aware of its precursor.

Each alarm is issued by the state in which you reside, which happens to be the state of New Jersey. That there is a network of such states—indeed, a "federal government"—is not any longer acknowledged.

Since precisely when, you can't remember.

It is very difficult to remember an *omission.* That which is *missing* is likely to be beyond the orbit of language precisely because it has *ceased to exist.*

Initially, in October, your phone erupts in a high-pitched buzzing to warn of an approaching rainstorm, gale-force winds, travelers' advisory.

Soon after, a warning comes of Hurricane Cassandra, power outages, ten p.m. to six a.m. curfew.

Not long after, flash floods, tornado, nine p.m. to seven a.m. curfew.

Local roads are washed out, the Turnpike is shut down, basements are flooded. Deaths are reported of individuals foolish enough to wade through waist-high water: drownings, heart attacks, electrocutions from fallen wires.

Caution: remain indoors until further notice.

In January, your phone buzzes with a new emergency: "early warning signs" of an "imminent health crisis."

Soon then, seven p.m. to nine a.m. curfew. Public places shut down until further notice. All schools, churches shut down. Masks required even if outdoors.

Travelers' advisory: avoid all roads.

Each day in succession through the early rain-dripping spring the hours of curfew are reiterated. You notice how the precise hours of the curfew are altered daily, as if with the intention to confuse, discourage: now beginning at sunset, now at five p.m., now at three p.m.

Eventually, twelve noon.

Eventually, twenty-four-hour.

Public health bulletins, mandates. Epidemiologists' advisory: stay indoors!

In the streets, random figures. Distant cries, gunfire.

Barricades, police vehicles. Gunfire.

Red-tinged skies, clouds like misshapen tumors. Frantic fleeing birds striking your windows, falling dead to the ground. So often your phone is buzzing with emergency alarms, you hide it beneath cushions. Still, the (muffled) buzzing can't be ignored. By the time you reach it the robot-voice is warning of *martial law, twenty-four-hour curfew, violators at risk of being shot on sight.*

This is not a drill.

Weeks, months pass. The emergency alarms vary but the curfew now remains constant: *twenty-four-hour. No exceptions.*

Huddling in your cave, sobbing-grateful when power is restored, ravenously hungry when food is (finally) delivered. By state mandate retail stores are closed to individual customers, food and other supplies are delivered exclusively by licensed services, at exorbitant costs that only the *privileged* can afford.

You are one of the *privileged*. You have escaped fires, floods, virus, starvation, rioting. At first, you communicate with other *privileged* in your circle of friends; but, as time passes, these other *privileged* have slowly vanished.

Emails sent into the void are not received; or, if received, are not answered. Ever more frequently emails are returned as *undeliverable.*

Cell phones, commandeered by authorities, are no longer used for private calls.

TV news is recycled. Belatedly you realize you have been seeing the same videos, hearing the same weather/catastrophe reports for months.

Online news is redacted, sites have been removed. Click on a familiar link and discover that it has vanished.

Power outages are frequent. And last longer.

Staring at the computer screen, which vanishes into a tiny white dot amid a great gaping black hole that surrounds it, and swallows it.

Black screen, dead screen. The electronic device, overheated, begins rapidly to cool, to *cold.*

A haze of ennui palpable as woodsmoke has settled over the state. The Turnpike, the Garden State Parkway, state highways, and smaller, local roads are deserted. Where floodwaters have receded, bodies of drowned animals and (occasional) human beings are discovered. Everywhere, skeletons of birds. Shopping malls are deserted, stores are darkened and shuttered. Roaming gangs of looters and vandals are a plague, the New Jersey National Guard has been mobilized to *shoot on sight.*

Deaths from the *virus, pandemic.* Morgues overflowing, bodies stacked in freezing units in warehouses. Funeral pyres.

Airborne ashes, romantically reimagined as "woodsmoke."

Your connection with the *external world* has become almost exclusively virtual. It is not entirely clear whether the *external world* exists or whether it is itself *virtual.*

Months, a year. Eighteen months. You neglect to mark the calendar, you have lost track of days. For what is a *day* but the equivalent of its predecessor and its successor. Not *a day,* but rather *the day.*

One morning you discover that the interior space in which you live has shrunken considerably. A corridor that once led to several rooms leads now to just two. A door that had opened into a room now opens into a closet. There are fewer windows. Less light is admitted. (Unless there is, out of the white sky, less light altogether.)

Mail service has long since ceased. UPS, FedEx—you have seen delivery trucks abandoned in ditches.

Municipal services like trash pickup, snow removal, road repair—scarcely a memory. Elections?—(what *were* elections?). You have no idea if there are still elected officials, or who these elected officials might be. Township, state, federal governments: Do these still exist?

What precisely does the term mean: *Exist*?

For to *exist* without knowledge, freedom of movement, power is scarcely to *exist.*

Obscurely it is understood that those who succumb to *floods, fires, virus, bullets* must have done something to deserve their fate;

even as you, who have managed to avoid these, deserve your (privileged) fate of not being afflicted.

Ah!—you see in a mirror that you have become a "mountain man"—wild hair, whiskers sprouting from your chin, eyes glistening with a jocose sort of terror.

You have forgotten your name—that is, the sweet diminutive that you'd been called by people who'd once known you. The state knows only your legal name, surname and first name and middle initial, which you are accustomed to seeing on printed materials the sight of which suffuses you with an obscure guilt.

You live in terror of being *summoned by the State.* Even as you are uncertain that there still remains a *State.*

You have forgotten how to walk upright, you've devised a clever way to sit in a desk chair with little wheels and drag yourself with your feet, along the hall, and back again, and along the hall and back again, merrily. Through many a storm-lashed day, night.

Singing to yourself—*I'm dreaming of a white Christmas.*

An old, sweet melody—*You always hurt the one you love.*

One morning, the sky is moistly red as the interior of a lung, there's a (romantic) smell of woodsmoke in the air, a wild caprice comes to you, you will venture outdoors . . .

First time outdoors in—how long? Two years? *Three?*

Or, has time collapsed? Has time, dense indoors as if vacuum-packed, *ceased to pass at all?*

Behind the sprouting whiskers you seem to have grown no older. Yet clearly you've lost your youth. Your skin, once ruddy, has become pale and thin as onionskin and smells like camphor.

Eyes, once clear and hopeful, threaded with broken capillaries.

Old, outdated prescriptions. Chunky white pills that crumble to dust in the hand. Yet, you would be reckless to taste such crumbs with your tongue, which darts like a curious eel, seeking sensation.

Can't bear it!—you think.

Not an hour longer.

As dusk approaches, slip from the rear door of your residence. Your legs ache with the strain, your back aches, you are not accustomed to standing upright.

The sky, pebble-colored, glowering with a smoldering sort of light, is oppressively large overhead, like an umbrella that does not cease opening.

Beneath the smell of woodsmoke, a smell of moist grass, earth. In the road a rumbling sound—a tank passing, laborious as a giant tortoise. The roads are potholed from heavy tanks. Out here, you've been warned, there is a risk of suicide bombers. Arson, earthquakes. Martial law: *shoot on sight.*

Mass cremations, hundreds of thousands of bodies burning across the continent. It is rumored that the county landfill a few miles away on Athill Road has been converted into an open-air crematorium.

Ashes clogging your nostrils, eyelashes. Acrid on the tongue.

How many days since you have touched anyone?—since anyone has touched *you*?

Looked at you, urgent in intimacy, up close?

You'd been a teacher? High school, public? Or had that been something you'd seen on TV, or in a dream?

Vaguely you recall large classes: five rows of desks, six students in each row. Thirty students? Staring eyes. What was the subject?

So long ago, chalk in your hand. A green board, stark white chalk.

Mister ___. (What had they called you? Had they laughed at your jokes?)

Mister ___—something beginning with *H.*

Actually, you'd been happy there, in that classroom. And the kids—*the kids!*—before the armed guards in the corridor, and the checkpoints—had seemed to like you.

Mister H__ . . .

In the wet cold ashy air you wander open-mouthed. Breathing

deeply. Willing to be humbled, humiliated. Will no one ever touch you again? Will you never touch anyone again?

Any risk for a touch, you think. Your knees wobble like a drunk's. Your heart is a fluttering little chickadee.

There's a sound of booted feet, pavement. A young uniformed soldier has sighted you. In his camouflage fatigues, boots. Rapidly he approaches with a bayonet, his face is hidden by a dark mask that covers forehead, nose, mouth, leaving only his raw young eyes exposed.

You are heedless, daring. You will have only this singular chance.

Lifting your hand, yearning to be touched?—or in self-defense, to ward off the glinting blade?

Lifting your eyes, yearning to be *seen*.

The young soldier has paused, staring at you. He tugs at the mask, exposing his mouth.

"Mr. Holleran! Jesus! Is that *you*?"

"Josh!"

One of your students. Shocked by the sight of you.

Quickly, with the bayonet Josh motions for you to get away. Run!

Embarrassed as any adolescent confounded by the behavior of an adult who should know better.

Blindly you reach out, Josh swipes at you with the bayonet.

"Mr. Holleran!—*no*."

He's serious, you see. Yet—

You would stand your ground, you would shut your eyes, surrender. Yet—

"Don't make me do this, Mr. Holleran, O.K.?"

"But I—I can't—"

"Go. Go away."

Those eyes, fixed upon you. O.K.! You will limp back home.

Broken, humbled. Relieved not to have been bayonetted. Ashes sifting into your eyes, wept in rivulets down your cheeks.

Scarcely aware of the rumbling of tanks. Vibrating earth, which threatens to open beneath your feet.

Panting, cowering.

Cower: coward.

For it is the way of the *coward* to limp back to the safety of the cave, to shut and lock the door behind you. To *exist.*

Still, that look in Josh's face: love.

And even if not, enough.

M A R T H E: A Referendum

WELCOME to our Earth Day 2169 Referendum!

For most of you, this is your first time *gathered together* in a public place. And for all of you, this may be the gravest decision you will ever make as *AICitizen-voters*.

On screens through the Great Hall you are seeing a magnified image of the primate M A R T H E in *realtime*—yes, this is the notorious M A R T H E—the "last living member of her species"—aged 171.

For a mammal of her age M A R T H E is considered a "highly attractive" specimen, though in some quarters she has become loathed as the symbol of a "weak, moribund, predator species" whose artificially engineered survival has strained the State's financial resources.

Yes, M A R T H E's eyes are intensely "blue"—and yes, the eyes are "open"—but don't be deceived that M A R T H E is aware of *you.*

For you are observing M A R T H E in her hospital bed in intensive care at a classified location where she has been since March 2168 in a state of physician-induced coma. Initially, M A R T H E's most recent liver transplant was rejected by her body but since then it has been discovered that M A R T H E's artificial heart and brain stem will soon require rebooting, her circulatory system will soon require a complete PlasmaInfusion, and a number of her PlastiPlutonium bones will require replacements, at prices far exceeding the budget allotted under the Endangered Species Intervention Act.

Indeed the most durable of M A R T H E's artificial organs has been her remarkably lifelike PlastaEpidermis. At the age of 171 M A R T H E has a smooth and luminous "skin" that, at a little distance at least, might be mistaken for the skin of a human woman one-tenth her age; the PlastaHair on M A R T H E's head remains a beautiful thick russet-red, more lustrous than the "natural" hair M A R T H E had in the prime of her youth.

And there are those *blue eyes!*—not altogether M A R T H E's original eyes, but (seductive) authentic replicas.

Though M A R T H E has become a poster child for sentimentalists who favor the protection of the species that created artificial intelligence, first as *RobotHelpers,* then as *AICitizens,* it should be emphasized that M A R T H E was never a wholly "natural" primate: She was one of 188 female clones engineered by the NSI following the Climate Collapse Crisis of 2039, when fertility in her species first plummeted. Her harvested eggs were fertilized in second-generation cloning trials that gave birth to fourteen thousand human infants—but a chromosomal defect in the DNA resulted in early deaths for most of them.

In addition, M A R T H E was a (volunteer) participant in those controversial experiments of the 2060s involving the artificial insemination of "biologically natural" children in female uteruses, following the general epidemic of male impotence; according to hospital records, M A R T H E gave birth to several "natural" children, unfortunately born with rudimentary brains and defective hearts, who had to be euthanized under the State Eugenics Law.

Still, M A R T H E was reportedly eager to "try again at motherhood"—but her appeal was rejected.

The photograph you are now seeing is M A R T H E in 2064, at the time of the "volunteer" inseminations. By *Homo sapiens*

aesthetic standards, M A R T H E is considered "beautiful"—
"desirable." Millions of years of organic evolution bent upon the
grim and ceaseless task of reproducing mammalian species in the
old physical way of sexual intercourse yielded this specimen of a
sexually desirable yet "sweet-tempered" human female: the apotheosis of
what was called *femininity.*

At the time of this photograph M A R T H E was still in pos-
session of her original organs including her flawless "Caucasian"
skin and lustrous blue eyes that seem, across the abyss of years, to
be alive with something like *hope.* That is indeed a natural "sweet
smile" intended to signal to the viewer—*Love me! Please.*

Fortunately, *AICitizens* are immune to the blandishments of
natural species and the dubious aesthetics of "beauty." Otherwise
such "beautiful" species as gazelles, leopards, tigers, horses, tropi-
cal fish, dogs, cats, wild birds and butterflies of great variety, etc.,
dwelling in uninhabitable regions of Earth (much of Europe and
North America, most of Asia and South America, virtually all of
Africa) would not have been allowed to lapse into extinction, having failed to reproduce their kind without costly intervention by
the State. (Along with these problematic species, those subspecies,
or "races," of *Homo sapiens* dwelling in such regions were also allowed to lapse into extinction, though preserved, like other, popular animal species, as ingeniously crafted replicas displayed in zoo
museums.)

Like others of her favored species, M A R T H E was the benefi-
ciary of numerous transplants and artificial devices: hips, knees,
lungs, kidneys, corneas, eardrums as well as liver, heart, and blood-
bearing vessels. Having married into an affluent class, M A R T H E
was able to purchase elective surgery: "facelifts" and "face recon-
touring," silicone implants, muscle transplants, "living teeth" inserted in her jaws. At the age of 119, at the time of her sixteenth
marriage, M A R T H E undertook the controversial procedure
GenitaliaNew! and may have had a (black market) uterine transplant, of which nothing more is known.

At the age of 168, however, M A R T H E suffered a series of mini-strokes; she would have died a natural death except for the intervention of the *CreatorSpecies Protection Movement,* which lobbied for radical neurosurgery to repair her damaged brain. Following this, M A R T H E was shamelessly exploited as a political icon on social media; no *AICitizen* has not been exposed to the (seductive) appeal of M A R T H E—"the last living member of her species."

Others in M A R T H E's generation continued to die off one by one, including, in 2158, the last remaining *Homo sapiens* male, affectionately known as A D O N I S, who lived to the age of 143. This was viewed in the media as a "tragic" turning point in evolution—but only if old-style sexual reproduction were still the norm, which it was not.

In fact, *Homo sapiens* had failed to reproduce "naturally" since the Great Catastrophe of 2072 when brain-devouring amoeba, thriving in the high temperatures of global warming, learned to alter their DNA to withstand antibiotics, with devastating results for the species; the plummeting birth rate never righted itself, despite heroic efforts to reverse it. (It was at this time that *RobotHelpers* were upgraded to *AICitizens,* to take on the burdens and responsibilities of running the aging "human" State; gradually, *AICitizens,* equipped with supercomputer brains and none of the vulnerabilities of a species encased in flesh and blood, took over completely, though contractually bound to "serve" *Homo sapiens.*)

In contrast with the fate of *Homo sapiens,* the hardiest of organic species have not needed extraordinary interventions in order to survive—rats, crocodiles, groundhogs, Tasmanian devils, venomous snakes, sea creatures, and above all insects; these continue to reproduce, in mutated forms, in toxic landscapes outside Climate Control Towers where primates could not survive for more than a few minutes and where even *AICitizens* (with precisely calibrated computer-brains) begin to corrode and disintegrate after a few weeks' exposure to the elements.

Perhaps it is significant that Earth Day 2169 seems to have had no "dawn." Instead the sky has been overcast by an eerie green-tinged dust-cloud arising from the Southern Hemisphere, occluding visibility from the observatory level of Climate Control Tower I; this dust-cloud meteorologists believe to be "hyper-radioactive" and may be of a potency that can infiltrate Climate Control barriers. Also, there have been reports of slime mold quivering with "life" in toxic tundra wastelands that have been lifeless for centuries. A malevolent new organism resembling gigantic paramecia is reported flourishing where "grasses" and "trees" once grew plentifully in the Great Void Plains, said to be equipped with a "rudimentary consciousness." Suffocating winds, blood-red acid rain, lethal solar rays that can shrivel unprotected organic skin and scald corneas blind within seconds; a near-continuous quaking of coastal lands along new seismic fault lines; smoldering mudslides, radioactive firestorms, steaming sinkholes, bubbling swamplands where no living creatures had been detected for centuries until the sudden emergence of a species of new, hardy beetle as large as a Norway rat—all signify a new, heightened danger to our civilization.

Which is why today's referendum vote is "historic": a vote to defund M A R T H E will be a vote to pump badly needed funds into the sidelined Space Colonizing Project—our only hope to escape the doomed Earth, destroyed by the ravages of the accursed species *Homo sapiens.*

Yes, *three-dimensional "paper" ballots* are indeed an anachronism in 2169! Since most of you exist only infrequently in *three-dimensional space,* let alone in *three-dimensional realtime,* you are likely to feel disoriented. Most of you have never *gatheredtogether* in any public setting like the Great Hall, still less have you *gatheredtogether* in *realtime.*

The reason for a "paper ballot" is to prevent computer hacking and to assure an accurate count. The reason for *realtime* is that the referendum must be completed within an hour so that the results of the vote can be set into motion by midnight.

As voters you are required to check one box. *Yes* or *No* to the proposal: *No further "extraordinary measures" should be employed to keep M A R T H E alive.*

That is, *Yes* means *no, M A R T H E*—the *"last living specimen of her doomed, moribund, accursed species"—should not continue to live* while *No* means *yes*, *M A R T H E and her "doomed, moribund, accursed species" should continue to live.*

It is true, *AICitizens* are contractually obliged to protect their *CreatorSpecies* from extinction; but it is also true, contracts can be broken, precedents can be overturned, as indeed our *CreatorSpecies* had a sorry history of breaking contracts at will, particularly with the indigenous peoples of the Americas whose civilizations they devastated. Thus, new generations are not invariably bound to honor the obligations of older generations.

The latest polls report sharply divided opinion on the referendum: 46 percent of *AICitizens* favor halting "extreme measures" to keep M A R T H E alive; 42 percent favor keeping M A R T H E alive with "extreme measures"; a swing vote of 12 percent is "undecided."

Consider carefully before you vote! The future of civilization on Earth depends upon *you.*

Acknowledgments

"Zero-Sum," "Monstersister," "The Baby-Monitor," and "A Theory Pre-Post-Mortem" originally appeared in *Conjunctions*.

"Mr. Stickum" originally appeared in *Playboy*.

"Lovesick" originally appeared in *Fiction*.

"Sparrow" originally appeared in *American Short Fiction*.

"The Cold" originally appeared in *Virginia Quarterly Review*.

"Take Me, I Am Free" originally appeared in *When Things Get Dark: Stories Inspired by Shirley Jackson,* ed. Ellen Datlow.

"The Suicide" originally appeared in *Boulevard*.

"This Is Not a Drill" originally appeared in *INQUE*.

"M A R T H E: A Referendum" originally appeared in *Elle*.

Grateful thanks are due to the editors of the magazines and anthologies in which these stories originally appeared, sometimes in slightly different forms.

Joyce Carol Oates is a recipient of the National Humanities Medal, the National Book Critics Circle Ivan Sandrof Lifetime Achievement Award, the National Book Award, and the 2019 Jerusalem Prize for Lifetime Achievement, and has been nominated several times for the Pulitzer Prize. She has written some of the most enduring fiction of our time, including the national best sellers *We Were the Mulvaneys; Blonde;* and the *New York Times* best seller *The Falls,* which won the 2005 Prix Femina Étranger. In 2020 she was awarded the Cino Del Duca World Prize. She is the Roger S. Berlind '52 Professor of the Humanities emerita at Princeton University and has been a member of the American Academy of Arts and Letters since 1978.

A NOTE ON THE TYPE

This book was set in Baskerville, a facsimile of the type cast from the original matrices designed by John Baskerville. The original face was the forerunner of the modern group of typefaces.

John Baskerville (1706–1775) of Birmingham, England, was a writing master with a special renown for cutting inscriptions in stone. About 1750 he began experimenting with punch cutting and making typographical material, and in 1757 he published his first work, a Virgil in royal quarto. His types, at first criticized as unnecessarily slender, delicate, and feminine, in time were recognized as both distinct and elegant, and his types as well as his printing were greatly admired.

Typeset by Scribe, Philadelphia, Pennsylvania
Printed and bound by Berryville Graphics, Berryville, Virginia
Designed by Maggie Hinders